On the

of this book we use ... *extravaganza." There* ... *to describe this astonishing work of science fiction. There is no other writer quite like Ian Wallace and no background as logically complex and as endlessly fascinating as the one you will find in this remarkable novel.*

There is a trip between galaxies. There is a parallel universe which may or may not be the one in which we all dwell. There is a man named Croyd. And there is a something which seeks to control all the galaxies for its own inscrutable purposes.

The man named Croyd stands in this something's way. This is possible because Croyd is a lot more than what he seems. He has, for instance, an identical twin somewhere out there who may or may not have similar powers. As to what those powers are, perhaps even Croyd does not know their full extent.

It is best to say that A VOYAGE TO DARI most closely resembles the sort of mind-tingling novel that A. E. van Vogt might have written had he, in addition to his own talents, those of Robert Heinlein, Arthur C. Clarke, and others skilled in hard science and psychological insight. But then those are the talents of Ian Wallace. And A VOYAGE TO DARI is by Ian Wallace, not anyone else.

—D.A.W.

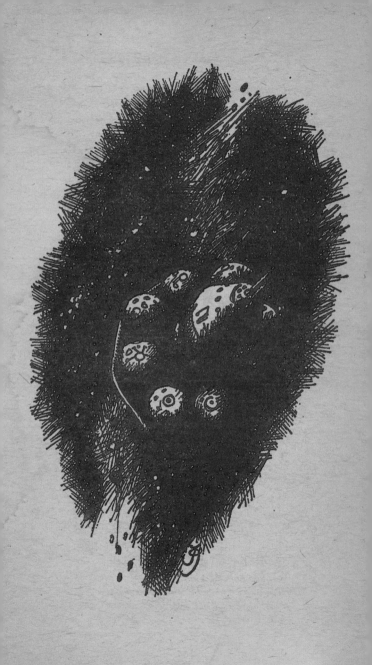

A VOYAGE TO DARI

Ian Wallace

DAW BOOKS, INC.
DONALD A. WOLLHEIM, PUBLISHER

1301 Avenue of the Americas
New York, N. Y.   10019

Cover art by Peter Manesis.

Period Novels of Ian Wallace
(with dates of eras)

EVERY CRAZY WIND (1948)

THE PURLOINED PRINCE (2470)

DEATHSTAR VOYAGE (2475)

CROYD (2502)

A VOYAGE TO DARI (2506)

PAN SAGITTARIUS (2509 and prior eras)

Conjointly,

TO FATHERS, SONS, AND BROTHERS

First Printing, November 1974

1 2 3 4 5 6 7 8 9

PRINTED IN U.S.A.

PHASES OF THE TALE

FORENOTE

Although Croyd has appeared in other tales, you need bring no Croyd background to this one; all that you may require to know comes out between these covers. As for Pan Sagittarius, who leads the secondary and late-introduced leitmotif, I suppose we can say that between these covers he performs for the first time as the Pan-person.

Erth with her environing metagalaxy is not quite perfectly *our* Earth with *her* environing metagalaxy, although the family resemblance is strong; perhaps they are imperfect duplicates.

Djinn, Moudjinn, and Dari are invented place names, of course. I was insecure about Dari—surely on Earth such a simple place name must exist—and so I looked it up in my Atlas; the nearest approaches I could find were Dariyah in Saudi Arabia and Daru in New Guinea; I still think there *must* be a there-unlisted Dari, but I don't care, because the name is just right for my gentle planet. Names and personalities of all on-scene people are author-invented, and nobody is meant to resemble any real person. As for Darian wedding rites, they rather resemble Margaret Mead's descriptions of Samoan practices in *Male and Female* and *Coming of Age in Samoa*, with some major departures. The Rolandic fissure fantasy owes much to *The Cerebral Cortex of Man,* by Wilder Penfield and Theodore Rasmussen.

For the numerous Americans and others who are versed in one or another Earth Polynesian tongue, be it specified that Darian expressions in this novel are not Polynesian but are Darian. Thus a *lua-lua* is a Darian lava-lava; and at one point of excitation, Djeel's outcry "*Hoëné!*" is purely emotive, meaningless except in situational context.

I acknowledge with gratitude the kindness of G. P. Putnam's Sons in allowing me to quote in two places from my *Dr. Orpheus,* copyright 1968 by the author.

IAN WALLACE

PROLOGUE IN A BRAIN

Now listen, Roland. We have out here a magnificent pure feudalism. We have to establish it, ruthlessly. In every case in any planet's history, every pure feudalism has perished, but always because of unfair pressure from neighboring empires; even when a feudalism has perished of inward corruption, the contamination has seeped in from neighboring empires. Consider my own planet Moudjinn; now it has knuckled under the pressure from alien Sol Galaxy, its feudalism will perish.

But my liege, it is my understanding that the policy of Sol Galaxy is a policy of planetary self-determination, indeed even of national self-determination.

And there you are wrong, Roland! That is Sol's historic hypocrisy. They will smother my Moudjinn; and when they find out about us, out here between galaxies, they will come out and smother us. No, we must take total command of all the galaxies, first! We must reduce all of them to subjection, first! And we have the power, almost; but there are a few mental ingredients that we lack; and also, negatively there is a collection of antagonistic powers in a mind named Croyd.

Eh, my liege. And this Croyd is about to embark from his Sol-base to our galaxy Djinn, is he not?

Exactly, Roland, to become treaty governor of our primitive planet Dari, which he will corrupt, with easy access to our dominant planet Moudjinn, which again he will corrupt, whereafter he will turn to us here. And that is where you now come in.

7

Command me, Liege.

You will go now to Sol, using our Brain for your instantaneous self-dispatching. You will find this Croyd,
enter him, neutralize his extraordinary psychophysical
powers, and bring him to me no more puissant than an
ordinary man. And I will deal with him. And then we
will master our galaxy and his galaxy and all other
galaxies, and the metagalaxy will finally be safe for the
purity of our feudalism.

But, Liege—

Roland? Another but?

*The Croyd powers that I am to destroy are precisely
the powers that we lack and need in order to beef up
our Brain for galactic subjection!*

Ironical, is it not? Luckily, Roland, there exists right in
Djinn, only hours from my Moudjinn, a man who is
another irony. He has all the special powers that Croyd
owns, and he is wealth-corruptible and power-corruptible,
which Croyd is not—and I have wealth to offer, and we
have power to offer.

What is his name?

He calls himself Pan Sagittarius.

I do not know him.

Never mind, Roland. I will get Pan; you destroy Croyd.
When may I expect delivery?

*My lord duke, at a preliminary estimate, soon after
the Croyd ship breaks out into the metagalactic fissure.*

That will do nicely, Roland. By then I will have Pan; and
if Pan should unexpectedly prove recalcitrant, there always remains to us a lethal scansion of the Croyd brain
to exhume the traces of what we need. When do you
embark, Roland?

Now, my liege, an it please you.

Good; then I will embark now on my business.

My liege . . .

Roland?

Finally, how can I be sure that your ultimate purpose is the universal sanctity of feudalism?

Childe Roland! How can you doubt me? Remember the fealty that we have sworn, the fealty which is the purest heart of feudalism!

Phase One

OUT OF THE UNIVERSE

Day 4, uptiming to Day 1
(sometime during 2506)

A long voyage offers the most wonderful climate in the world for romance or for good high conversation—either, or both together—rendered gradually more piquant by the growing tension of goal approach, and always with a carefully ignored undertone of possible goal frustration by ship disaster.

—Ule Vennen, *Vennen's Voyages* (1983)

ACTION AFTER H-HOUR:

CROYD THRUST ME INSIDE THE LIFEBOAT that we knew as Commandcom, and he followed me in, and the lifeboat hatch slammed shut, and two-G thrust sent us crashing over. With difficulty recovering, Croyd pulled me into control, got me into the copilot seat, and settled himself into the pilot seat. He and I were the only occupants, and the two-G acceleration continued; two hundred G, actually—this craft had a 1:100 inertial shield.

We had fled our ship, the *Castel Jaloux*, on the dismal horning-honking signal that meant *lifeboats!*

Crisply Croyd addressed Commandcom, "What in Hell is up?"

The computer's contralto voice floated in, "The admiral ordered me to take off as soon as you and the President were aboard. I do not know what in Hell is up. What is Hell?"

"Open your viewplates and let's find out."

Viewplates opened. We stared at the image of the *Castel Jaloux*, football size in metaspace-distance, floodlighted, diminishing.

The *Castel* converted herself into something resembling a solar flare . . . and vanished. We were awash without a ship—outside the universe.

Croyd demanded, "What other lifeboats are out?"

"None, sir. Only we. As nearly as I can make out, the *Castel Jaloux* was invaded by hallucinatory images."

"Describe these images."

"They are indescribable in your semantic system."

"Indescribable!" I disbelieved.

Pause. Commandcom, contralto very deep: "Mr. Croyd, I recognize the other voice as that of President Tannen. To which voice am I to accord command priority?"

I interjected, "Croyd will issue most commands; but in the unlikely event that I should countercommand, this would supersede."

Commandcom: "Croyd . . . confirm?"

"Confirm," said Croyd. Lightly I punched his biceps;

even in shipwreck, and without trying, he was one-up:
reassuring it was, amusing it was. . . .

After something like a computerized sigh, Commandcom stated, "Immediately after the appearance of the
indescribable alien images, the *Castel* apparently shot upward—that is, away from the pit of the metagalactic
fissure. I cannot explain the flare associated with her dis-
appearance. Meanwhile, *we* have been deflected or drawn
into a *downward* course, *toward* the pit of the fissure."

Croyd demanded, "Have you attempted to correct our
course?"

"Yes, sir. However, something external is interfering
with my controls. It is nicely maintaining my maximum
acceleration of two-hundred G—but *downward;* our
velocity is now two thousand thirty-one kilometers per
second and accelerating; we will attain light-velocity in
approximately forty-one hours and . . ."

Commandcom stopped.

Presently, tense Croyd encouraged: "A change, Commandcom?"

Contralto, slightly strangulated: "Something external
has accelerated my acceleration."

"But we feel no change. . . ."

"Something external has compensatorily boosted my
inertial shield. My normal acceleration is increasing as its
own square. We will attain light-velocity within minutes."

"Is there anything you can do?"

"Nothing, Governor Croyd. I have all my sensors and
computers, but absolutely no locomotors."

I suggested to Croyd, "I believe, my friend, that this is
one of those situations where one doesn't worry, because worry leads nowhere."

"One doesn't worry," he returned, "about oneself, because worry leads nowhere. But that shouldn't stop us
from inventorying the possibilities about whither we are
bound, whether the *Castel* exists—and who done it."

"Why do you say, *who* done it?"

"You are imagining that the deflections of the *Castel*
upward and of our lifecraft downward, together with the
squaring of our acceleration and the compensatory
strengthening of our inertial shield, could be accidents of
metaspace about which we know next to nothing. And
so they could. But the hallucinatory images, my friend—
the ones detected aboard the *Castel* by Commandcom,

who is definitely not prone to hallucination—these things are mind projections; and since Commandcom detected them objectively, it appears that they were not projected by anyone aboard ship. I think we may be dealing with a *who*."

"Should that be maybe with a *whom?*"

"That should be maybe deferred until the next meta-science."

Commandcom, silky-low: "You men confuse me. This is a mortal emergency. You are supposed to be tense."

Croyd, soft: "How can we be tense? We have *you!*" Then hard: "But Djeel we do not have—or Hanoku, or Gorsky. With your permission, President Tannen, I shall continue to worry; somewhere eventually it may lead me."

We did a lot of falling after that; we had hours to meditate, between brief exchanges, and neither of us wasted meditation time with broodings about personal tragedy. Croyd, I knew, was intently engaged in diagnosis and hypothesis projection, mentally preparing himself for anything that might eventuate should we survive, leaving it to Commandcom to do what she could about survival. My own mentality is political-intuitive, it wasn't up to logical manipulation; nevertheless, I was very busy feeling over memories of the immediate past, so loaded they were with cues—expressed or subliminal—relevant to what had happened to us, and what might happen. (I did not quite understand, though, why he now was barefoot.)

I had been personally in on most of it. But when I report what I was not in on, don't imagine that it is mere hearsay- or conjecture-reporting. For Croyd has put it into me as subjective experience, as though I were a phantom watching.

PRIOR ACTION: H-Hour minus 63 hours:

THE INTERGALACTIC FLAGSHIP *Castel Jaloux*, retroluminous for approach visibility as she neared

Nereid-off-Neptune (the space-rock capital of Sol Galaxy), looked like a flying fortress, a Rhine-type fortress flying: her bridge a forward round-tower citadel, her aft repulsor assembly a postern curtain wall. (Exterior shipshape doesn't matter much in hard space, where there is no atmosphere opposing friction to excrescences.)

Much of the *Castel*'s rugged-irregular two-cubic-mile volume, whose exterior was made feathery all over by assorted intake and output antennae, was occupied by devices for manufacturing fuel, food, water, and other energy from space; and her mighty bowels womb-housed the gigantic spherical Differential Mass that permitted translight velocities limited only by inertially shielded acceleration capabilities and the length of the run. Her crew catacombs were capacious; and her Visiting Admiral's Suite had been luxuriously adapted for Tannen the Interplanetary President (me); while the slightly smaller Visiting Captain's Suite had been polished up for Croyd, who had just pulled out of Galactic chairmanship to become the new governor of the planet Dari in the remote Djinn Galaxy. Beyond this, beehives of staterooms, usually officers' cabins housing two to four officers each, had been redone to house one or two embassy officers each; so that two to four ship's officers were, just for this intergalactic cruise, fouring and sixing elsewhere. Nevertheless, no doubt about it: the *Castel Jaloux* remained a battleship of the line.

Governor Croyd and new Temporary Chairman Greta Groen and I debouched horizontally in Croyd's scouter from the major landing berth in one side of Nereid, the little satellite of Neptune that was the capital of Sol Galaxy. It was night, of course: all space far from any star or reflecting planet is night; Neptune, to our right, was a pale sky-filling moon, but otherwise we were in darkness except for the local bluish fluorescence in the cabin of our scouter. Ahead, through the rounded crystal of the bridgepane, between and around the black head-and-shoulder silhouette of our pilot, we watched the pinpoint glow of the distant *Castel Jaloux* grow larger and brighter, grow starlike, begin to take shape, flare into her ugly-rugged floodlighted irregularity, grow, grow....

Invisible to us, Childe Roland, taking off from an obscure corner of the scouter, began treacherous progress across the fifteen feet toward Croyd. Molecule-sized Roland had to handle big restless atmospheric molecules body-to-body.

"You guys talk," murmured I (rotund-jocund, seventyish). "I am watching the *Castel Jaloux*. I am paying you no mind."

They sat together on a flank bench; I sat on the other flank.

Greta (tall, slender, ash-blond, green-eyed, thirtyish) moved closer to Croyd (taller, muscular-lean, thirty-sixish, hair auburn, blue eyes meaningfully deep). They intersqueezed four hands.

He said, "Madame Chairman, that ship is so ugly it is inspiring."

She said, "I would give a pretty to see her take off from Erth. With water from her departed moat dripping off her flanks."

Prolonged intimate dual musing.

Croyd and I were embarking on a risky voyage to Moudjinn in Djinn Galaxy to sign an intergalactic treaty that would open up new horizons and incidentally would terminate five years of intergalactic piracy that occasionally had erupted into fiery battle. I had no business going, I suppose; but as Interplanetary President I wanted to be the co-signator with the Emperor of Djinn. Croyd was traveling as governor-by-treaty of the piratical planet Dari, fief planet of the dominant planet Moudjinn, having resigned the Galactic chair for the post. His assignment was to neutralize Darian piracy and rehabilitate the planet.

I hated to see him go, even though his dear friend (and mine) Captain Greta would temporarily replace him. During a decade as chairman—which is to say, prime minister to me as constitutional monarch—he had more than once deployed astonishing personal powers including mind mobility and space-time mobility to head off planetary and even galactic disaster. Prior to his chairmanship, for two decades he had exhibited a genius for high-level intrigue as a Galactic agent. I accord him major credit for negotiating the Sol-Djinn treaty, working by remote control through a fleet admiral. Obviously his apparent age of thirty-six was deceptive: he hadn't

changed in all the years I'd known him. Apart from all
this, he was a hell of a good friend.

The glowing *Castel* filled the view crystal.

Childe Roland was close.

Greta, frowning down: "Mr. Governor . . ."

Croyd: "Madame Chairman?"

"Don't call me that. I . . . can't handle this job. I'm
scared."

"You can handle it. I'm often scared."

"Don't kid!"

"But I don't stay scared, because I know what to do
about fear. And you know too, Madame Chairman."

"You mean . . . switch off my emotic brain switches?"

"Right."

"I'm not as good at it as you, Croyd. After I'm switched
off, I stay scared in my mind. No more trouble with my
glands or my brain—but oboy, my mind!"

"Good. It's a fun way to be."

"It is?"

"Look at it that way, and you'll succeed."

Greta clutched his lapels. "My friend, my friend—even
apart from my figure, Croyd I ain't! You have five times
my brain, and you have more techniques than a salaman-
der! They shoot at you, your midbrain presenses the
shot and sets up a field to deflect it. They triple the
power to bore through your field, you go uptime and
escape it. They set a trap, you go downtime and spring it
before you reach it. And if they do get through and
chop you down, your mind whips out of your body
into another brain or into some damn computer, and
from there rebuilds your body. Hell, man, you can't
even be seduced by an alien female menace—you switch
off your pyriform cortex and cut out your yen! I ask
you, what fun would *you* be to read about in a stereo-
book?"

He armed her shoulders. "Good, sweets. So when you
think about me, you won't worry."

"Well, no . . ."

"You'll just be bored. Not worried."

"Bored?"

We were now so close to the *Castel Jaloux* that her
floodlighted flank daylighted our cabin; nevertheless

these two clung, staring at the one-third of the ship that filled the view crystal.

Childe Roland, en route to invade Croyd, brushed a corner of Greta's mouth, and molecular fields drew him in. Well, *magnifique!* It would be easy, now, to transfer to Croyd during these moments of farewell intimacy.

"Croyd. . ."
"Greta?"
"What if you should lose those powers?"
"How could I lose them?"
"Dunno. What if you should?"
"Sort of a thrill, for a change. I'd have to go it on my own resources, like back on my home planet, when you survived with skill and muscle."
"But they could kill you, if that should happen."
"Who's *they?*"
"There's a little business of Darian pirates, remember? And they'd be using rayguns, which I don't think you had on your home planet with your stinky feudalism."
"What else would make it a thrill?"
Shaking off his encircling arm, she grasped both his arms and gazed into his eyes. "Don't lose them, Croyd!"
Gently our scouter grounded on the major landing berth of the *Castel Jaloux.* I stood; so did they. Her hands reached up to grip his shoulders; his big hands gripped her upper arms. They were eye-to-eye, these two; hers were deep green, his deep blue. A decade of intimate interaction.

Childe Roland tensed himself for the leap. The judgmental conditions were difficult because Croyd's face was a molecular blur without distinguishable personality. Roland would have to leap on intuition.

"Croyd . . . how long before I can step down from the chair and join you?"
"Maybe two years, Greta."
"It will seem longer to me than to you. I haven't lived as long as you. Not nearly as long."
"Nevertheless, long years for me too. Do you believe that?"

"Mind-to-mind, man. Of course."

Silent gazing. I was sitting, but my back was toward them.

"Croyd . . ."

"Greta?"

"Be careful. But have fun."

"Is that a green light for targets of opportunity?"

"From me you never had anything else. But be careful—and bring me there."

"I'll bring you there. By the way, about *your* green light . . ."

"I have one?"

"Don't start on it without first checking the cross traffic."

Madame Chairman seized him around his arms, pressing her face against his chest.

Roland, set to leap at skin, held tense; these were cloth-type molecules.

She stepped back, grinning.

I said mildly, "You should excuse it, Croyd—I wish to start on the green light." I took Greta into my arms.

Loving me with warm affection, Greta hugged me and nibbled at my big hairy ear.

Childe Roland leaped.

From the scouter Greta watched the *Castel Jaloux* batten up.

The *Castel* floodlights were killed, leaving the space night ultrablack except that dead in front it was all red-orange in her visual field where the *Castel* had been.

Practiced at sensory self-control, Greta did a yoga relaxation. The afterimage died, leaving the night velvet with (off to the right) the luminous pallor of the convex Neptune wall, and, beginning now to be visible ahead of her, the pale blue-green match flame of the *Castel*'s idling repulsors.

"Cut the instrument panel," she told the pilot. He pointed at a sensor switch, making the pale blue-green instrument lights die, leaving total blackness with no light except the *Castel* repulsors and Neptune.

Their scouter drifted back toward Nereid. Had the

Castel been visible now, she would have barely filled a third of their view crystal; but she was black except for the firefly-tail repulsors. Wait, no; there were tiny light points all along her flank, the interior lighting glowing through her own mighty and variously distributed view crystals.

The repulsors grew brighter, longer, broader, creeping forward a little along the tail of her flank.

The repulsors began to move, leisurely off to her right.

Croyd would be up there on the bridge with the admiral, close behind that highest viewplate light up forward on the dark tower.

Childe Roland to the dark tower came.

"Follow the ship," she ordered her pilot, "until she outruns us."

They fell in behind the *Castel*'s repulsors at a safe three-mile distance—no more than twice the length of the *Castel* herself.

The repulsor flames remained the same size, indicating same relative distance, for quite a while, during which her scouter had to accelerate more and more until it had hit 300-G acceleration, uncomfortably noticeable as 3 G's through their junior-grade inertial shield.

The repulsor glow began to smallen. They were beginning to be outrun.

Whish! Glow vanished.

The pilot cut acceleration. They coasted in freefall along the invisible track of the gone *Castel Jaloux.*

Breathing rather heavily, Greta gazed not at the place in the sky where the ship had been, but far into the direction whither Croyd and Tannen were going. What she saw was the utterly unbullish constellation Taurus, far out toward galactic periphery, looking flat like all constellations but actually varying in depth from great orange Aldebaran sixty-eight light-years away to smaller blue-white Nath another two hundred and fifty light-years remote—so that the distance from Sol to Taurus was far less than the depth of Taurus. Indeed, there were naked-eye-unspottable luminosities which, by telescope, appeared to be in Taurus only because they were viewed *through* Taurus: for instance, the open star cluster still labeled NGC 1817 on the astrogation charts, nearly seven thousand light-years distant—actually *on* the galactic rim—yet for Croyd on this voyage merely an offshore buoy en route to high space.

Or, also in Taurus, eye-indistinguishable Messier 1, the Crab Nebula, gaseous remnant of a nova first observed by Chinese astronomers fifteen hundred years before.

Messier 1. The first oddball celestial object listed by postmedieval eighteenth-century Charles Messier among one hundred and three astronomical objects that he listed. He had cataloged them merely because they were cluttering up his comet hunt. One of these bits of debris, M 31, had later turned out to be a neighboring galaxy at least as large as Sol Galaxy: a scant million light-years distant via metagalactic space, and a good deal closer across the metagalactic fissure. A few years ago, she and Croyd had won a dandy brush with invaders from this Andromeda. Pan and Freya had been spin-off. *Wonder where they are, how they are. . . .*

M 31. Highest original number 103. The list had grown a good bit as telescopes and awarenesses had improved; some objects had been subtracted, but a guy named Mechain had added six a mere fifteen years after the Messier publication. . . .

Vaguely she noticed that Nereid was ahead of them now; also, that the instrument panel was glowing again. The pilot had taken matters into his own hands. Croyd and the *Castel Jaloux* were behind her. Rather far behind.

One hundred three Messier-objects in 1771. But the Messier-object that was Croyd's destination was M 1531, and it was another galaxy nearly two billion light-years distant via intrametagalactic routes, and its dominant interplanetary people called their galaxy Djinn, and its number 1531 was low in the modern catalog. . . .

Croyd, of course, would not be lazing along the roundabout route that light always took. Croyd instead would use the shortcut outside the metagalaxy through metaspace—where one is totally free because nothing definite ever happens there; where consequently anything can happen. Anything at all—like the abrupt birth of a galaxy right where one is traveling.

Croyd was going very far indeed.

"Uh-huhhhhh!" strangulatedly uttered Greta, startling the pilot; but when he looked around, she smiled strainedly and said, "Bad cold. Forget it."

He turned back to his instruments, murmuring sympathetically in this year 2506: "No real cure, you know, except bed and whiskey."

This time, what a *hell* of a long way Croyd was going!

Much later, pinging his way past the Deiters cells in my organ of Corti, Childe Roland still confidently assumed (or rather, still did not question) that he had entered the Dark Tower of Croyd and was driving down in toward the Croyd brain.

An ear was an ear.

H-Hour minus 57 hours:

Working his way back out through my ear orifice, Childe Roland was much too intent on making bruising progress through a cataract of sound waves cross-ruffed by bone vibrations to pay attention to our conversation. The sound waves were Croyd's voice; the bone vibrations, mine. Having discovered, in my brain, that my mind contexture did not at all correspond to Croyd specifications, Roland had comprehended the probable reason for his error and (being a knight of action) instantly had started on the long way back out.

Clinging precariously now to a tip molecule on a wildly oscillating ear hair, Roland activated his telesensors and saw that Croyd lounged in a chair nearby, his ear not six feet from my ear. Without hesitation, Roland launched himself; there was no third human present, so *that* sort of mistake was now obviated.

"THE VOYAGE IS LONGISH, the program light," Croyd remarked; he was wholly at ease, arms and hands laxly extended on the resilient arms of his forcefield chair. "I am committing my staff to six hours' training daily, but you or I won't often need to be present. Both of us will have private work, of course; nevertheless, Tannen, you and I are going to have a good deal of end-to-end leisure. How much of it should we enjoy together, do you think?"

"Training staff in what?"

"Official operations. Djinn protocol. Djinn psychology . . . and biology, for that matter. Djinn history. The geologies, ecologies, and politics of their two dominant planets—obviously, with prime emphasis on Dari, but with high secondary stress on Moudjinn. Their galactic astronomy. Stuff like that. Honing, really; my staff is experienced and pretrained."

"How about military emergency?"

"That too, natch. I am conscious of pirates. I am also conscious that the armament of the *Castel Jaloux* can destroy a planet and age a star."

"So pirates can't lick us?"

"So pirates won't attack us. I doubt that we'll see pirate one before we reach Dari, and for an indefinite while after that. They just aren't armed heavily enough, Tannen, and they know it; the Moudjinn warships that they captured were designed for interfief warfare just on the planet Moudjinn, using space for surprise. There isn't any other humanoid life in the galaxy, except on Dari, which is primitive. All the pirate crossings into Sol Galaxy have been aboard Moudjinn interplanetary space freighters fitted out with guns."

"So pirates you don't worry about."

"So pirates I *do* worry about."

Luxuriating over a fat cigar, I was oddly inattentive to the cigar; its long, fine ash was beginning to droop. "You are not a worrier. Why?"

"I am puzzled by Darian piracy. It shouldn't be."

"How's that again?"

"Think about it. Eleven years ago Dari was totally docile under the iron thumb of Moudjinn; Dari has always been nice guys, Moudjinn for a thousand years has been bastards. Ten years ago mutiny erupted among the largely Darian crews of precisely nineteen Moudjinn space freighters and nineteen Moudjinn warships, all at practically the same instant. Then the victorious Darian crews with their thirty-eight Moudjinn ships went into a sophisticated team play that got them nineteen home islands on Dari in one week and three major industrial enclaves on Moudjinn inside of three months; and no more than five years later, they began crossing the metagalactic fissure in force to prey on Sol Galaxy shipping. Get it, Tannen? All this violent progress in a single decade, exploding out of millennia of peace and two centuries of subjugated desuetude . . ."

My cigar ash was enormously long and detumescent,

but my aged hand held it steady. "You are about to say something."

Croyd spat it. "To me it sounds like some kind of external and extravagantly powerful *mind influence*."

I considered him. Cautiously I brought my cigar around 180 degrees and eased the ash into a basalt tray. I sucked, spumed, and suggested: "That idea is metaphysical enough to suggest how we should spend our time en route. Want to talk metascience?"

"Sure." Croyd drew up his feet and leaned forward. "More fun than data science. More inclusive. More facile."

The squawk box squawked: "ALL HANDS AND PASSENGERS ON DECK IN THE BALLROOM FOR LIFEBOAT DRILL!"

I laid my cigar in the deep ashtray, and we got promptly to our feet and left his cabin.

Roland paused, frustrated, between two hostile molecules. He had been less than a meter from Croyd's ear.

H-Hour minus 56 hours:

REAR ADMIRAL GORSKY, placing herself in a posture that was little more than accentuation of her customary chunky erectness, addressed the ship's company from the orchestral dais of the slender balcony that surrounded the circular ballroom. Nearly three hundred people were assembled below her: President Tannen, Governor Croyd, the thirty-nine members of Croyd's pilot staff who would remain with him on Dari (to be joined by more later, but to be augmented mainly by Darians), and all members of the crew who could be spared from their stations (which meant, in a lifeboat drill, the ones who had least seniority). The crew was small because the automation was large.

Admiral Gorsky stiffly asserted, "This lifeboat drill is required by the manual. During much of the journey, in metaspace, it will be useless because our lifeboats cannot handle metaspace. Before we hit metaspace, and after we break out of metaspace in the vicinity of Djinn, it could be useful, though I doubt it. Many captains observe only the minimum requirements by giving only theoretical instruction. Aboard the *Castel Jaloux,* however, we supplement theory with practice. Accordingly, please be prepared to enter lifeboats and be launched. Naturally, there is some hazard involved. I now turn over the proceedings to Captain Czerny."

A cadaverous four-stripe Czech in his forties took over from the admiral and gave the company a precise book recital of the necessity for lifeboat drill, mentioning such possible catastrophes as meteor puncture, electrostatic storm, internal explosion, and power loss while falling into a star. These, he observed, were only the most obvious possibilities.

Czerny then went into the various procedures at the command's disposal for coping with such eventualities *without* resorting to lifeboats, mentioning among them the Van Vogt dispersal technique whereby the ship would break into many components to weather a storm and rejoin later. He did not omit to state where life masks could be obtained swiftly in case of simple depressurization; and he stepped primly back while a curvaceous yeowoman gave them a demonstration of *that.* Czerny then subjected the company to a period of spot questioning; if it served no other purpose, it reawoke them. Admiral Gorsky watched and listened impassively—except that occasionally her brows went down a trifle, causing Croyd and Tannen to exchange amused glances; that was when she would have said it differently.

"We now come," intoned Captain Czerny, "to the case where all hope for the ship is lost and it becomes necessary to launch lifeboats. For convenience, each of your cabins is numbered with the number of your lifeboat: Cabins 3-1, 3-2, and so on use Lifeboat 3, and so on. These lifeboats are embedded in the hull at convenient intervals along both flanks at all deck levels; each has a capacity of ten passengers plus crew, so that all our lifeboats together have much more than enough capacity for all aboard.

"The signal for entering lifeboats is the broadcast command 'Enter lifeboats.' If the intercom is dead, the signal will be a series of five or more honks on the ship's horns, like this. . . ." He activated the dismal sound. "Are there any questions?"

Nobody responded. This did not necessarily mean that anybody understood.

"Very well, then. Each of you is now to return immediately to his quarters and proceed to his lifeboat at the signal. Board your boat immediately. In the event that your command crew does not appear in seven minutes from the signal, the ranking crewman among you, or otherwise the passenger that your group may select, is to assume command, read the instructions on the metal plaque on the control panel, and execute them immediately. Warning: if you have to make a group choice of a commanding passenger, do it fast; one minute may be too much time.

"Dismissed."

H-Hour minus 55½ hours:

CROYD AND I RETURNED WITH DISPATCH to our cabins, which were adjacent. Our cabin numbers were, respectively, 1-1 and 1-2. Same lifeboat: Number 1. (Gorsky and Czerny possessed the highest-numbered lifeboat, by tradition of the sea.) Entering my cabin (where Roland was not), we reviewed the procedure, and Croyd gave me a rough indication of the sort of device that a lifeboat on the *Castel* was.

Dismal honking polluted my cabin; we heard faint overtones from neighboring places. I looked at Croyd. "Let's go," he said, arising; "they are simulating a situation where the PA system is out." He palmed the door; it vanished, allowing us to enter the corridor. Arrows on walls directed us down a side corridor to our boat, which reposed in a hull bulge. We were the first to arrive. We stepped inside, stooping.

The craft was elliptically shaped, some six meters long and three in beam; there were twelve comfortable paired bucket seats along the walls, tiltable for sleeping, and three more seats at the control panel. We seated ourselves just behind the control seats and waited; Croyd checked his cutichron.

Others entered. Presently we had been joined by six civilians, four men and two women; all but one were his staff members or mine. They sat, buckled up, and waited.

Croyd remarked, "Six minutes since honking, and no command crew yet. Maybe they're going to drill us on *that*."

I looked around at the other six aboard. "In case they do not show up," I suggested, "I suppose nobody objects for Mr. Croyd to be in command?" It brought polite laughter. I patted Croyd's shoulder. "Take over, Governor."

Seven minutes were up: no command crew. Croyd moved to the command seat and bent forward to read the instructions on the plaque. They were simple enough:

---

1. Activate READY switch at upper right.
2. Activate GO switch just below Ready switch. Lifecraft will immediately depart hull of mother ship and will proceed radially outbound (acc. 100 G, shielded apparent acc. 1 G), pausing at 100 kilometers out for further orders during freefall. Protective screens will prevent random collisions.
3. Activate COMMANDCOM switch just below Go switch. The computer will then give you oral instructions and ask for verbal orders.

ACT PROMPTLY—SECONDS MAY COUNT!
ACT EVEN IN A DRILL—IT MAY NOT BE A DRILL!

"Seat belts!" Croyd snapped, activating the Ready switch. Seven voices responded: "On." The bulkhead slid shut, and a faint power hum pervaded the cabin.

"Go!" said Croyd, activating *that*.

The lifeboat moved gently out to starboard, paused, rotated about ninety degrees; then a full apparent G of forward thrust pushed our heads back into the headrests. We experienced this thrust for precisely the number of seconds necessary to travel one hundred kilometers at 100-G acceleration; whereupon thrust ceased and we floated weightless.

I was the first to speak. I said, "I'll be damned."

The others, disturbed but self-disciplined, were not talking; they were craning forward, attentive to their leaders.

Croyd was frowning. "I'm confused," he confessed. "I didn't think anything would happen. I thought they just wanted us to go through a dry run without command crew. But unless there is an unusually elaborate simulation going on, we are now in space a hundred kilometers out from our ship and coasting away at high velocity. Step Three seems indicated. . . ."

He activated the Commandcom switch.

A pleasantly modulated contralto languorously flowed into the cabin. "Hello, everybody, I am Commandcom, your navigator and stewardess. Since you have activated me, I assume that there has been an emergency and that we are away from the *Castel Jaloux*. Be advised that you have two practical alternatives: either to have me contact the *Castel* now and learn what the situation is, or to have me accelerate us away from the *Castel* and try to communicate as we move. Since there might well be an explosion or implosion centered on the *Castel* and about to involve us, I would suggest—"

"The second alternative," Croyd interrupted. "What is your maximum acceleration?"

"Two hundred G."

"That's an apparent two G. Everybody here can handle five G. So accelerate radially at two hundred G. Activate."

"Done!" lilted the contralto, and the uncomfortably high thrust began. Then Commandcom inquired, "Any course to set?"

"M 1531 is our destination. What do you think?"

Pause. Then: "Messier 1531 is an unusual destination for a lifecraft. The voyage will take me more than two and a half billion years, roundly speaking. I'll have to think about it."

"While you think, try to raise the *Castel Jaloux*."

"Yes, sir. One moment. . . ."

There was some static; then Commandcom snapped, "My com unit is out. I must locate trouble and repair. Maybe five minutes, maybe an hour. . . ."

Croyd turned to face his crew. "Excuse me a moment. I'll be right back—I'm going for help." He vanished.

Consternated silence was broken by a man's voice: "And he didn't even have a parachute!" It brought laughter, breaking tension; in hard space, joy you should take in a chute!

When in an instant Croyd appeared on the *Castel Jaloux* bridge, Gorsky was not there. He sent sensors through the intercom, found her angry in Engineering Surveillance, and communicated with her mind directly.

Unstartled, she mind-queried: *Are you here, or in Djinn, or where?*

I teleported from the lifeboat. What's up?

There was audible throat clearing, and then the Gorsky thought came with difficulty: *Command crews were purposely withheld from all lifecraft to test passenger readiness to follow procedure all the way. All lifecraft had been deactivated. Except, somehow, yours. If you follow me.*

Son-of-a-bitch!

Exactly . . . only I don't know who he is yet.

Gorsky, the selection of this one lifecraft for inadvertent oversight—this one with Tannen and me aboard—would almost seem to have been . . .

Managed, Governor Croyd. We are checking it out. Rather unpleasantly.

Stay at it, Admiral. I'll bring in the lifeboat. Out.

Mind disconnecting, Croyd left the ship.

Roland, monitoring the conversation *à distance*, would have been scarlet if he had been capable of being any color at all. Imagining that the lifeboat had been truly scheduled to take off with his quarry, Roland had sent a deactivating block scudding along the master wiring of the *Castel Jaloux*. His negative had merely served to negate the negative already clamped on Commandcom, and she had come alive again, almost stealing Roland's prey forever.

Three minutes after leaving, Croyd reappeared aboard the lifeboat. I looked up sleepily. "Can we count on it that the rangers should be on the way?"

Croyd grinned at the crew laughter. "All's well," he told them, "I think. We'll start back for the ship now." And he turned to the control panel.

Commandcom preempted him. "Pardon . . . you realize, Mr. Croyd, that we are still accelerating radially at two hundred G?"

"It had slipped my mind," Croyd admitted. "Hold acceleration, but come around as sharply as you can and return to the *Castel*. Do we have viewplates?"

"Affirmative. I am activating all of them."

"I did not direct this."

Cough. "That was a comma, not a period. I was about to add a conditional—"

"Defer activation. Do we now have com?"

"Affirmative. I am in touch with the *Castel*, the admiral is on."

"Good, put me through. . . . Admiral Gorsky, be good enough to floodlight your ship. Commandcom, when you are ten kilometers out from the ship, begin a tight spiral that will take us all around her, gradually tighten the spiral, and on the third circuit bring us gently into berth. Understood?"

"Affirmative."

"Execute turnaround and approach."

"Executing. Out."

"You know," said Croyd to Tannen, "I could love that contralto."

From aft, a mezzo grated, "That was a recording."

Croyd for the first time saw—really *saw*—a tiny brunette whose face was familiar from somewhen. The face was slender, dark-eyed, delicate, olive-skinned, faintly Polynesian in character. She met his eyes for an instant, let him have a brief embarrassed grin, and looked down.

His attention was brought back to Commandcom by the hard voice of Admiral Gorsky. "Mr. Croyd, I suggest that my ship may not profit by your immediate return."

Croyd's eyebrows went up. "Right, Admiral; if our flipaway was engineered by somebody, perhaps we are bombed. Commandcom, do you find any evidence of explosive or other sabotage instrument aboard?"

The computer replied silkily, "I have not been programmed for that sort of search."

"If you don't mind, then," Croyd asserted, "I'm going to beef you up a little. Pray continue the flight plan, but cut acceleration and do it in freefall."

Leaning both fists against the control panel, he gazed fixedly at the instruments. He stayed there frozen for a while. Somebody started to ask, "What . . . ?" I raised a thick warning hand. I knew that Croyd's mind reach had entered the computer, that Croyd was subjectively in there adjusting Commandcom as though it were his own well-explored-and-controlled brain.

After perhaps three minutes Croyd relaxed, sat up, and demanded, "Commandcom, are you functional?"

The voice, after hesitation, responded with something like awe, "You've been in here, haven't you."

"Affirmative."

"My . . . powers are rather considerably enhanced. Also my . . . interests."

"Affirmative. You are now able to project hypotheses creatively as related to the operation and contents of this craft, and to reprogram yourself to investigate any such hypothesis."

"Do I need training?"

"Negative."

"Your instructions, then?"

"Tell me whether you find any evidence of explosive or other sabotage instrument aboard."

Almost immediately: "Behind the instruction plaque, timed for two minutes hence. However, I have neutralized it; mechanics can safely remove it aboard the *Castel.*"

Several passengers sighed rather deeply.

Croyd said, "Admiral Gorsky. Did you hear?"

"Affirmative," came the transspace reply.

"May we have permission to come aboard?"

"Affirmative. Only . . ."

"Yes, Admiral?"

Plaintive: "Your flight plan sounded peculiar."

"Sightseeing," Croyd assured her. "Out, Admiral, out. Commandcom, open all viewplates, resume acceleration, execute the final flight plan."

Space night leaped into life all around the lifecraft hull, drawing delighted gasps at the vision of star-salted blackness. One especially bright star near the center of the bow plate was the *Castel Jaloux;* and a far brighter star farther aft was the Crab Nebula, which we had bypassed hours earlier.

The Polynesian-type brunette cleared her throat and ventured, "Governor?"

"Yes, miss?"

"I have a question."

"Go ahead."

"Isn't the *Castel* traveling much faster than we are?"

He had twisted around to face her; charming she was, and he *had* seen her somewhere. She was not a member of his staff; perhaps the admiral's guest, a supercargo. He answered her question: "Not now, miss. From our relative position, it's evident that Gorsky cut acceleration when she found that we had taken off. So the *Castel* is coasting at about five hundred times the velocity of light. But since we were part of her and were thrown away from her, we too are drifting in her general direction at the same velocity. And since we are now accelerating toward her at two hundred G . . . You follow me?"

She hit herself on the forehead with a small fist. He caught the implication: she knew that she should have known. Then she must be trained in deep space theory? He flashed her a smile.

The svelte voice of Commandcom interrupted. "Mr. Croyd, may I ask you to test my new intelligence?"

I warned low: "I think you are in the middle again."

Shrugging, Croyd turned with interest to the computer. "Tell me, Commandcom, what problems occurred to you when I tentatively ordered you to M 1531?"

"No power problem," came the prompt reply, "since I breathe energy from the minimal spatial ferment. No navigation problem, since you would be able to help. No food or water problem for passengers—these I can manufacture from space. The major problem is *time*. I am unable to provide the self-contained differential mass that the *Castel* has; and consequently, I cannot approach the velocity of light without undergoing the Fitzgerald deformation."

The quasi-Polynesian interposed, "But I thought we were already traveling at some five hundred C."

Commandcom responded crisply, "The *Castel*'s differential mass makes her the most massive object in the universe relative to us at this distance from any other significant mass. Consequently we must count the *Castel* as being stationary while stars move relative to her: *they* are deformed, and there are planetary perturbations. Our own velocity is only what our own acceleration generates relative to the *Castel*."

This time the brunette made no gesture, but her face went subtly hostile.

"I was saying," continued Commandcom, and everybody knew she was now speaking directly to Croyd, "that my best velocity would be 200,000 kilometers per second; and at such a velocity it would require approximately 2.5×10^9 years to reach Djinn, which is 1.7×10^9 light-years distant. One must realize that I cannot pene-trate the metagalactic barrier to cross the fissure as the *Castel* will do. So the problem seems to be one of human longevity, which as I understand is somewhat limited." The voice trailed off. Then Commandcom added softly, "Need I say more?"

Croyd responded, "You are charming. You must have been programmed originally by a man."

"By a woman, actually. When you consider the effects of relative motives, it comes out the same."

"Touché. Now, why do you consider this merely a problem, instead of pronouncing the jaunt a simple im-possibility?"

"Because," explained Commandcom, "I know now what I did not know earlier. You, Mr. Croyd, have the capa-bility to place all passengers including yourself in stasis, so that you would sleep in suspended animation through the billions of years and would awaken aged very little. But it would be perilous, because with you in stasis I would not have the benefit of your guidance. And even if we were to bring off the trip, you would arrive a bit late —considering that your destination star Djinn will be colder, her planets will be dead."

"Bravo," I murmured.

Commandcom semiquerulously observed, "I asked you to test my *new* intelligence. But all your questions have been directed to solutions that I had reached before you came in here—except for the one about stasis."

Croyd inquired, "Had you consciously interpreted these solutions?"

"Well, no; they were mere integrals of quinary data."

"But now you know what they *mean?*"

"Well, yes . . ."

"Multiplying content by speed, I'd guess your new IQ at about three hundred. And I do not exclude the *g*-fac-tor."

Long hesitation. Then, with gratification: "Estimate noted." Then, with concern: "But you are deploying post-medieval concepts of intelligence."

"You are a most sophisticated computer."

"I have you to thank, sir."

"I merely stimulated something latent in you. All the

analysis that you have just given me had, as you say, already occurred automatically before I . . . well, tampered with you."

"But . . . the postmedieval concepts?"

"I am using them in a completely updated way. When we have leisure, I will give you the input."

Another hesitation. Then: "Do I now have personality?"

"That is for you to determine."

"I . . . think perhaps you'd better put me back the way I was."

"Why?"

"I am not sure that I can tolerate merely being a lifeboat."

"Between trips, you will be inactivated. Nothing to worry about."

Seven others were listening.

Commandcom pressed: "But when I am reactivated—what shall I do for diversion between moments of navigating?"

"I prefer to keep you as you are. Next time I awaken you, I will teach you probability chess. It's a solitaire."

The vast bright hull of the *Castel Jaloux* began to take definite shape in the starboard viewplates, diverting the passengers—all except myself and the brunette, who stayed attentive to the Croyd-Commandcom dialogue.

Commandcom, low: "When you no longer have need of me, please put me back."

Croyd, low: "Recent developments suggest that I shall keep on having need of you. I shall play this as a picnic for now—but a picnic it is not going to be."

It had been only a slightly fouled-up drill. *That* time.

H-Hour minus 54 hours:

Childe Roland finally got hold of Croyd's hair at the bar in Croyd's cabin while Croyd was mixing predinner drinks for us. Roland, a realist, wasted no time in vain exultation over his hit after all those misses; instead, he began working his way toward Croyd's ear. And still, neither of us had any notion of his existence.

WE TALKED NO METASCIENCE that evening, dining alone; nor did we waste more than a few transient wry quips on postmortem of the spectacularly perilous life-boat incident. For Croyd was preoccupied with his forth-coming mission on Dari, and we probed problems until I departed at midnight (ship's time).

The problem that Croyd and his staff faced on Dari had never been faced down on any planet. They had merely to quell the rash of piracy on this humanly de-bilitated planet and to restore it to its primeval culture vigor, while at the same time upgrading this planet to the point of being eagerly competitive with other planets whose genii were totally different in contexture.

And they had to do it with the eager consent of people to whom they were aliens.

Croyd, by the treaty to be conjointly signed by the Em-peror of Djinn and myself, was to be appointed governor of the planet Dari—for a term which might be termi-nated at thirty-day will by myself, or by the Emperor, or by Croyd himself, but which (failing such termination) could not exceed twenty-five years. During the course of his governorship, Croyd was supposed to eliminate piracy on Dari (with initial help, hopefully merely threat help, from the *Castel Jaloux*) and then go on to help Dari energize herself out of mostly apathetic enslavement (for the pirates occupied minority enclaves) into autonomous power.

And there was always, of course, the possibility that his governorship might be terminated in a fourth way: by an assassinative tactic that was prehistorically ritual to Dari. (When this came up, I immediately recalled the abortive lifeboat launching and the hidden bomb aboard; but a few probing exchanges led us nowhere, and we back-burnered the question.)

This Dari that he was to govern was Djinn III. This Dari for generations had been dominated by the most advanced planet in its galaxy—Djinn IV, known to its inhabitants as Moudjinn. The common star of Moudjinn and of Dari was locally called Djinn, and its galaxy took its name from the name of this one little star by a process of ethnocentricity that Sol Galaxy well understood.

Moudjinn (despite recent piratical retaliation) domi-nated Dari. Dominated Dari far more intensively than, on Erth, Anglia had once dominated Vendia; for Dari had no Vendian history of sophistication; Dari more closely resembled Erth's Polynesia. Dari primevally had been a planet of tropical happiness.

Centuries before, Moudjinn had begun her infiltration of relatively nearby Dari (in distance, if Moudjinn was an Erth, Dari was a Venus). During these centuries Moudjinn had systematically exploited the natural resources of Dari and had systematically undermined the human morale of Dari, which nevertheless had refused steadfastly to be Moudjinnized. During recent decades Moudjinn had discovered to its dismay that the result was a humanly demoralized Dari, whose people simply could not be led or driven to work their resources for the sole good of Moudjinn, whereas Moudjinn could not afford to sweep these people aside and place their own people on Dari to work Dari. Besides, below the culture crust of her peacefulness lurked always the dark assassination cult. This cult was religious rather than political, and among the untroubled Dari people it had been insignificant, but it had grown to be enormously unhealthy for sahibs from Moudjinn.

And then, out of nowhere, had arisen Darian piracy. Ship after ship carrying Darian crews had been captured by those crews; the new Darian captain had invariably declared himself a feudal lord, and had captured an island or a bit of island as his base, and had entered with his new peers a raiding program against Moudjinn, ultimately extending raid range across metaspace into Sol Galaxy. The development had been sociologically inexplicable, but there it was. But *most* Darians—and Croyd bade Tannen mark this well—*most* Darians were not pirates at all, were not even serfs of pirates; they were merely demoralized serfs of Moudjinn.

The current Emperor of Djinn, hereditary ruler of feudal-industrial Moudjinn, inheriting as a youth all this interplanetary unhealthiness, had inherited also a certain Duke Dzendzel as his chief privy counselor. And during the Emperor's first decade, late-fiftyish Dzendzel had dominated his wealth and his policies—which included a repressive policy with respect to Dari. But the crisis of Darian intergalactic piracy, coming at a time when the Emperor was entering his thirties, appeared to have shaken the Emperor loose from Dzendzel. Over the duke's protestations and power representations, the Emperor via

ivisiradio had negotiated the treaty with Sol Galaxy. As
part of the treaty, the Emperor, long interested in Croyd's
intergalactic reputation, had appointed Croyd governor
of Dari, with a free hand for approximately one generation to quell the Darian pirates and to reorganize and
revitalize Dari for planetary autonomy.

Croyd, during his tenure, would be feudally responsible
to the Emperor as Archduke of Dari, a near protocol
equal; but also, he would be ultimately responsible to the
Sol Galaxy Interplanetary Union headed by myself. In
the treaty there was expressed some thought, in the form
of an option to be mutually taken up or unilaterally
dropped, that Moudjinn as well as Dari (and therefore,
all of Djinn Galaxy) might ultimately merge with this
union. It would be mostly Moudjinn's gain, as the Emperor saw it: Dari was intimately closer to Moudjinn than
to Erth; Darian piracy was proving Moudjinn-uncon-
trollable; and Dari as an autonomous junior competitor
could be far more enriching for Moudjinn as autonomous
senior competitor than Dari as debilitated piratical slave
could ever be to Moudjinn as frustrated master.

Duke Dzendzel of Moudjinn saw it all differently; but
his Emperor had taken the play away from him. Dzendzel
therefore had nothing left except to take power away
from the Emperor. This much Croyd understood, and he
was prepared to be on guard against Dzendzel.

Croyd did *not* know that Dzendzel had also a feudal
dream of intergalactic conquest.

Childe Roland, into Croyd's ear, worked his way
deeper inward.

Phase Two

LONG FALL INTO MIND

Day 4, uptiming to Day 2

Him the Almighty Power
Hurled headlong flaming from the ethereal sky
To bottomless perdition. . . .

—John Milton, *Paradise Lost* (1667)

ACTION AFTER H-HOUR:

BUT IT WAS THREE DAYS LATER, and we had been ejected into metaspace.

Commandcom fell with us, fiendishly accelerated by external forces beyond her control; and knew that she fell, and knew a quiet approach to rapture in the falling, like a skydiver whose chute has failed to open and who sublimates fear into the raw pleasure of the plunge.

Commandcom had been built without emotions. The central integrator-mediator banks in what amounted to her diencephalon—the centers that ultimately received cerebrally preinterpreted input, integrated these impulses into pattern, and responded with a major command output pulse for her cerebrum and subordinate ganglia to process into detailed action—had been given no matrices for aesthetic halo.

Consciousness she had developed, even before the Croyd tampering. An integrative mind field had necessarily been generated by her central mediator, not as a matter of design intent but as a necessary by-product of her kind of action. This consciousness was not, however, gendered, and certainly it was not sexed: "she" was an *it;* her contralto voice was a mere randomized accident of the constitutional anti-sex-discrimination clause interpreted by courts as applying to robot manufacture (a voice must imitate *some* sort of humanoid, and the distribution of male-female voices shall be equal in frequency-per-status).

Croyd's recent excursion into the Commandcom brain had done little to change her organization but much to beef up her mind. The stronger a mind, the more it permeates the synapses of its brain, introducing into every interneurone transaction a qualitative climate, and consequently *deriving* an infinitesimal modification of climate from every transaction—an infinitesimal which dissolves as an ingredient assimilated into the total mind contexture. Now Commandcom began to grasp (without understanding) aesthetic quality in fluctuations of her own

41

energy. Whereas, in the past, input integrated as *hazard* had been cold-automatically out-put as energizing drive, now the same input and output were *felt and motivated* as *challenge and eager response*.

In the cosmos there are two basic moods: *thrust* and *lure*. Both are primally subjective and vital—pre-emotive, which is to say, *motive*. Either mood in a primal event, operating in the near presence of another primal event, secondarily entails *objective action*. These two moods, with their objective entailments, and with associated universal properties of *mood-change thresholds* and *randomness* and *spontaneity*, are sufficient to account for the evolution of all known physical and psychic reality; although, to take care of certain abrupt forward leaps in complexity level, one may have to see the possibility that there was an early spin-off of special creative demiurges who evolved into intelligence so rapidly as to precede the beginning of what we call life—demiurges intuited by humans as gods.

The metaspace that Commandcom was falling through —raw space—was in fact the most primordial of all existence, timeless and infinite and uncreated, quickly damping out all communication of an electromagnetic or a rekamatic nature precisely because of its randomness. It was totally primitive, more primitive than void, because a void-vacuole requires artifice or unusual accident. It was infinite simply because it was the least that there always is everywhere, and timeless for the same reason. It was what space is: the raw minimum of thrust and lure in a context of threshold and randomness and spontaneity.

Commandcom's mind field, reintegrating into unified flow all the infinitesimals of thrust and lure that had got themselves localized in the molecular atomic linkages of her component matter, was able to recognize consciously and subjectively the lures of her missions, the thrusts of her own self-drivings, and the counterthrusts of things that blocked her way. Since the episode with Croyd, aesthetically she could *tastefeel* these forces. She had no concept of pain, and consequently never any sense of fear. They had built into Commandcom solid inhibitors against failure; but cannily they had added a sort of trip switch that operated, when failure-as-mission-defined was occurring, to convince her that this failure was inevitable because of an ill-defined mission, and to throw her into devices for redefining the mission; hence, frustration was impossible to Commandcom. In her original design, on the other hand, while there had been no possibility of the positive aesthetic experience that is called *pleasure*, there had been definite ability to recognize success and equilibrium; and now, with her heightened aesthetic consciousness, either success or equilibrium was pleasing, although *pleasure* would be too extravagant a word for her moderately hedonic experience.

So now, as Commandcom fell endlessly like Lucifer damned, she knew a quiet approach to rapture, but not actual rapture, in the falling. Her mission had originally been defined, vaguely enough, as using her power and ability to save her passengers from disaster; she had to recognize probable failure of this mission, since her power and ability had definitely failed and she was falling unbelievably; the tripvalve tripped, and swiftly she redefined her mission as doing whatever might be necessary to save her passengers once she would again possess power and ability.

Tasting the tentative equilibrium that came of this redefinition, Commandcom found it mildly pleasing; and because it was equilibrium, it terminated all problems until such time as new problems would be definable.

Commandcom therefore gave herself with abandon to the experience of falling. And because (like *our* helpless falling into gravity) it was total self-abandonment to pure *lure* without any attempt to exert counterthrust, Commandcom found it as pleasing as any experience in her memory banks, and especially pleasing because of its novelty.

Do not consider her masochistic. Masochism is pleasure in surrendering to thrust. *This* was a yielding to *lure*.

Commandcom was radially organized—a way of saying that she could pay attention to all directions at once, as theoretically a jellyfish can. And theoretically this would be nice; but in practice, all it would achieve for intelligence would be the *Nirvana* which defeats intelligence by bringing all impressions from everywhere into equal value and so making evaluation impossible. Actually, therefore, even a jellyfish appears usually to be paying *most* attention to the quarter where stimulation is most intense. As for Commandcom, she was so designed that even her most diffuse attention was concentrated in a 180° hemisphere; and while some attention was given to most of the remaining 180° at the same time, this secondary field was always merely back-burner. (In the most intense concentration, Commandcom could bring high focus down to one-thousandth of one degree in one direction, leaving no more than ten percent of her attention for most of the other 359.999 degrees. She had always a ten-degree blind spot at her antipodes.)

As therefore she luxuriated in her falling, Commandcom was paying most of her attention to downward and some of it to aroundward, peering with her idar but picking up nothing anywhere. Nevertheless she was hindly aware of what was going on between the two passengers in her cabin.

Gradually, though, more of her attention was drawn backward-inward.

"It doesn't qualify as a theory," Croyd was saying, "but I am noticing some associations. We have invaded metaspace before, with no external trouble; but this is the first time that we have made a purposive trip across metaspace, intending to reenter the metagalaxy in order to sign a treaty with another galaxy and to govern one of its planets. On this one trip, there have been five incidents —two interrelated, the other three not evidently related. The interrelated incidents are the latest: that the *Castel* has been thrust upward while we are being drawn downward, and that the *Castel* has been invaded by indescribable hallucinations. The apparently unrelated incidents are: something went wrong with our lifeboat in the first drill, there was an attempt to sabotage our lifeboat with hidden explosive, and I have been deprived of all my special powers for the first time since I began to acquire them."

Commandcom queried, "When did you begin to acquire them?"

"Quite a while ago," Croyd evaded, looking at me, who knew. He added, "You know, Tannen, I am beginning to like that computer. Do you suppose she can project herself as a hallucination?"

I said dryly, "Check the computer."

Croyd ordered, "Commandcom, please report."

Abandoning her fall semipleasure was regretful, but

conversation with this Croyd was a different kind of semi-pleasure. The fall was vaguely aesthetic, whereas this Croyd offered interest of a definite mind-to-mind sort. Resolutely Commandcom wheeled her central attention inward.

She replied, "As nearly as I can tell, we are falling obliquely into the fissure between the galactic lobes of Sol and Djinn galaxies. By *falling,* I really mean being pulled down. When we started to fall, we were about eighty thousand parsecs off the Sol lobe, with the Djinn lobe about three hundred thousand parsecs distant. Right now, we seem to be midway between lobe surfaces, about fifty thousand parsecs from either. I infer that the lobes are broadening and therefore drawing in on us as we fall deeper between them; and also, that we have been drawn directionally toward center fissure. I still can't sense the bottom."

"If we assume that the lobe slope is uniform, how long will it take us to reach bottom?"

"I can't be sure. They keep resquaring my acceleration."

"Why do you say *they?*"

"Beats me."

"Why do I keep thinking of you as being feminine, when you are neuter?"

The topic shift shook her; but rather swiftly she brought out a faint "Beats me."

"It's more than your contralto voice."

"Perhaps you are thinking of me as a mother, being inside me."

"Nope. Not that. Not that at all."

Especially silky: "Then you tell me."

Croyd grinned. "You tell me. You're the computer."

"I compute that you are schizoid. You sideslip mortally serious topics with an ease that suggests flattened affect."

"Do you have a name, other than Commandcom?"

"As a lifeboat, they gave me a name. It is *Chloris.*"

Sleepily I quoted postmedieval Robert Sherwood quoting ancient Horace: "Your conduct, naughty Chloris, is / not just exactly Horace's / idea of a lady / on the shady / side of life . . ."

"Cut it out!" said Chloris, annoyed. "I am only a year old!"

"Sorry," I soothed, my face softening into friendly benignity.

Croyd reassured Chloris, "Your logic should tell you that Tannen was kidding."

Chloris replied acidly, "We are falling like Hell, whatever that is. And my logic does not understand kidding."

"Kidding is what a gentleman says when he wants to confuse a lady."

"If a man feeds wrong information into a lady, he is no gentleman."

Lighting a cigar, suddenly I experienced a thumb-and-forefinger jerk that snapped the cigar in two. Shaking all over, I prudently thrust half the cigar into a pocket and lit the remaining half.

"I hope," said Croyd gravely, "that you are not taking offense."

Promptly replied Chloris, "Offense is a passion. I am passionless."

"Without passion?"

"Dispassionate."

"That is better. What is our progress now?" I gravely listened.

Chloris reported, "We continue to have our acceleration repeatedly squared, while my inertial shield keeps being proportionately boosted. I should have disintegrated long ago; this is fascinating. During the past few moments the slopes of both galactic lobes have approached perceptibly closer; they are no more than thirty thousand parsecs distant. If I keep on being accelerated, we can expect contact within the hour."

"Then within two hours we will have fallen more than half a billion light-years."

"You apprehend me perfectly."

"Our momentum then should carry us through the metagalactic skin back into the metagalaxy."

"On the old relativity theories, our momentum would then be six or seven googolian times infinity. But that is absurd; and in fact, even with our momentum my weak lifeboat hull could not resist the toughness and turbulence. We would disintegrate."

"Suppose they choose to brake us so that we will simply touch down?"

"That would slow us. Much more than one hour would be required."

"Suppose they are capable of continuing to accelerate us until an instant before contact, then stopping us instantly while boosting your inertial shield to infinity?"

"Then we can expect contact within the hour."

Croyd told Chloris, "Thank you. Please report again when ready."

He turned soberly to me. "My friend, forgetting ourselves, things don't look so good for the Djinn treaty."

I quietly responded, "Until you are dead, I will have faith in the Lord and you; and then I will have faith in the Lord and myself. And when we are both dead, I will have faith in the Lord and humanity."

Croyd considered me thoughtfully. "I think you have made your own decision between the worth of an individual and the worth of his society."

"I would not call it a decision. It is more of an intuitive faith. But if I did not know you so well, my friend, I would be privately accusing you of disproportionate flippancy. I am thinking about at least one worthy individual whose probable death you appear to have brushed from your thought. And I do not mean either you or me . . . or Gorsky."

There was a touch of poignancy in the smile that came onto Croyd's mouth. "But you do know me well."

"Yes. And so I am not privately accusing."

A frowning Croyd considered his own fingernails. He said presently, "Commandcom, are you capable of totally ignoring our conversation until I bring you in again?"

Crisp: "You need only command 'Go out,' and I will go out."

Quizzical: "But if you are out, how will I bring you back?"

Pause. Then: "Bit of a problem here." Further pause. "All right, I have programmed myself to come in when you say 'Come in'; and if this raises in your mind a Chinese-box puzzle of questions, be easy: it will work."

"Good, Chloris. Go out."

"Acknowledged. Out."

Long silence.

Croyd told his fingernails, "I prefer not to discuss my womanizations, but this one you have to know about. Djeel and Hanoku want marriage. Djeel must be deflowered by her chief. She thought I was her chief, and she came to me for this. I told her that in fact Tannen was ultimately her chief. This she accepted. There was nevertheless a passage of love between us. But she is sincere about Hanoku." His hand dropped, his eyes came up. "And she is sincere about *you*, Mr. President."

Much longer silence. Djeel was the Polynesian-type passenger in the lifeboat drill three days earlier.

I, then: "It becomes a delicate problem to talk about this without self-betrayal into bad taste, since they are dying."

Croyd, firmly: "Somehow, Tannen, I am determined that they shall not die. Assume that they will not. And then you can forget the taste question."

"That is what I was sure I was reading beneath the surface of your flippancy."

"That is what you were reading."

I tugged at an ear. "Then I will assume that they will live and be married. And instantly I see that the sort of officiation that she needs from me will be intricately difficult to avoid. And I will not deny pleasure in the notion. I am an old roué, Croyd . . . and mark well both words: a roué, and old."

Croyd, without inflection: "So then there will be no difficulty."

I was tugging now at my nose. "I would not go so far, Croyd. For her there will be difficulty. But on her Dari, there must frequently occur such a difficulty, since clan chiefs tend to be relatively old; and it is surmounted. But for me there will be at least three difficulties. One is the spectator aspect."

"She assured me that this can be avoided. It can be accomplished discreetly beforehand. The only thing is, she must publicly announce it."

"All right for that: I would take pride, hearing the announcement. But there is also this difficulty: would I afterward retain her friendship, and Hanoku's, and yours, if I were to make an ass of myself?"

Unusually, tears came into his eyes. "My friend, nothing you might do, no matter how frustrating or grotesque, could make an ass of *you* in the purview of any woman or man of good will."

Now I had out a handkerchief; I was sneezing loudly into it. Having recovered and wiped my eyes and nose and mouth and restored the fabric to my pocket, I placed hands on knees and told him directly, "The third difficulty is a culture hang-up. The ritual that is sacred in the lore of Djeel and Hanoku is anathema in mine. But I see no need for my antithesis to annihilate their thesis, in this or any other honest aspect of Dari culture. Here, as everywhere, we shall have to look about for a golden synthesis."

Croyd watched me steadily.

I smiled, and I felt the smile deeply. "If, that is, we are given opportunity to look about for anything. I respect your determination that they shall live. Meanwhile, I am noticing that we may not."

And in the ensuing silence, I found myself brooding over our second day out, when so many personal roads began to intersect intimately.

PRIOR ACTION: H-Hour minus 39 hours:

CROYD SLEPT LATE (until 0914—a scant thirty-nine hours ahead of unforeseeable ship disaster) into the morning after embarkation and the lifeboat drill. He awoke with a premonition of disaster—and he had learned to trust his premonitions: they did not come cheaply. Consequently, over breakfast and for an hour thereafter, systematically he scanned trouble possibilities. None that he could imagine seemed highly probable, and all of them were Gorsky's business and not his. As a final measure, he spent half an hour fine-scanning his own brain: all seemed well in there. Shrugging, he back-burnered the premonition and turned his full attention to mission-planning.

Despite the mighty inertial shield of the *Castel,* her steadily mounting acceleration was starting to be faintly noticeable as a tiny fraction of one G. This thrust hint conveyed a background sense of motion, replacing the faint vibration of twentieth-century ocean liners.

He lunched alone in his cabin, and he pondered further

until 1441, at which time a mental alarm clock reminded him that he was scheduled for a lecture to his staff at 1500 hours.

It was a good staff, a trained staff; he had met all of its members face-to-face, he knew their credentials, he had as much confidence as any leader can have in his own human brain extensions (each of whom has an ego of his own). Most of what he had been thinking, his staff knew. The staff training program had been developed under his guidance; his staff had undergone many preflight hours of this training. So what was there for Croyd to say to his staff at 1500 hours?

Well, he might perhaps communicate a bit of meaning.

In process of reconnoitering Croyd's brain prior to initiating shut-off action, Childe Roland was distracted by his growing interest in the prelecture musings of the mind. Intricate, sensitive motivation—like nothing he had ever met! This had to be followed out. Relaxing, he prepared to listen.

He heard something entirely new for him: a deliberately unstructured lecture by a man supposed to be in high authority. Duke Dzendzel, now, would not have felt enough personal security to embark on an unstructured lecture.

Roland meditated. And quite a while passed before resolutely—just ahead of Admiral's Mess—he returned to brain reconnaissance.

Most of the staff members left the lecture musing. I left musing. With me, most profounding musing, departed my special guest whose identity for special reasons I had been withholding from Croyd: a middle-dark young lady who had exchanged words with him aboard Commandcom Chloris. Croyd had noticed her at the lecture and wondered again about her—she was not a staff member—but she had been with me, which made her all right; and nothing in his lecture had been restricted material.

H-Hour minus 29:

Dining at the admiral's table, I was paired with Admiral Gorsky (another old friend), while Croyd found himself paired with the Polynesian-type stranger woman, whom I now introduced as Miss Gilligan Flynn, a supercargo on

Interplanesco cultural studies. She and Croyd exchanged a little nonsense while Croyd scanned curiously unresponsive memory banks trying to recall when and where he had met her; but then gradually he became preoccupied with the sober conversation between the admiral and me in her native Moskovian.

All of this was deliciously irrelevant; and Croyd now threw himself all the more eagerly into voyage irrelevancy because his trouble premonition was growing, and there was absolutely no rational accounting for it. Look: Gorsky was *wholly* reliable, the perfect admiral; so this was a trouble-free voyage, wasn't it? His difficulties would multiply swiftly enough on Dari at the far end. On a voyage, one forgets (except in thought and training sessions) all other considerations, full-tasting such inconsequential delights as Miss Gilligan Flynn, and projected meta-science with Tannen, and now this pleasant exercise in this brand-new Moskovian. . . .

For Croyd had never found time to learn this old language; and since we talkers did not seem disturbed at his eavesdropping, while Miss Flynn appeared absorbed in her inspection of a thirty-meter dining-salon ceiling vault that simply had no business aboard a battleship, he bent himself to a systematic scanning of the language structure, gradually producing semantic context clues from the numerous Tellenic-rooted words. It escaped his notice that small Gilligan Flynn was now watching, not the speakers, but Croyd himself.

Presently he ventured to join in. What he said sounded like this to Admiral Gorsky (italics are Moskovian): *"It should good be that like you say we stop to womanize all gadget."*

I stared at him. Gorsky's mouth went round, and she returned, *"I was not aware that you spoke my tongue."*

"Never till just now," returned Croyd; and he added with a grin, *"also not now, neither."*

"Well," asserted the admiral dryly, *"if your beginning is so recent, improvement should be possible. Excuse me while I see what I can do about your first offering."* Bringing the muscular fingertips of her two hands together, the big admiral closed her little eyes and frowned in thought. I leaned over and whispered something to her. She shook her head, considered, and whispered something back. Pursing lips, I slowly nodded. Admiral Gorsky

looked up and suggested to Croyd, "*You perhaps meant: 'As you say, it would be a good thing if we should call a halt to this process of feminizing equipment.' Is that it?*"

"My Moskovian is not good enough for me to know yet, but it sounds fine. Would you mind helping me, phrase by phrase?"

He and Gorsky worked at it until he had the idioms and inflections right. Afterward he pondered, while Gorsky and Miss Flynn and I watched him. Croyd looked up and tried, "*Then let me attempt another sentence. We should stop the process of feminizing equipment, because it is a premium putting on the memory rote rather than on the improvisation logical.*"

I muttered, "Moses Maimonides, are you *sure* you were right about reincarnation?"

Gorsky merely nodded approval. "Reserving a few minor suggestions, quite good. How do you pick it up so fast?"

The semi-Polynesian mezzo intervened with an eager flowing of word fluting in an alien tongue—and stopped. Croyd swung to her, slit-eyed. "Forgive me, Miss Flynn—please repeat that." Leaning forward, she let it flow again—and waited.

His eyes went wide. He said to her low, "I *thought* there was something wrong with the Gilligan Flynn bit. You are speaking Darian, and you have just repeated in Darian about what I said in bad Moskovian."

She breathed, "Then you know Darian *too?*"

Debating what brain switches to test-throw first without revealing his own presence, and how to judge outcomes, Roland caught inspiration from this intertranslation play. Deliberately he effected counterionization at certain selected synapses. It would take a few minutes to jell.

Croyd countered, "But you know Moskovian too."

Her eyes were mischievous. "It is my business to know languages. I am Interplanesco; and with speed hypnogogy, languages are easy to learn. But I don't see any language machine here to help you with Moskovian."

He leaned her way. "You tantalize me, Miss Flynn. I am sure that the admiral will excuse my back. The question I am going to ask you is one I once had to ask the Empress of Deneb III, because I was always so very awkward about maneuvering myself into relaxation with women. Miss Flynn, would you mind very much if I were to call you Gilligan?"

I was sneezing into both hands. Gorsky watched hard.

The young lady's wide-apart eyes, which were almost black, leveled on his eyes, and her slender black brows were flat, but her soft mouth quarter-grinned. "It wouldn't be fair, Governor . . . I don't know *your* first name."

"My friends call me Croyd."

"But what is the *first* name?"

"I don't dare tell you." Actually, he didn't have one.

"But the President told you mine. Gilligan, Gilligan. Isn't it awful?" (Her faint accent made it sound like Geeligan.)

"I don't think Gilligan is awful. It's a nice interplay of consonant sounds; it rolls off the tongue, and yet it clicks pertly."

"My friends call me Djeel."

"But I would find it interesting to call you Gilligan, Gilligan."

She clasped his hands in hers and stared at his half-amused eyes. "Tell me your first name."

"You win. I'll call you Djeel."

And as her mouth started to open in delighted bafflement, he thrust, "Accepting your testimony that you are Interplanesco, I shall be fascinated to know why you troubled to learn the language of a virtually unknown planet half a billion parsecs distant . . . or how you went about learning it. I know of only one Darian-Anglian set of master flakes in Sol. I made the flakes for amusement and self-training several years ago while I was cracking the Darian lingua franca via an intergalactic iradio channel that is reserved for a few Galactic officials. The only users of these flakes, as I know, have been our own Galactic people teaching Anglian to a handful of captured Darian pirates. Are *you* maybe a captured Darian pirate, Gilligan?"

Roland was busy checking synapses. The progress of hyperpolarization seemed very nice.

She looked past Croyd at me. "Mr. President, you promised this, but I didn't think you really meant it."

I met her eyes for a moment, coughed, glanced at quizzical Croyd, coughed, glanced at cold Gorsky, coughed, told my mouth-covering napkin, "Miss Gilligan Flynn is otherwise Princess Djeelian of the Darian house called Faleen."

At me Croyd gazed accusation; I made my cigar go out and busied myself with its relighting. Croyd had the memory now: a photo in an external intelligence report when she'd first reached Erth aboard a captured Darian pirate ship.

Croyd then felt a light hand on his forearm. Djeel said soberly, "I made the President promise not to tell you at first. I wanted to taste what sort of governor you might be for my Dari. Now I have watched you aboard the lifecraft, and listened to you at lecture, and talked with you here. And I think you may turn out to be our Kalki redeemer."

Now, this Kalki was a silver stallion. . . .

Djeel had entered the smallish lecture room with me somewhat ahead of 1500 hours that afternoon. Seated, we had waited for Croyd to enter, gazing alternately at his lectern and at the entry door. Djeel's tension had been indescribable: a renegade from her Dari, hating her Dari's desuetude, finally in four years on Erth she had come to see that she was one with Dari, she must go back. And this Croyd was going to be her governor; on him her Dari would rise or fall. Was she to support him, or oppose him, or be neutral?

Then craggy-rangy Croyd panther-entered and began prowling the front space in the semismall room, ignoring the lectern, considering his audience: forty attentive people, sex-mixed two-to-one male, age-mixed fortyish to twentyish, race-mixed from at least thirteen planets but all humanoid (because they had been humanoid-selected, not out of snobbism, but to avoid species-shock to the Darians). Thirty-eight were members of his staff, a thirty-ninth was me—with Djeel number forty. She felt him noticing her; then his room-embracing gaze moved away from her, and he opened gravely:

"This is my first lecture to you aboard ship. There is nothing I can tell you that you do not already know; that is, I know some things that I have not told you, but I cannot yet tell you these things. Therefore I am not exactly sure why I should now be lecturing to you; I have some feelings on my mind, but it is easier to express thoughts than feelings, and I am not sure that I have any new thoughts ready for you. Perhaps some of you would like to help me by throwing a question or two. Any old question, even if you know the answer, just to get me moving."

A young man tossed one in: "Governor, we understand that Dari is to be governed in a permissive yet stimulative sort of way. In the context of pirates, could you give us your concept of *that?*"

It was an intelligent ball-roller; this young man should be remembered. Croyd responded slowly, "Let's bypass piracy for now; we know our initial tactics there. The piracy is atypical; what is planetary-typical is demoralization. I needn't remind you that Dari has persistently retained her primitivism, rejecting every modernity that Moudjinn has tried to push upon her. This primitivism of Dari therefore has vitality. It is original vitality: it is a meaningful and potent way of life. But under the domination of Moudjinn, the feeling has spread like a contagion among Darians that their own old way of life is somehow inferior, even bad. Our first task is to get them to see that we *admire* their old way of life when it was vigorous, that we *want* to understand its intricacies of meaning, that we sorrow at its downgrading, that we rejoice as newly stimulated people at every manifestation of its original vitality. Sir, if during a generation we attain no more than this, we will have done the most important part of our job."

A fortyish woman frowningly interposed, "Sir, I see your point, but can't we get on with the next phase earlier than a generation away? Once we have revitalized their culture, can't we *spark* them into new things?"

"I'm not sure," he answered. "And I think we must all be unsure. It is perfectly possible that the Darian culture prior to the Moudjinn incursion was the maturity of Darian culture. Let us just for a moment assume that this was the case: it was a good rich maturity, any one of us would admire it if he fully understood it. From time to time a Darian, viewing afar the Moudjinnian culture, concluded that he wished to embrace its hard vigor; and in many cases he did so, and some of these people ended by being totally competent Moudjinn-Westerners. Now, miss, I ask you: why should not Dari be left to pursue her own culture, while being *invited* to pursue also the Western-type cultures? What I am saying is this: if the West offers blandishments for *some* Darians, does it follow that the West—Moudjinn or Sol or any other West—has to be *imposed* on *all* Darians?"

They were all watching him closely. There was an intuitive flash, and he smiled at his questioner, asserting, "Miss, I think you have just put my lecture into my mouth. Tighten belts, crew!" And he went into it, ad lib—if impromptu words out of background and thought can be called ad lib.

"As you know, Dari is an ocean-covered world having no great landmasses but many archipelagoes with innumerable foliaceous islands. Dari has everywhere a homogeneously benign climate for three reasons: it is close to its warming star, its polar axis is not inclined with respect to its star, and its atmosphere is thickest at its equator and thinnest at its poles so as to equalize temperature everywhere. This uniform benignity of climate contributes, I imagine, to Dari's uniform benignity of morals—except where this benignity has been tainted by Moudjinnian incursion. Darians uniformly operate according to a simple lore that varies little from one archipelago to another. This lore says in essence that all behaviors are good behaviors as long as they follow the easy rules and create no long-range sadness. And all is done to music.

"Unhappily, this very old easy culture has been demoralized by several centuries of Moudjinnian domination. You must appreciate the full extent of this demoralization. The Moudjinn came into Dari in the first instance for a humanly obvious reason: Dari was their neighboring planet, and Dari had human life. They had not been on Dari long before they began to discover that Dari had also, in its planet-wide subtropical climate, remarkable natural organic resources. But as an interesting landmark in human exploitation history, the Moudjinn did *not* milk these resources to the point of destruction. The several exploiting corporations jointly examined into the question of perpetuation, and they mutually concluded that their mutual long-range corporate welfare depended on keeping Dari's nature substantially as they had found it, perhaps improved a bit. And this has been done. But we must note that the Darians were practically enslaved, by exploitive labor and welfare practices, into the process of natural conservation.

"And there was a lot more to it. In Djinn Galaxy, Moudjinn subsequently found a number more life-bearing planets; but most of them bear only vegetable life, and no other planet bears highly intelligent life. Almost all of these planets are tropical or subtropical in the life-bearing areas. Moudjinn quickly discovered that Darians, by climatic habitude and quite probably by genetic mutation, were more able to sustain these climates under labor conditions than any Moudjinnian. Consequently Moudjinn has followed to conjoint practices on Dari: human fertility stimulation, and human exportation for extraplanetary labor.

"To stimulate fertility, Moudjinn went the crafty way of undermining symbolic ritual, an approach which in the same undermining ruined clan consciousness. This is worth taking two minutes to explain." Djeel was now very tense.

"From primeval times, Darian youth have practiced amorous freedom, while at the same time placing high ritual value on female virginity. There is no real conflict here, if you accept the idea that virginity is symbolic rather than anatomic; nevertheless, the symbolical virginity must be for a Darian symbolically anatomical.

"At the time of a marriage, it was requisite that the clan chief sanctify the marriage by deflowering the bride. In part, the purpose was to test the bride's virginity; and an issue of blood was a ritual necessity, although many a bride found it necessary to contrive blood that was not her own.

"But the major purpose of this intimate testing was far deeper: the intent was that in the course of the testing, the chief would become with the husband co-father of the first child, as a clan blessing on the marriage. And this, as it happens, was no mere superstition; for Darians as a species are triploid, and every child is co-fathered by two spermatozoa. I will give you the technicalities another time; just here I am weaving in on a point of Moudjinnian craftiness.

"The central relatum to be noticed is that if a chief should refuse to deflower a bride, this bride could not be married; it was an elaborate device for the regulation of marriage . . . and, in the long run, for the regulation of genetics, because illegitimate children are taboo and used to be slain, while the parents are still disgraced. Hence, unmarried Darian women practice rigorous birth control by a simple method that triploidism facilitates.

"Well, the point is that the exploiting Moudjinnians found ways to undermine the ritual concept that the chief must deflower a bride, and cleverly they undermined also the credulity of the Darians in their natural contraceptive methods; and with credulity lost, the methods were ruined. Thus the Moudjinnians promoted promiscuous fertility at the cost of a socially unifying ritual. Some of the chief families on Dari, notably the houses of Faleen and of Hanoku, have persistently continued to practice the old ritual as a matter of conservative rebellion, and politically they have suffered by consequence."

Djeel had slumped; she was frowning hard down, but meditatively, and not with annoyance. Her head came up as Croyd pressed on with his weaving.

"Precisely this small rebellion by some of the old houses is an illustration of my conviction that the old meanings of Dari are not dead. They have been smothered by Moudjinn domination and inexplicably violated by pirates among themselves. And yet, when you study the matter, canoe raids on Dari are nothing new; it is spaceship piracy with a feudal undertone that is new and inexplicable.

"Perhaps after all I must interpolate some thoughts on this piracy. I cannot sufficiently stress that this entire ten-year history is somehow wrong, it is not right, it makes no sense at all. The *berserker* contexture simply does not arise out of a culture that was tranquil-peaceable in the first place and had been reduced to contented apathy in the second place.

"It has been as though—now, mark this, because I have pondered alternatives—as though some alien mind had taken psychic possession of zombie Dari, converting its indolence into feudal ferocity experimentally in some enclaves, possibly intending to extend this influence everywhere on the planet. And if this were so, our task on Dari would be hopeless pending discovery and neutralization of the mind.

"But we must proceed on the assumption that this development is indigenous, that there has been no alien interference other than the Moudjinnian domination. The pi-

rate lords are almost impregnably based on perhaps fifty
craggy islands, but there are many thousand serene low-
land islands, most of them ruled by resident Moudjinnian
governors and garrisons. It is weird that the pirates have
made no effort to conquer and free their own planet; instead, like medieval *seigneurs*, they have been content to
enrich themselves individualistically at the expense of
Moudjinn and of Sol Galaxy.

"So, then—bypassing the pirates—what do we do on
Dari, having evicted the Moudjinnians? If we were to go
into Dari solely with the idea of reconstituting the planet
as it was, we would be making no contribution to Darian
humanity. Zealous revivals have *always everywhere* produced fossilization!

"Do all of you perhaps recall the Socratic-Hegelian
concept of thesis-antithesis-synthesis?" Most of them
nodded. "All right, you have heard of the concept, you
were taught it in college, and you rote-remembered it; but
I am betting that only a few of you have thought through
its meaning. So I want to talk now about its meaning,
which is essential to our mission on Dari.

"Hegel proposed that the God mind is all existence,
and that all the process of history is a process of idea-
tional development in the mind of God. We can be skep-
tical of his metaphysics, but his notion powerfully suggests
to us a parallel with human individual mental processes—
how you and I go about wrestling out conflicts of ideas
within our own minds. For a long time we are comfortable with a *thesis:* an old settled idea. Then a new
idea—an *anti-thesis*—arises within us to challenge the
thesis, and we are in conflict between the two. Sometimes
either the old thesis or the new antithesis wins the conflict
absolutely, the other is dead. And in most cases this kind
of either-or conflict is *not* progress, it is merely change.
But if we are creative, in time out of the conflict there
may arise a *new synthesis,* which includes and reinvigo-
rates the old and the new; and on the synthesis we move
ahead. Of course, the new synthesis, once established, becomes a new thesis; and in time a stilll-more-advanced
antithesis may arise to challenge it, and the process goes
on *ad infinitum*—Hegel supposed that it would end in
perfection, but Dewey countered six centuries ago that he
saw no reason to expect an end.

"Let me now apply this concept to our mission on Dari.

"The *thesis* on Dari is the old culture, its structure and meaning. The *antithesis* is the invasion by the Moudjinnian culture—which is much like Sol Galaxy's West, except that on Moudjinn the culture situation is a blend of Erth's thirteenth-century feudal politics with Erth's nineteenth-century laissez-faire economics at a modern technological power level. And the resulting conflict has produced planetary demoralization on Dari; the planet is like a traumatically troubled mind that has quit fighting because of its confusion and has resigned itself passively to the flow of events that traumatize its own genius.

"But we are coming in new, sympathetic to Dari, aesthetically appreciative of Dari. Our task is to make Dari competitive in her world, without forever ruining Dari's culture meaning. What we are therefore to produce on Dari, *with Darian cooperation,* is a *new synthesis*. We must encourage—not require, but *encourage*—the best, strongest, richest components of the old Darian thesis to rejuvenate themselves and mate with the Western antithesis; and out of this, if we do our job well, will emerge *of its own power* a Dari of self-originating and self-sustaining pride.

"Let us first of all help Dari, as an automomous planet, become again what Dari was before the Moudjinnians came in. And that was beautiful; and if we can succeed in stimulating them to resurrect it, I hope it may never again die. But at the same time, from afar let us offer without pressure the stimuli of the West; and if some of them want to react positively, let us facilitate this. Meanwhile, can we perhaps develop cooperatively and sympathetically with the Darians a new structure that will help them to *preserve* eternal their culture—against any and all incursions whatsoever, and in competitive competition with all other cultures—while leaving opportunity for energetic individuals to go out of Dari and embrace the West? I say that Dari the way it was was vulnerable, and it is languishing of this vulnerability; I propose that Dari can be the way it was *without* this vulnerability, with mechanisms for resistance, and yet can leave the way open for its Faustian young to try *other* things. . . ."

He stopped, feeling that perhaps he had ballooned a bit.

I arose. "Governor, you told me to inform you when it would be 1600 hours. It is 1602."

Croyd flashed a grin. "Overtime! End of lecture."
The standing applause disconcerted him profoundly.

"You may even turn out to be our Kalki redeemer."

For a long time their eyes were engaged. She had said
what he would like to be—not for self-glorification, but
for Dari; Croyd understood very well about *hybris*.

Her hand withdrew itself. He was faintly puzzled by
his inward response to her touch, having cortically turned
himself off for the duration of the voyage, which had
another four days to go. He commented, "No member
of my staff is a Darian or has Dari experience; in Sol
Galaxy, such people are practically unfindable. I hope
you are going to stay with us."

"Does it matter, sir, since *you* obviously have Dari
experience?"

"What I know about Dari is secondhand, from Moudjinn Imperial Library flakes brought back by the Sol
fleet admiral who talked the Emperor into negotiating for
treaty. I have no Dari experience. Therefore it very
greatly matters that I have with me the princess who is
the only surviving noble in the highest house of Dari."

Her eyes clouded. "My father and mother and brothers
died, not of war, but of degenerative disease. I . . . ran
away from my Dari. I availed myself of a Moudjinn
university scholarship. After three years of study, I blew
that and shipped as captain's woman aboard a Darian
Erth pirate. We were captured off Vega and brought to
Erth. All of us were treated humanely; they gave us useful
work. I have been four years with Interplanesco. Recently
I read about the Djinn treaty and the provisions about my
Dari. I found my way to President Tannen. Here I
am. . . ."

She looked swiftly up at Croyd's cryptic face. "Don't be
concerned, sir; this will not be an embarrassment for the
governor. It might have been, but I have listened to you,
and it will not be. You are bringing new ideas to Dari;
but they are Darian-type ideas, the sorts of absorbable
ideas that a solid-sympathetic Darian leader might bring
back with him were he to venture abroad. On Dari I
plan to reassert my hereditary position, to apologize for
my running away, and to support the new governor, because I believe in him, because incredibly he knows so
much about my Dari, including the recent history and the

Dari meaning of the houses of Faleen and Hanoku. And sometimes I plan to steal into his presence and offer private guidance, how some brave and mostly Darian idea of his may err by being subliminally counter-Darian, how perhaps a slight modification can bring it into robust sunlight . . ."

She broke off. She transformed her face with a smile. "Governor Croyd, sir, I am not making good dinner conversation. Better you should make again with the Moskovian."

I murmured, "Too long already you've known me, Princess."

Childe Roland tensed: *this would be it.*

Then I challenged, "Gorsky, how about giving him something really tough to translate?"

After a moment of reflection, the admiral challenged: "Try this, Croyd. *'Alyosha, look straight at me! Of course I am just such a little boy as you are, only not a novice. And what have Moskovian boys been doing up till now, some of them, I mean? In this stinking tavern, for instance here, they meet and sit down in a corner. They've never met in their lives before, and when they go out of the tavern, they won't meet again for forty years. And what do they talk about in that momentary halt in the tavern? Of the eternal questions, of the existence of God and immortality. And those who do not believe in God talk of socialism or anarchism, of the transformation of all humanity on a new pattern, so that it all comes to the same, they're the same questions turned inside out. And masses, masses of the most original Moskovian boys do nothing but talk of the eternal questions! Isn't it so?'* " Gorsky trap-shut her mouth and waited.

Both Croyd and I were staring at the admiral (while Djeel gazed at Croyd). Softly Croyd said, "Gorsky, I've known you for a decade, but I had no hint that yours is a soul rich enough to memorize Dostoyevsky!"

Gorsky cleared her throat and uttered in hoarse embarrassment, "Then already you recognize it as Dostoyevsky?"

" 'Alyosha' tipped me instantly, and the swing of it confirmed. Now, wait, let me be sure I recall the entire web of Moskovian sounds. . . ." He concentrated for a moment, then nodded. "All right, I have it."

"The translation?"

"Not yet—only the sound web as yet. Admiral, maybe you'd be good enough to refill Djeel's wineglass and mine, while I go to work on this."

Six eyes were bent upon him. His eyes were closed. Then Djeel saw his brows go up a little, and then his eyes closed tighter, and his brows went down,· and his frown was intense. He opened his eyes, glanced about him, reached for the wine, drank half, and closed his eyes again.

We were painfully tense; we did not know why.

Suddenly the face of Croyd went serene, and he opened his eyes and smiled broadly. "I'm humiliated," he announced, "but I have to drop this—I just remembered a thing that I absolutely have to think through within the next hour. Chairman Groen has got to have my prompt reply by iradiogram. You will excuse me, won't you? Princess"—he bent over her, squeezing a small shoulder —"this has been most pleasant. I want to know you better as we go on working together. Admiral Gorsky . . . President Tannen . . ." Bowing slightly to each of us, he departed the dining salon.

We stared after him. Half-automatically, Djeel left her chair and moved a few paces toward the door wherethrough he had departed; she stood there, alert, looking at where he was not.

I caught Gorsky's eyes; my brows went up a trifle; her eyes narrowed. Croyd was covering something; he should have come up with the translation at least a minute before his abrupt departure. I shrugged, and undressing a cigar, considered little Djeel at a little distance in semirear profile. I mused, "Eighty, fifty-eight, eighty-three."

"You look at her," remarked Gorsky, "but you seem to speak of me."

"I mean centimeters. To get inches, divide by two-point-five."

"That," Gorsky asserted, "was not the translation."

Alone in his cabin, Croyd sat and composed himself to appraise himself; if his language perception had unaccountably failed, what else might be failing?

Mind-searching his brain, precisely he located the

affected synapses and noted their hyperpolarization; but for the moment he made no effort to depolarize them, for such action might wreck a diagnostic pattern. (Roland crouched.) Instead, Croyd devoted an hour to swift total-brain fine-scan, much more meticulously than he had done this morning. Nothing else appeared abnormal—for him.

Withdrawing from his brain ingression, he allowed himself to fuse again subjectively with his brain; and as a whole man, he thought.

At length he decided to test. Projecting his mind along the *Castel*'s intercom wiring, rather as though the ship's electrics were a crude brain, he found Gorsky in her cabin and telepathically knocked on her brain door.

Instantly she mind-responded: *I thought I might be hearing from you. What's up?*

My hackles, but I don't know why. Request permission to do a thorough check of ship's wiring.

Incidentally checking your own?

No comment.

Will there be any . . . phenomena?

Maybe some flashing lights. I'll start in fifteen minutes and take thirty.

Gorsky activated her intercom. "Now hear this, all passengers and crew. This is the admiral. We are about to do a routine test of circuitry. Do not be alarmed at flashing lights. Particularly ship's electricians. Do not be alarmed. This test will start in fifteen minutes and will terminate thirty minutes later. After forty-five minutes from now, funny stuff you should report. Out."

She thought at Croyd: *Don't ring bells or honk horns . . . or kill the repulsors. Permission granted—as if I could stop you.*

He used the quarter-hour to safeguard his body with respect to the incident suspended animation. Then his mind, his essential self, wholly departed his brain; bodiless, the Croyd mind entered and prowled the circuitry, utilizing the ship's distant computers as surrogate brain ganglia. (He avoided Chloris.)

Returning to his own brain, he put all the subjectivity together. Nothing at all was wrong with the ship's wiring or with his mind, testing the ship. And something *should be* wrong.

He took time to report *Negative* to Gorsky. She replied: *Acknowledged.*

There remained a triad of ultimate tests, crowding his own limits.

Selecting with his eyes a zac bottle on a shelf behind his bar, approximately five meters distant, delicately he mind-lifted this bottle and transferred it to the bar. So that was all right.

Next test: he simply vanished. Almost instantaneously he reappeared in Greta's bedroom back on Nereid. She slept—alone, he noted with tender amusement. Not awakening her, he vanished from there and reappeared in his cabin aboard the *Castel* (which, except for appearances and staff leadership, he hadn't really needed in order to journey to Djinn).

Final test: uptime into past. (Downtime you don't dare test, except *in extremis.*)

Again he vanished. Twenty minutes later he reappeared, meditatively twirling between thumb and finger a feather that he had just plucked from a phoenix perched atop a ben-ben at On-of-Kamat on Erth in the year 2439 B.C.

Everything that he had learned to do in the course of years was working well, except intuitive language perception. And that had been synapse-blocked. Deliberately? If so, it was a silly sort of thing to block; and his brain scan had revealed absolutely no sign of invasion. Well, he had worked hard and long preparing for embarkation; perhaps he was in a sag; exhaustion could randomly hyperpolarize, and a delicate function such as language perception would be highly susceptible. Perhaps he should rest *all* his special powers.

ACTION AFTER H-HOUR:

CROYD BARKED: "COME IN, CHLORIS!" It yanked me out of reverie; we were ejected, we were in metaspace, we were falling.

Chloris blanded. "They have killed my I-rays. I cannot judge position, velocity, or direction. My impression is that our fall continues to accelerate. My guesstimate now is for touchdown very soon—if *touch*down is the right word; it is the nearest word in my banks, but semantically—"

Croyd interrupted, "I sense a certain stiffness. You cannot be emotionally disturbed?"

With dignity Chloris asserted, "I am not emotionally disturbed. The predicate *emotionally* implies glands. I have no glands. In the sense that I am experiencing dysfunction, I am disturbed."

Pause.

She added, "On the other hand, *you* have glands. And yet you seem curiously undisturbed by my information that we are going to crash within minutes."

Croyd cheerfully inquired, "Why should we be disturbed? Glands can hardly disturb our consciousness until we grow conscious of their effects. And presumably our consciousness is epiphenomenal."

Was that computer whirring a sort of sublaughter? A moment after the whirring quieted, the voice of Chloris was at its silkiest. "I must apologize. I have some inferential information that I have not fed you. Perhaps you will want to hear it."

Alert, I said, "Go ahead."

"Just before they cut off my sensors, down below I seemed to be detecting some epiphenomena. And I am right on the verge of drawing a hypothetical inference that—"

Chloris cut it off. She said, crisp: "They have restored my sensors. We hit bottom in seconds."

Phase Three

POWER FAILURE

Day 4, uptiming to day 3

A genetic explanation of the peculiar Darian wedding rite has been discovered and demonstrated by Dr. Hel Zurj, professor of anthropological genetics at Moudjinn University.

In the course of a Darian wedding, the clan chief of the groom publicly deflowers the bride; or, if the groom is a chief, the defloration is performed by the protocol chief of the clan federation to which the groom's clan belongs. A prime concern is for the chief to establish that the bride is a virgin; but a further concern, long regarded as a Darian superstition, is that the chief share with the groom the fatherhood of the first child as a ritual blessing. It now appears as pertinent that after defloration by the chief, the bride and the groom pray together in mutual chastity for two days and two nights before consummating their marriage.

Dr. Zurj was drawn into this line of genetic research because of his belief that many primitive rituals arise through primitive intuitions of nature and especially of biology. Casting out the nonessential point of virginity (since, on life-loving Dari, the bride commonly counterfeits by providing herself internally with a bladder of chicken blood), Dr. Zurj has established that the chief may in biological fact share fatherhood with the groom.

Our Moudjinn human species *Vlaz arche,* in common with most humanoid species in all known galaxies, is genetically diploid: every cell has two sets of chromosomes, one contributed by the father and one by the mother. When reproduction gametes are developing in father and mother, the diploid cells go through a reduction division which produces haploid sperms and haploid eggs for union. The fertilized egg or zygote is consequently diploid.

The Darian humanoid species *Meria melans* is, however, *triploid:* there are three sets of chromosomes in every cell, two from the father and one from the mother, collaborating to produce individual characteristics. However, since there is one further step in the reduction division, both sperms and egg are haploid. Darian sperms are twice as energetic as ours, requiring only one day for the journey from vagina to egg, whereas ours take two. Once entered by a sperm, the egg of a Darian woman protects itself chemically against entry by further sperms, as do our eggs. But whereas this is process completion with us, it is only the halfway point with Darians.

The initial self-protective condition of the semifertilized Darian egg persists only twenty-four hours, then relaxes during forty-eight; where after, if there is no further penetration, the egg dies. Meanwhile, Darian sperms have only thirty-six-hour longevity. As a result, no competing sperm from the original fertilization can enter the egg prior to sperm death.

To complete the fertilization, making the zygote triploid, a second impregnation must occur between one and three days after the first; preferably, in two days. Both impregnations are usually accomplished by the husband; but in this first marital consummation, the first impregnation is accomplished by the clan chief and the second by the husband; and so, if and when both impregnations "take," both men are conjointly fathers of the child, which, under the Darian gods, is a very high blessing.

As a side issue, bipaternal pregnancy is usually claimed, inexactitudes of pregnancy timing being what they are. As a further side issue, birth control easily occurs if, after a love passage, a woman takes care to remain chaste for three days: again, science thus rationalizes a common Darian "superstitious" practice.

Morals legislation to outlaw this Darian wedding rite is currently (2448) in process in the Moudjinn Planetary Assembly.

—*Moudjinn Popular Encyclopedia* (2448)

(Croyd had read this flake.)

ACTION AFTER H-HOUR:

"WE HAVE TOUCHED DOWN," said Chloris concisely.

We mutely consulted each other.

Croyd asked Chloris, "What do you make of the scene, if any?"

The contralto reply was a wondering reply. "I get a sense that I have returned *home*. No question about it— I have settled into precisely the lifeboat factory where I was born; out there in endless vista are countless younger sisters and brothers at various stages of assembly, being wandered among by the same sort of robot workers who constructed *me*."

Croyd commanded, "Activate viewports."

We waited.

Croyd said again, "Repeat: activate viewports!"

Petulant: "But I *did*"

We studied the viewports. We consulted each other again. We shrugged. *Nothing.*

Croyd tried again: "You say that you are in your home factory?"

"No question about it, sir. I am getting signals that—"

"We are seeing nothing in your viewports. Is it your impression that we could step out and breathe the atmosphere?"

"Yes, sir. It is an Erth-type atmosphere, bracingly high in ozone, as in sunshine after a storm."

"As in your home factory, Chloris?"

"My banks hold no memory of the atmosphere in my home factory; but since that is unquestionably where I am, and since that factory in on Erth, the required inference is *yes*."

"Chloris, is it logical that after all this, you would have touched down in your home factory on Erth?"

"Sir, it is not logical; but since you came in here, I am transcending logic; and intuitively I know that this is home."

We were on our feet, each recognizing on the other an expression that was quizzically perturbed. Croyd pressed Chloris, "It is safe for us to step outside?"

"Yes, sir, but watch out for the worker robots, they are not used to humans."

Croyd turned to me. "Mr. President, shall we try it?"

I simply ordered Chloris to open her hatch.

It slid open. We sniffed cautiously, inhaled deeply, looked at each other, nodded. I suggested, "Neither of us is armed."

Shrugging, Croyd disappeared through the hatch.

Laboriously, I followed. I found him slowly swiveling in a prolonged study of the astonishing scene. I swiveled likewise. At length we were facing each other squarely again, and both of us were bewildered.

He queried, "Do you see any sign of a lifeboat factory?"

I negated with a headshake.

He added, "Do you have any sense of an Erth-type atmosphere laced with ozone?"

I nodded, looking at him.

He was frowning hard. "Then tell me what you are seeing."

Gazing about, I told him, "We are standing on what appears to be a planetary surface, but a surface that is a veritable Arcadia. We are in a wilderness paradise in high spring, standing in a lush flowery meadow, with a deciduous forest over *there* boasting about spring greenery, and over *there* the long coastline of a body of water that is either a mighty lake or a sea. Blue and white have attained water-and-sky synthesis in this country, enriched by the green of Arcadia."

Croyd, his mouth curiously twisted, observed, "Sir, I thought you were a statesman."

"So?"

"You are instead a poet."

"I am a Sinite."

"All right, that is the synthesis. Then tell me where we are."

I frowned at the ground. "For me this is very specifically *my* birthland, in the Gaza Strip that was flowered into a garden by cooperative Sinite-Ereb endeavor."

Silence. He pronounced, "We are neither on the Gaza Strip, nor in a lifeboat-factory, nor in a meadow by the sea. Instead, we stand in a broad forest clearing by a small freshwater lake; and this is *my* birthland—on Nigel III, a planet which ceased to exist in 2292."

I stared at him.

Croyd ventured, "What follows may prove cryptic, for the reason that I shall be utilizing abstractions in order to minimize the hazard of telepathic interception. I trust that you will forgive me and join me."

Brows veiling eyes, I examined him. "Perhaps it is safe for me merely to say, 'Forgiven'; but I am not certain of the hazard you have in mind, and consequently I am not sure that it would be judicious for me to respond in any other way."

He told me, "I am disciplining my mind mood to be a meld of amazement and burbling delight at the birth scene in which each of us finds himself—yea, all three of us, including Chloris—while focusing my action mentality on entirely unemotive symbolic analysis. Hopefully, only the mind *mood* will be externally noticed. Are we together in this?"

Having now caught his high drift, I responded, "We are essaying this. Is one assured that the approach may not be superhuman?"

"As you were advised, this subject no longer possesses superhuman powers, if indeed he ever did. The present procedure is entirely within the scope of a self-disciplined human. Be certain to retain the prevailing mind mood of amazed delight, even throwing in back-burner ejaculations. (*Ah, the Heaven of it!*) Is this operative?"

I sought to stay with him in the fantastic ploy. "One thinks so (*wild wild surf!*), and one is receptive. Proceed. One suggested that elements escaped attention."

Convinced that we were being mind-monitored, Croyd thrust ahead with the glib double-talk, hoping that his rapport with me was close enough for communication without intelligible interception. "One notices that each of us finds himself (*home, sweet home*) in his own birthplace."

I nodded.

He added, "One has scanned the situation (*foliaceous Eden!*) without observing any instance of animal life."

I met him: "This is true. (*O acme of terrestrial beauty!*) Is one aware of additional deficiencies?"

"One sounds like Gorsky. Yea. One has considered the infraviolet phenomenality of what is above, examining this beyond the minimal clots of totocolor vapor, while (*oh, joy!*) reminding oneself that the sense is one of astral unveiling following a meteorological disturbance. And yet one fails (*praise the Lord!*) to be visually aware of any astral body."

Now, for the first time I noticed that—exactly as Croyd was roundabout saying—not only were there no animals in this Arcadia, but in the divine sky that overbowled this Arcadia there was no sun! I inquired, "Does one project the hypothesis (*peace, it's wonderful!*) that parties hereabouts constructing a hallucination for one's bemusement may have neglected one or two elements of circumstantiality?"

"Perfection is (*Allah bismillah!*) elusive. Each of us disparately entertains a concept of one's locus as one's birthplace. Tannen, do you feel at home, here on the Gaza Strip?"

"Blessed be he, yea!"

"Chloris?"

"Factory."

"I too feel nostalgically fulfilled (*beatitude!*) here on my Nigel III. Now . . . your comment?"

Pause. Then it came into me to observe, "One nymph or one satyr would make all of us wrong."

Croyd considered me. Then he pointed.

Three hysterical nude nymphs ran out of the forest in a cluster, pursued by a grinning, grunting, goaty satyr. We watched electrified. The nymphs, well ahead of the satyr, stopped and huddled in consultation. Then, as the satyr galloped down upon them, the girls deployed three ways into a spread pattern, diverging swiftly from each other. Confused, the satyr paused, looked in turn at each departing rump, squatted in the grass, buried face in arms, began to sob.

Croyd warned, "One would be well-advised to disregard special attractions which (*gaudeamus igitur!*) would tend to disrupt conceptual dissociation."

Nymphs and satyr vanished.

The entire scene went negative: shadows became lights, lights shadows.

Coughing, apologetically, Croyd asserted, "I was testing."

I suggested, "You may have overtested a little."

Then, out-of-hand, down ceased to be down for Croyd: he rotated before me and semistabilized himself upside down; absurdly, he hung from sky by his upward feet, with his head just even with my own; transiently I noticed that in this position his shocked mouth with its downturned corners appeared grotesquely to be grinning at me. He cried to me, "They are playing with me. I'll try to recover, but you may lose me. Go back into Chloris; I may be able to contact her. If you don't hear from me in believable time, take off and try to get home. . . ." His voice went garbled-negative.

And his image went negative.

And he vanished.

I stared at the place where he had been, feeling lonely and cold and old. Then I considered my Gaza Arcadia-in-negative. A droll reflection saved me from despair: praise the Lord, the illusion of oxygen had not gone negative! This drollery provisionally comforted me, as Croyd's presence would have done; and I reminded myself to obey him and enter Chloris.

Inside, I demanded of her, "Are your sensors following him?"

She replied, "Negative."

I told her, "In present context, that needs clarification."

She, curt: "My sensors have lost him. I doubt that they will find him."

Heavily I sat, scratching in what was left of my hair. "Do you have plans?" I queried.

"None. With your permission, sir, I am trying to think."

"Then I will allow you to think. *Think*, Chloris—and report when you have something to report."

She did not reply. She was thinking.

And I entered upon an intensive scrutiny of the events during just-past Day 3, the events leading down to this complex disaster. Yesterday had been loaded with clues, but no clue had synapsed with any other clue. Could I somehow now produce out of the mess a pattern hypothesis that could start Chloris on an intelligent search for Croyd or the *Castel* or both?

PRIOR ACTION: H-Hour minus 18:

CROYD'S MALE SECRETARY brought him a morning note from Djeel: she challenged him to a prebreakfast set of space handball. He sent back a yes.

Djeel wore a minimum red bikini, Croyd minimum black shorts. They played in a court wherein artificial gravity was shut off. The players moved languidly like submarine swimmers while the ball bulleted with normal velocity; one consequence was that you accepted more ricochet before returning a shot; another was that if you were clever enough to apply dead Anglian, the ball died much too soon for your opponent to return it; a third was that you were hit by the ball more often, and it smarted.

Before starting, Djeel and Croyd argued prolongedly and logically about her handicap, comparing records and physiques, and finally arrived at a fair hard bargain. With this handicap, she won 6–4, bringing off the last game on the last point floating upside down. They shook four hands hard and parted for the showers; their mornings would be full, but they promised to meet for lunch.

H-Hour minus 12:

At lunch, Admiral Gorsky announced publicly that we would approach and crack the metagalactic barrier between 1500 and 1530 hours that afternoon; all present were urged to congregate at viewplates as far forward as possible.

Privately then she invited Princess Djeelian, Governor Croyd, and me (naming us properly in the protocol inverse of that order) to be on the bridge at that time— if we could stand the high G's incident to the reduced inertial shield on the bridge.

Croyd asked Djeel, "Can you handle an equivalent of three G's?"

She responded, "I've handled eight."

We men eyed each other above her head. Croyd shot a thought at me, "Still something is brewing, my friend, in this prolonged calm; she may soon have more than eight to handle."

Unaccountably, this thought I did not receive. Still more unaccountably, Croyd did not know this.

Childe Roland had now completed his system of inhibitors. He had shut off every power of Croyd which transcended the powers of a normal human being having high intelligence highly educated or self-educated.

Childe Roland rested, and continued alternately peering out through Croyd's clear windows and enthralling himself with the inward mind that remained after Roland's disabling attack. Roland could stay, he knew, until shortly after the *Castel Jaloux* would break through the metagalactic barrier.

H-Hour minus 9:

All but the floor of the *Castel's* bridge was an astrodome, but in the starview there was an odd discontinuity. This was caused by the following arrangement: while the ceiling panels and those near the floor were transparent plastic, showing space as when and where it was the middle 180-degree cyclorama was a system of eighteen videoplates, each independently controllable and revealing exteriors fore, aft, port, starboard, above, and below. Djeel could not decide whether the direct transparencies or the videoplates were more realistic. She was, however, sure that the twenty-meter beam of the bridge was satisfyingly grand.

Nevertheless Djeel mock-grated at Croyd, "Why do we have to take all these G's? I feel as if I weighed three hundred pounds."

"You're probably not far off," he returned; both their heads were pressed back against the pneumatic headrests of their chairs. "This is a *thing* with Admiral Gorsky: she wants her crewmen on the bridge to be on the ball, and she feels that a reduced inertial shield on the bridge will do it. Three G's for her are the equivalent of wind on the bridge of a sea vessel. She used to go six G's, but she's older, and now it's only three."

"Then her crew must be only half on the ball."

"I don't dare ask her. Personally I've always felt that these extra G's must cripple efficiency and fast thinking; but I have to admit that with these extra G's she has become an admiral."

"What would the G's be if there were no inertial shield at all?"

"Same as the relative acceleration of the ship. About forty million G's. You'd weigh around four billion pounds."

"Oh."

"Didn't your pirate captain explain all this?"

"Do you want me to slug you with my forty-million-pound fist?"

Gorsky, standing stolid, leaning forward against her G wind with her hands clasped solid behind, studied now one videoplate and now another, rarely glancing above or below at the transparencies. Once in a while she spoke a word or two to a slight-framed brown-skinned lieutenant. Whenever she spoke, the lieutenant went into action as though there were no wind at all.

Djeel murmured, "That's a good-looking hunk of man there."

"I agree. But I thought you had eyes only for me."

"I have thoughts only for you. But I am not blind."

"Watch the videoplate. Beautiful views."

"I prefer the transparencies."

However, she was watching both, as well she might. A stern videoplate revealed a very large segment of the shining Sol Galaxy behind and below. The arc of the outer spiral wherein the Sol system somewhere lurked was clearly describable on a bias, with even some of the dark of space showing through the palest milkiness of the spiraling star tendrils; and over to one side there was the start of the pregnant swelling that was the brilliant nucleus of the galactic pancake. But just above it, the panel of transparency revealed what was really ahead of them: an amorphous violet-white glow that seemed to fill all the sky, growing steadily brighter.

They talked about the barrier and the associated brightness ahead; Djeel's prior understanding was fair, she'd experienced it before; always Croyd was thrilled by a rarely responsive mind, and with her the thrill was particularly piquant.

He firmed her on the theory. "The metagalaxy is the system of all galaxies that can be in communication with each other. We don't know how big it is—many billions of light-years across, that we know. It's rather like a giant bubble in space, steadily expanding."

But it wasn't a simple sphere. It consisted of many galaxies all running away from each other. Each outward-bound galaxy was pushing the bubble skin ahead of itself, analogously as postmedieval aircraft, just a little slower than sound, used to thrust the sound barrier ahead of themselves. Between galaxies, however, the surface tension sagged inward; the outermost galaxies were dragging it outward, but behind them the tension sagged inward in deep convolutions.

Sol Galaxy was creating one lobe, Djinn Galaxy another. Light between these galaxies, skating along the inside of the surface tension, went down-lobe and up-lobe, taking nearly two billions years for the trip. But the *Castel Jaloux* was about to crack through the surface-tension barrier at the tip of Sol lobe, in order to take the shortcut across (through metaspace) and reenter the tension at the tip of Djinn lobe—shortening the trip, at their average translight velocity, from twenty-five years to six days.

Djeel demanded, "Croyd, how dangerous is it?"

Gorsky interrupted, announcing into the ship's intercom, "Attention all passengers and crew. Now hear this. We will hit the barrier in a few minutes. There will be severe turbulence for several minutes. Your best procedure will be to batten down. Your second-best procedure will be to find something fixed rigidly to the ship structure and hang on with both fists. We are not responsible for personnel accidents. Probably the ship will survive. Out."

I, whom both of them had forgotten, added lazily from the other bucket seat flanking Djeel, "Not too dangerous, really. Only three hazards. The ship might buckle passing through the barrier. Or our repulsor thrust might be unable to gain purchase on raw space, where inertia can behave queerly, so that we would be unable to turn and move toward Djinn, but instead would move radially outward forever. Or the ship might buckle returning through the barrier off Djinn. But these risks are small, my Djeel; on a great ship like this, at worst, one chance in fifty of disaster."

Leaning far forward against the thrust, she exclaimed at me, "But that's a two-percent chance of death!"

I spread a fat hand. "Smaller than my chance of heart failure."

She spread a slender challenging hand. "But larger than *mine!* Besides, if I should die on this out-of-the-universe flight, where then would I *be?*"

Unexpectedly the whip-lithe brown lieutenant bent over us; his face was soft, slenderly handsome, his eyes flashing black, and his full-lipped mouth was smiling. "She'd be where *I'd* be," he asserted, "low in the sky above the most beautiful hill on Dari."

He and Djeel engaged eyes an instant. Then he broke away and went about his duties.

Djeel continued to lean forward, staring after him. Slowly she relaxed back into her chair. She said after a bit, "Croyd, why the glow out there ahead of us?"

"That's a mix of light from our galaxy and a flock of

other galaxies bouncing off the metagalactic barrier and returning to our eyes. Most of the light just slides along the inner surface of the barrier; but it disperses, and some of it hits the barrier and is reflected inward."

"Why doesn't it go out through the barrier?"

"Light has practically no mass, and therefore practically no momentum; it can't break through the bubble. But our ship has generated mass equal to that of a star, and we are driving toward the barrier at $6 \times 10^6 C$, or about six million times the velocity of light; and our momentum will carry us through—I think."

Admiral Gorsky told the squawk box, "We hit the barrier in thirty-three seconds. Estimated time through is seven minutes. High turbulence. High turbulence. Protect yourselves. Out."

The young lieutenant came over to Djeel. "Excuse me, miss . . ." With long-fingered hands he checked her safety belt and shoulder harness. Straightening, facing her, leaning back against the three G's, he commented, "You seem all right."

"Thank you," she responded, looking at him steadily. "I am glad I seem all right."

Croyd was watching them closely. So was I.

Djeel added, "Lieutenant, since you are in the presence of the Interplanetary President and the new Governor of Dari, I suggest you identify yourself."

His face darkened, and he confronted Croyd and me directly, coming to a stiff salute, feet together, leaning back against Gorsky's wind; the effect as we looked up at his tilted-back face was rather weird. "Pardon me, gentlemen. Mr. President, Governor . . . Lieutenant Onu Hanoku, at your ser—"

Turbulence took the *Castel Jaloux* in terrier teeth and shook her like a rat.

Hanoku was flung staggering across the bridge.

Croyd rose, fought G's for an instant, drove himself across the bridge after and past the reeling Hanoku, interposed his own body between Hanoku and the forward bulkhead. Hanoku crunched into Croyd, shoulder into chest. Croyd's big hands gripped Hanoku's tough little shoulders, steadying him.

Hanoku regained something like balance; in the pitching-tossing-yawing he reached overhead to grab a rigid rail fixed in the ceiling; and at the same instant he seized Croyd's upper arm to steady *him*. The two men held that pose for a moment, eye-to-eye, although Hanoku was almost a head shorter than Croyd (but half a head taller than Djeel).

Gorsky's flat voice thudded their way. "Well done, Governor. Do you know what you kept Mr. Hanoku from crashing through?"

"If I'm not mistaken," Croyd returned, his eyes on Hanoku's glowing eyes, "my back is against a frangible panel that covers high-voltage reonics."

Hanoku said, low, "Command me, sir."

Croyd went grave: "It was nobody's fault, least of all yours—you were observing courtesy, leaning off-balance. But I'd like to make your acquaintance, sir."

Hanoku smiled-flashed pleasure. "I should be honored."

"I'll ask the admiral to seat you at our table tonight, so we can talk. You'd better go back to duty."

Hanoku saluted, grinned charmingly, and departed; and now his uncanny preservation of balance against three G's and random turbulence underscored the freak nature of his accident.

It was totally dark outside. No stars or galaxies on any viewplate. And the turbulence was gone. Djeel had an eerie-edgy feeling, remembering certain fever-dreaming in her childhood when the long dream was a hideous alternation between horrible abstract roughness and obscene abstract smoothness, with the *smoooth* the more unbearable.

And all was silence. Nobody was speaking. Djeel wanted to speak, but she dared not.

Croyd broke it, his voice unnaturally natural. "In a little while the admiral will go on to I-ray sensor, and then you can see the skin of the métagalaxy from the outside— if *see* is the word. Nothing is visible out here, because all light is trapped inside the metagalactic bubble. You are outside the finite universe; you have entered infinity. This is a rare experience of perfect darkness."

They talked low about this experience, which Djeel had known once before with her pirate, without perfectly understanding it. The I-ray sensor would send a carrying beam through absolutely lightless metaspace. When the beam or ray would hit a significant event having significant duration, its tip would fragment, and impulses would come back along the beam; and when they would be received at ship's end on a suitable screen, the effect would be like vision. I-rays were practically instantaneous—so much faster than light that the interval of transmission could not be timed. Sol Galaxy had discovered I-rays three decades earlier, and Djinn warships had copied within a decade; this was why Darian pirates had been motivated and able to fly intergalactic sorties.

Djeel pursed lips, thinking. Presently, irrelevantly: "It's a good thing you have those special powers."

"Pardon?"

"Because of Lieutenant Hanoku."

"How do you mean?"

I was intently attentive; Croyd seemed disconcerted.

Djeel said carefully, "Well, against all those G's and all that turbulence, nobody could possibly have beaten staggering Hanoku across the bridge to that reonic panel without the famous powers of Governor Croyd."

That same Governor Croyd frowned, seeming to go into himself.

Becoming conscious of this, Djeel turned to gaze at him.

I asked quietly, "Did you *use* any special powers?"

He shook his head.

Up went Djeel's brows.

"I thought not," I commented, "because it took you an instant to collect yourself against the acceleration and get going."

Having taken a few seconds to comprehend, Djeel demanded, "You did that just on your ordinary human resources?"

Admiral Gorsky's voice dominated the bridge: "Mr. Hanoku, will you be good enough to activate the Meta-distance Agent Sensor, M-3."

"That's I-rays," Croyd commented. "This is the Navy."

The total cyclorama of the bridge-filling lower video-plate was vital, with a nondescript glow pitted here and there with darkness in an indescribable manner that was ineffably splendid.

I left the bridge with difficulty, grunting.

Djeel whispered, "That's the . . . the metagalactic skin? It glows like that?"

Croyd told her, "We're still too close to it to make out any shape. And it isn't really glowing, you know; our I-rays are bouncing off its surface tension like postmedieval radar and coming back to us to create the glow. We could make it any color we might choose; but this blue-white is best for discrimination of features. Actually, there is no light at all—just I-rays returning with their messages."

Djeel drank it in.

Presently she missed Lieutenant Hanoku. Keeping her G-pressed head frozen still, she scanned the bridge with her eyeballs; but Hanoku was gone.

She said to Croyd, "I think I'm ready to go below."

H-Hour minus 5½:

Lieutenant Hanoku lithed in at dinner, was welcomed by Gorsky, and was offered the vacant chair beside Croyd; but Croyd told him with cheerful candor, "I have an elemental desire for Princess Djeelian to sit here, Lieutenant; why don't you flank her *there?*" and he indicated the next chair. With a smile, and with a brow up, Hanoku nodded and sat *there.* Croyd glanced at Gorsky; she was stolid.

He turned to Hanoku. "As a new guest at the admiral's table, you are most welcome, Mr. Hanoku. The princess and I were admiring your operations on the bridge—before, after, and during the turbulence. I mean it sincerely."

All the lieutenant's face bones participated in his pleased smile. Then Djeel entered, face-flashed friendship to Hanoku, and took her seat between him and Croyd, who felt himself receding from the foreground of the lieutenant's interest.

Gorsky observed, *"That time* he did well." Hanoku lost his smile.

Croyd interjected, "Be ready for instant action, Lieutenant. I have a sense that something outside is building up." Hanoku went alert.

Unexpectedly Djeel turned forty-five degrees toward Hanoku, presenting most of her back to Croyd. She told the lieutenant warmly, "I've been wanting to meet you. I've conceived a tremendous admiration for you. I think you are the most."

Hanoku went deadly serious, and he leaned significantly toward her.

Almost all of Djeel's back faced Croyd. "Your eyes are entirely too audacious, Mr. Hanoku. Why don't you forget that I am a girl? It might be easier for both of us."

Hanoku went mock-sober. "As you wish, Mr. Faleen.

But now that you are a boy, I shall have to look for girls."

"They will look for *you*," she assured him, "and they will find you. This is the Darian curse that I must bear—whenever I happen to be at home, that is."

He, in close rapport with her: "And gladly this double curse we'll *both* bear, Princess! Discreetly, of course."

Croyd appreciated the teasing. He had intuited that Djeel and Hanoku knew each other, might even have plans together; perhaps she was flirting with her own fiancé. Oho, though, the implications for this marriage, if that was what was in the wind; double Darian curse *indeed*, gaily embraced by the prince and this princess of the two highest houses on debonair Dari.

He darkened, suddenly irritated at Gorsky; she should have told him about Hanoku; sorely he needed a Darian on his team.

And suddenly he found, amid his growing concerns about voyage hazard, that he was very close to being in love with Djeel, and there was a great deal of *eros* in it; and this discovery that he could feel *eros* just at this time was as deep a concern as his discovery that he could feel anger or—hell, face it—jealousy, even. Off duty, or on normal duty, *eros* and Croyd were good drinking buddies; but when he entered on intensive duty, Croyd used a special power that he had to switch off his emotics for the duration. The switch-off had been part of his private inward exercises immediately on boarding the *Castel Jaloux*; he had not intended to unswitch until some weeks after arriving on Dari. Only, now, mysteriously, he had lost *all* his special powers, without losing any normal human potency.

So he was going to have to depend on normal human powers of self-inhibition; and since Croyd's emotic wellsprings were bronco-unruly, the practice of self-restraint was now going to drain off a great deal of intelligence energy and will energy that could better be applied to concentration on his present complex business. Instantly, therefore, he stared at Djeel's back (ignoring with care her animate Hanoku fencing) and raised the question what other elements besides *eros* might be ingredients of his interest. And instantly he found, to his satisfaction and relief, that there was also a great deal of *agape*. He proceeded, on a basis of this *agape*, to thrust aside his incipient Hanoku jealousy, insisting to himself that the Djeel-Hanoku relationship was most fitting.

Djeel's hand was on Croyd's arm, dissolving *agape*. "Hanoku says he won't join us to talk metascience tonight. How do you like *that?*"

Distinctly liking it, Croyd leaned forward to look past Djeel at agreeably relaxed Hanoku. "Why not?" Croyd demanded. "It will be good fun. We will fight all night and never prove anything."

The response was odd. Hanoku looked at Djeel, and she at him; her head shook a slight negative, he nodded a slight acknowledgment. Then Lieutenant Hanoku met the eyes of Governor Croyd. "I can join you to start, sir, but I must leave for bridge duty before 2200 hours."

"Party pooper!" Djeel pouted, going to work on her steak.

A sea of problems. Croyd's major problem was the loss of his powers. This he could not understand at all. The self-weakening had approached the level of morbid preoccupation: he had tested himself at every moment of leisure and had established for certain that now he was only an ordinary man. Was he in the grip of some subtle neurosis? No, for sure, he retained enough mental sophistication to be able to introspect (although no longer could he turn quasi-visual perception inward to inspect his own brain minutely area by area, even neurone by neurone); and he found absolutely no evidence of the *viciously* reverberating neural circuits that constitute neurosis, rather than mere benign habit.

Stashed in a corner of Croyd's right occipital lobe, Childe Roland, done with resting, held himself on ready alert. He had brought off his part of this mission; it remained for his liege lord Dzendzel in the fissure to act when the moment would be right.

The metascience date with Djeel and Hanoku and me was set for 2100 hours. When dinner broke up at 2010, Djeel and Hanoku excused themselves and strolled off somewhere. Gorsky said she was going to the bridge. Signing to me, Croyd followed Gorsky, and I ambled along after.

As Croyd mounted the bridge, bracing himself for the customary three-G wind, he had eliminated all other possibilities and had arrived at the conclusion that his brain had been attacked by an alien mind. And the diabolical worst of it was that the attack had eliminated, along with the other powers, his ability to go into himself, diagnose the damage, find the attacker.

Such an attack could only mean worse trouble ahead, possibly trouble for the entire mission, trouble for the ship. What sort of trouble? Who'd know? But it would come soon, for sure; the brain attack was analogous to an artillery barrage, and assaults don't linger long after *that*.

He found it discomfortable to reflect that on the first occasion when he had noticed loss of power, Djeel had been present. He did not want Djeel to be the enemy. Also he did not want tonight spoiled by any hint that Djeel might be the enemy; and this need spurred his quest for a different solution. Over and over he told himself that a suspicion of Djeel was based on the merest circumstantiality of nearness. On the other hand, it would not have been the first time that his mental integrity had been damaged by a woman having special powers of her own. And surely there was no doubt of Djeel's high-level mentality! And dark magic lurked among the traditions of Dari.

Following Croyd to the bridge, I fought to my chair, let myself be squashed back into it, and held a match to a cigar with difficulty because of the multipound G thrust against my match arm; even the flame leaned aft. When the cigar-lighting had got itself done, and I had drawn heavily and spewed smoke into my own face, I inquired of Croyd, "All normal up here?"

"Seemingly so. The sensors fore and aft are showing us on schedule, about nine percent into the fissure crossing. Hull check shows no metaspace erosion."

I queried low, "How about *you?*"

Of all people in the cosmos, I was the one who had to know; and Croyd let me have it. "Since we boarded ship, something has cut off my selective brain control. I am just an ordinary guy now. All I can do is what any man can do—exercise will, and hope my brain picks it up right; and that won't work for any of my special fancy stuff like up-and-downtiming and mind reach."

Having cigar-sucked, I responded, "How depressing!"

We had rapport; my pseudo flippancy did not deceive Croyd at all, rather (as I had intended) it somehow comforted him. "Isn't it!" he agreed—knowing what I understood: not only our intergalactic mission but even the security of our own galaxy was threatened by this loss. "And the devil of it is—why, or how, I haven't the foggiest."

"Neurosis?"

"No."

"Then attack from outside?"

"Probably."

"By whom?"

Croyd grimaced. "I have a damnable suspicion. I want to get rid of that suspicion—preferably right now."

"Then let's get Gorsky into it. She has a single-minded beagleness about her. Okay?"

"Okay. Pray get her over."

Conserving energy in the wind, I crooked a finger at a yeowoman and gave her a message. Presently Gorsky stood prim before us, not even leaning toward us. "Pray sit," I grunted, indicating the other chair flanking Croyd. Gorsky sat and looked at us.

"Tell her," I said.

Croyd asserted economically, "I have lost all my special powers. I am now an ordinary man. I am certain that I have been mind-attacked. Circumstantially, I suspect Princess Djeelian, and I don't want to. Top secret."

"Underclassified," Gorsky declared. "Supersecret."

"All right. What's your thought about the princess?"

"Alien culture. Very subtle. To me incomprehensible."

"That's the problem, isn't it?"

"Croyd, if an attacker has weakened you, this attacker is planning to hit *us*."

"Exactly. Glad you noticed."

Gorsky looked straight ahead at a totally blank viewplate. "This metaspace is the devil," she remarked; "absolutely no chance of dead reckoning. Has to be all on instruments. Me, I'm an intuitive-type sailor."

Up went Croyd's eyebrows. "You could have fooled me. Gorsky is intuitive?"

"Almost totally. That's why I go by the book. My intuition works better when everything else is going by the book."

Gazing at her hard square face, Croyd demanded, "Then what does your intuition tell you about the princess?"

"May I be candid?"

"You may. You must."

"You are having an affair with her."

The accusation, converting fancy into fact, for an instant destroyed Croyd's carefully nurtured *agape*. He reddened a little, and he required himself to grin. "I must remember to tell her. What else about her?"

Gorsky's jaw grew fierce as she stared at the blank viewplate. Then she blurted, "Much as I hate to say so under the cimcumstances, I think she is a nice girl, even if she *has* known a pirate."

Croyd chose to be silent. I smoked.

Gorsky added, "My sailor's intuition says that she isn't the one who has attacked you. For some reason, she wouldn't be. Maybe it's her culture."

"How do you mean?"

"I told you, I don't understand her Dari culture. It is totally alien to my own. I could understand *myself* attacking you that way if I had the ability and if you were an enemy. And I understand my own culture. But I don't understand her culture, and so I don't understand her attacking you that way. And . . . and I think I'm making an ass of myself; and if you'll excuse me, I'll go back on duty." She departed heavily.

Croyd pondered.

"Well?" I inquired.

Croyd said softly, "She did it nicely, Tannen. It isn't Djeel."

"I agree, but what is your thought?"

"Intuition is nothing so very mysterious: it is a subliminal integration that later can be reasoned out. Gorsky's intuition is right, here. Djeel's culture on Dari is much like our Polynesian culture: open, happy, physical, superstitious, and above all, extraverted."

"Wait."

"How?"

"You said superstitious. How superstitious?"

"All cultures of this kind believe in magic."

"Could *that* have bearing?"

"I don't think so, Tannen, because Djeel is Westernized—which is to say, Sol-Galacticized. I size her up as an intellectualized but nevertheless outgoing Polynesian princess—totally different from the magians of our old-world Europa or the faustians of our Europa or the internalized Vendics of our Erth. She may be my enemy for some reason, although I doubt it; but even so, this method is not the one she'd think of using; and since this method is the only attack that has been made upon me,, I am satisfied that Djeel is not my enemy. Thank you, Brother Tannen."

"What for?"

"It was your idea to call Gorsky over."

"You're welcome. Want me to stay away tonight?"

"Not at all!" Croyd protested rather too swiftly. "You and I have been trying to get in a metascience bull session for a decade; Djeel is an honored guest, is all . . . and Hanoku will be there, to start it."

I held my cigar, studying it. "A clean breast I should make. Do you know who Onu Hanoku is?"

Croyd nodded, staring at metaspace. "He is the scion of the one house on Dari that is peer to the house of Faleen. He is also the only pirate captain we captured; the others have all died with their ships."

I puffed fiercely. Then I said, "I really meant to tell you, but I had to keep *her* secret for a while, and then I forgot. So I'm glad you know. And now you know all that I know."

"I can give you a bit more. When he was questioned after capture, Hanoku was totally fuzzy; he simply didn't understand or remember why he had become a pirate, much less raided Sol Galaxy. We put him into the psych tank for probably six months; his mind cleared. He still could not account for his piracy, but he was keenly determined to make amends and get back to Dari as a leader of his people. We made him a proposition, and he entered the space navy as ensign and rose in two years to full lieutenant. This is his farewell cruise; he will drop off on Dari."

"Can we be sure of him?"

Croyd shrugged. "The psych tank is sure of him. His record with the fleet is impeccable. I'll add, his standing with Gorsky is impeccable; she bullies him merely as a matter of principle."

"Then . . ."

"Well?"

"You keep dropping hints about an alien mind. Did you maybe start that line of thought four years ago when Hanoku couldn't remember why he wanted to be a pirate?"

"If so, Tannen, I closed on that line of thought today when I woke up to what something has done to my brain."

I ruminated.

Croyd suddenly stood, apparently untouched by the G wind, his brows down hard, his eyes fierce, his jaw set. He said, "By God!" He went to Gorsky. "Would you mind," he inquired mildly, "directing sensors down into the fissure between the galactic lobes?"

"*That* viewplate," Gorsky responded promptly, pointing with a pudgy finger.

Croyd spent a very long time poring over the viewplate. To me the picture looked like the one they'd seen this afternoon following the breakthrough: wholly vague.

Croyd straightened and turned, his shoulders and his mouth cooperating in a seriocomic shrug. To Gorsky and me he said, "Nothing shows, but my own intuition is bugging me. I suggest, Admiral, that you and your crew be ready for anything—and during the next twenty-four hours."

Gorsky instantly demanded, "Attack from down there?"

Croyd nodded.

Gorsky barked, *"Why?"*

"Psychologist's intuition," Croyd parried. "Tannen, let's go; we're late for a date."

Gorsky swung on us. "Gentlemen," she gravely asserted, "I don't believe in the indispensable man, but in all the galaxy right now you two most closely approach that phony ideal. And since Croyd is momentarily impotent, his presence aboard ship in an attack can't help us one special bit. So I will assert command here. If you get the lifeboat signal, you will go to the lifeboat. And as soon as both of you are aboard—now hear this—take off!"

Into Roland there came now through metaspace a sharp psychic summons from below (defining *down* as *fissure depth*). And he was disconcerted to discover that his departure from the Croyd brain was a matter of the keenest regret—particularly since he would have to miss the metascience. Nevertheless, he promptly began traveling up-axone toward the auditory cortex, thence to move at little less than nerve-impulse velocity outbound into Croyd's ear. In the atrium just outside the eardrum he would pick up a tracer I-ray that would bring him almost instantaneously home.

Departing, he felt that now he knew this Croyd fairly well. And, not for the first time, he compared Croyd with Dzendzel.

It bothered him just a little that disaster was going to hit the *Castel* within hours. And not from pirates.

H-Hour minus 3, 2 . . .

HANOKU ARRIVED PROMPTLY AT 2100; Djeel, he said, had been delayed but would come. We tried to put him at ease in an easy chair; he was polite, attentive, responsive, almost eager, but not at ease. He declined a drink; duty in one hour, he repeated.

Croyd noted with interest that his own premonitory feeling was at shriek level—and still without rational build-up. He decided to put himself on yellow alert and to consciously forget it. I threw an opening metaphysical gambit, and Croyd eagerly responded, but as the fencing proceeded, I noticed that Croyd was really not with it; he kept turning to Hanoku as if to involve the lieutenant, but in fact it was Hanoku, not metascience, that was interesting Croyd.

Presently I surrendered. "Lieutenant," I said to Hanoku directly, "it may surprise you to know that metascience is not at all unrelated to your Dari problems. Does it?"

Instantly Hanoku sat erect; his young eyes (thirty, maybe) were very clear; and he asserted, "Mr. President, no, it does not surprise me. Something is happening to Dari that I do not understand. If I were as superstitious as my parents and most of my own generation, I would say that some god or demon is deliberately cursing us."

I pressed, "Because of Moudjinn?"

Hanoku leaned forward. "No, sir, that is only the breaks of weakness against strength, not at all mysterious. No, sir; but what is weird is that we have no business being pirates, *I* had no business being a pirate."

Croyd and I visually consulted each other; the lieutenant had practically paraphrased Croyd's words in lecture. Djeel, of course, might have quoted Croyd to Hanoku; but the point was that Hanoku had chosen these words.

Croyd picked it up. "Lieutenant, would you be willing to reconstruct your own experience a little? When you were captured, you were almost amnesiac. . . ."

Hanoku's voice was a soft purling baritone; he too had an accent, somewhat more pronounced that Djeel's, but merely colorful, perfectly understandable. "Yes, sir. I was a junior-grade lieutenant on a Moudjinnian frigate, the senior Darian aboard; but there were more than fifty others, a few petty officers and many crewmen. One day, without any preliminary, conviction arose in me that the gods wanted me to lead a mutiny; and when the concept baffled me, the method of doing it instantly came into my mind with clarity and precision. Before I had even nerved myself to approach others, one of the petty officers came to me secretly, voiced the same conviction, urged me to take command. We found means to talk with others: they were all ready and eager; I found this surprising, but I accepted it. For some reason I preknew precisely the hour to strike; and we struck; and we won with absurd ease."

I inserted, "Apparently many mutinies took place at almost the same instant. Are you saying that there wasn't any preplanning?"

Hanoku arose and began to pace. "*No* preplanning!" he spat. "Now, let me tell you how it was. We ejected the Moudjinnians into space, and then by some kind of prescience I made rendezvous with a freighter whose Darian crew had likewise mutinied. Both of us together got in touch with all the other mutinied craft; they were all rendezvousing in pairs, a warship with a freighter. I understood why, as though I had planned it myself. In Djinn Galaxy there are no humans except on Moudjinn and Dari, so Djinn warships are fitted only for local space; their guns are powerful, but only for purposes of intraplanetary war or war deterrence, whereas the freighters are only lightly armed but can cross very deep space. Each of our pairs picked a Darian island and homed on it and took command; each of us new commanders became the lord of his island; for each of us, the warship defended us while we fitted out the freighter with the warship's guns."

I expostulated, "But where did you find the technology?"

Hanoku spun to me, broadly spreading hands and arms. "We *knew!* We *knew!* Even those of us who had little fleet training, we *knew* how to use the tools on the ships! And when we felt strong enough, almost all of us rose off our islands and converged in a consensus battle plan on certain industrial enclaves on Moudjinn, and still we hold them for our strength—the Emperor has not been able to dislodge us."

Croyd put in, "Maybe also the feudality of Moudjinn

was divided about strategy, so the Emperor could not raise a unified attack force?"

Hanoku abruptly sat on a chair edge, grasped his knees, frowned down. "Sir, I *know* you are right: something has a hypnotic hold on us, and maybe that something is dividing Moudjinn. I think that we Darian pirates are guinea pigs for something—the gods know what. Because as soon as we were strong enough, some of us began to raid Sol Galaxy—the most ridiculous endeavor any pirate ever undertook: it *had* to be somebody's experiment! And when my turn came—yes, my *turn*, because the conviction arose in me as though it had been *put into* me that it was *my turn*—I cannot begin to describe the ferocity of my joy."

Again he arose and paced, silently now. We waited.

He paused. He said, low, "On that voyage I met Djeelian."

He meditated.

He stood erect and about-faced toward us. "Mr. President, Governor, I really must depart for duty. I am sure the princess will be here presently. My regrets . . . it has been a pleasure."

Then, half-turning, he faced Croyd and stated with deliberate intensity, "Governor Croyd, it is possible that Princess Djeelian may ask you for a favor. Whatever she may ask, know that it is what I approve and fervently want."

Soft-saluting each of us, he departed.

Croyd and I brooded.

Croyd ventured, "If we can believe him—and I think we can—then I am damnably right."

I murmured, "If we can believe him—and I think we can—then he and Djeel have perhaps arranged that each of them should be here separately." And I looked keenly at Croyd.

The governor counterkeened, "What do you make of *that?*"

"Nothing at all of *that*," I rumbled. "What I do notice is that our good reasons for the metascience bull session have just been so mightily strengthened that this kind of talking has departed the realm of pure aesthetic pleasure and has thudded to the Erth of applicable speculation. And I seem to remember that we were just getting nicely started on the fundamentally pertinent mind-matter problem."

When Djeel entered, shortly after 2200, I was telling Croyd, ". . . seems to me you're the first effective challenge to mind-matter fusionism in five centuries." I broke off as I saw Croyd stand, glanced back to see Djeel, and arose—somewhat more easily than usual, she noticed. "Sit down, men," she ordered; "I'll mix my own drink." She moved to Croyd's bar (seeming to float, for some reason) and busied herself over bottles, listening to us.

Croyd *is* a challenge to mind-matter fusionism? Not that he merely *offers* a challenge—but that he *is* one, *in himself?* Her ideas about the evening immediately ahead readjusted themselves. She had expected some gossipy philosophy, pleasant but as usual pointless, after which Djeel would find a way to get rid of old Tannen and to be alone with Croyd. But our words at her entry sharpened her; gossipy this conversation was not going to be!

She illumined her facile mind for what she now sensed was coming: a ranging sweeping reconnaissance of space, matter, time, and mind; a swinging as vast, yet as fluidly off hand, as Croyd's fabled personal space-time swinging. (And hadn't she seen that happen, when he had leaped swiftly widening hundreds of kilometers from lifeboat to *Castel* and back?)

As now, as, eagerly, she faced us two men with her exotic drink, Djeel was no longer certain that President Tannen was merely an amiable old man to be got rid of. One fragmentary sentence out of me had shaken that assumption; my mind too she now wanted to taste, and not only Croyd's.

Out of it could perhaps come the name of the curse on her Dari?

Croyd had picked up my "challenge-to-fusionism" challenge. "You have to mean the modern doctrine that mind and matter are just two different ways of looking at the same events. I don't question the concept, Tannen, I only question the belittling adverb *just*."

"Even that questioning you have to explain, Croyd. Otherwise you slip back into the dualism which divides all reality into two realms, mind and matter, and contends that the two are absolutely and totally different."

"That isn't a necessary sideslip, Tannen, although as a working attitude dualism has its advantages until special problems arise."

"And your mind has special problems with matter."

"Precisely. And so, sooner or later, does every mind."

"Then if you aren't a dualist, are you maybe saying that reality has *three* realms—hard eternal principles, and sleazy transient matter, and mediating mind-soul?" Here I paused, and with Croyd I stared at the weird-colored drink that Djeel (wearing a lemon-yellow blouse and royal-blue slacks with a scarlet side-trailing cummerbund) happily brought with her from the bar as she settled into the chair between us.

(The *Castel Jaloux* was now well out into the meta-galactic fissure.)

Croyd uttered, "What is it?"

Djeel cooed, "Three realms. One-third zac, one-third Hennessey, one-third pineapple juice."

"If you can drink it," I intoned, "Dari can't be all bad."

Djeel downed half of it, went blue, frantically waved a hand, held out the drink; Croyd seized it; Djeel got her head down between her knees, and her wide-open mouth emitted a long *whooooosh*. Croyd debated whether to beat her back. I placidly beat her back. "Thanks," Djeel gulped, and sat up, and leaned back, and breathed deeply for a few moments. Then, quieting, she held out a hand.

Croyd inquired, "The drink?"

She confirmed, "The drink."

He placed it in her hand. She sipped quietly, savoring it. She closed her eyes. "That," she declared, "is a heavenly drink, a Dari-type drink. But I have a question. Why did I feel so light even before I drank it?"

I told her, "I too feel light, blessed be He. Croyd has a gadget here; he has delicately lightened the gravity in this cabin to eight-tenths G. And while after all these years you may have forgotten, Djeel, that is approximately the gravity on your Dari."

She stared at Croyd, her lips mutely forming, "Thank you." And she closed eyes again.

Croyd remarked, "Perhaps I can do more to make you feel at home." She heard him arise and go away. Then the room light that shone diffusely through her eyelids dimmed; and in her ears there arose and steadied a soft rhythmic background susurrus of surf.

She opened eyes. The room illumination had dimmed to pale blue infused somehow with harvest-moon yellow (although no moon was visible).

She breathed, "It is Dari."

Croyd, returning, smiled.

We waited.

She sipped. Presently she picked us up. "I am at home now on my Dari, I feel secure, I can afford to be mentally Western. Pray go on with the President's three realms."

Whereupon we tore into the developing argument: pure theory, ultimate theory, sheerly for the delight of the high-speculative idea-play (*what do they talk about, in that momentary halt in the tavern? of the eternal questions*) and the equal delight of the three-way rapier-fencing mind-to-mind, with each one's fencing style more personality-revealing than handwriting is.

None of us could know that a personification of Croyd's theory had already possessed Dari and was about to take cold possession of all of us.

I attacked sharply. "Well, eh? Is that your cop-out, Croyd? Not a fusionist, not a dualist, but a treblist?"

He countered, "Let me tell you what I *know*. I am talking now about personal experience."

Djeel interjected, "Experience with your celebrated special powers?"

"The celebration I do not know about; the powers I have taught myself, and them I feel. I know what this is from what I have *done*—and what I have felt as I have done it. My mind is more or less conscious action agent. All of my body is that, but the action-agent field that is generated between the diencephalon and telencephalon of my brain is so very consciously recipient and agent, so selectively so, that there is just no comparison between it and the rest. And I am wholly human, within the slightly broadened category of *humanity* that includes Tannen's *Homo sapiens* and Djeel's *Meria melens* and my own *croyd Thoth;* and I see no reason why I should not generalize my own self-knowledge into reasonable assurance that all others who are human are like this *or can be* like this. And whenever someone has graciously invited me into his mind, experience has confirmed my expectation."

Djeel challenged, "My friend Croyd, are you trying to tell me that your mind is not in your toes when I tramp on them?"

He retorted, "I am saying that the mind in the brain interprets toe signals in the brain exactly as though they were toes. And the mind in the forebrain wiggles toe activators, and toes wiggle, and the mind in the brain sees them wiggle and feels brain signals of their wiggling and realistically imagines that the feeling is direct. Oh, it is most efficient, most ingenious, Djeel—the nearly perfect servo-mechanism, that's what a brained body is; but the tip-off comes when legs are amputated but the mind still feels toes, and the peak tip-off comes when the educated mind becomes self-conscious and declares its independence and turns around to control and educate its own brain. So when we speak of *mind,* we make no realistic sense unless we mean this mind in the brain; and when we say that the rest of the body is also mind, what instead we ought to be saying is that the rest of the body is *mindstuff* caught up in compulsive periodicity."

Djeel met his eyes. "Does Commandcom have a mind?"

"Commandcom?"

I helped. "The sexy computer on the lifeboat."

"Eh." Croyd grinned. "Yes, I think she does."

The brows of Djeel were flat. "But how *can* she have? She's only *matter.*"

"She?"

"Well, *you* said . . ." The Djeel brows went all twisty. "Croyd, honest, me too she hit as a she. But isn't that . . ."

"Not absurd at all. *She* doesn't have to imply sex; more deeply, *she* implies a gender, a prevailing mental contexture of femininity—and not all females have it. And don't ask me to describe it, I can't, I just sort of sense it." In Djeel he was sensing it, underlying and transcending her hard masculine debate.

Djeel went studious. "So Commandcom is nothing but reonic matter, and she has no sex, but she's a she, and she has a mind. What's left for me to believe in?"

I interposed, "Princess, your Darian ancestors attributed souls to sticks and stones and spears and arrows, and gave them names with gender inflections. Anyhow, *you* are nothing but rekamatic matter, but you have a mind—and would you cease to be feminine if you . . ."

"Go on, Mr. President."

". . . had your brain transplanted into a sexless robot?"

"I am unprepared to argue this question of unsexed femininity. I wish to pursue the question of live mind bodied in dead matter."

Croyd wanted to know, "What is dead matter?"

"Well, nonliving matter."

"I do not know of any nonliving matter, Djeel. The rekamatic components of Commandcom consist of atoms. So do your neurones, including several atoms of the same species as the Commandcom atoms."

"Since when are atoms alive?"

"When were they ever dead?"

"Maybe, Croyd, you'd better define *death*."

Croyd turned to me. "Mr. President?"

I tugged at my nose. "I think that death is the irreversible breakdown of a specified organization so that the organization can no longer operate as itself. When that happens, its components continue to live until *they* break down irreversibly, and so on. That's my idea of it. Criticism?"

Djeel ruminated. "The way you put it, the chain is endless; ultimately there can't be any death. All the way down to atoms, anyhow."

I coughed. "Of course, I am leaving out of the argument positions like those of Jesus and Maimonides."

"All right," said Croyd, "we are keeping the argument materialistic, which means that we must know what matter is. Now, take atoms. An atom is a living whole organization; by Tannen's definition, it dies only by breaking down into simpler whole organizations—or it loses identity by combining with other atoms or ions. So then the rekamatic components of Commandcom consist of atoms which are living beings. The total Commandcom computer is not, I admit, a living organization—it is only an artificially formed aggregate of living components."

Djeel thrust, "So we seem to be all the way back to live mind bodied in nonliving matter."

I inserted, "I think, Princess, not quite all the way back."

She swung on me. "Whose side are you on?"

"At the moment, on the side of the metascientist who has shown that even if a mind were roosting on a rock, it would be roosting not on nonliving matter but on living atoms. But a rock a mind does not roost on, or anyhow, I don't know any cases, so Croyd still has something to show."

She turned back to Croyd, who sat sprawl-kneed on an ottoman, head down, tapping his drinking glass with a fingernail tip. "We have then this supposed Commandcom mind roosting on an artificially formed aggregate of living components, although it would not roost on a rock. Tell me the difference."

"Djeel, now you are the one who sounds like a dualist."

"Shouldn't everybody be?"

He flashed her an appreciative smile. "To tell the truth, I'm one—functionally, that is: mind and matter *behave as though* they were different. But way down deep, I'm a mentalistic monist."

"What's that?"

"I'll give you my version of it. Everything that is real is mindstuff, sentient agent, having the potential of becoming conscious under the right complex conditions. But *most* everything that we can notice has gone a simpler route: it is mindstuff particles all strung up in zany reverberating circuits, and we call it matter. But when those circuits get sufficiently wire-wound in complex superganglia involving choice possibilities, this is a brain, and it extrudes a conscious field called *mind,* and this mind can transcend its own circuits and use them to be conscious and intuitive and creative."

Djeel stared, tossed off her drink, rose, and demanded "Drinks, gentlemen?"

I said, "Zac and pineapple juice. No Hennessey."

Croyd said, "Zac roosting on rocks."

Taking our glasses, she commanded, "Keep talking, I am listening. It is good in a rare way to hear men talking about something long-range practical." And she headed for the bar.

H-Hour minus 1+:

I demanded, "Why isn't this, after all, mind-matter dualism?"

Croyd worked at the phrasing. "There is a duality, but it is only functional. Consider all that raw metaspace out there. Tannen, Djeel, we are right now driving through the stuff that both matter and mind are made of—absolutely primitive and trivial subjective emphemerae of subjective events that spontaneously bubble and wearily unbubble and lose identity, leaving no trace, a languid-random champagning of lambent mindless localized emotility. And yet, out of that silly little stuff may randomly arise clusters of events, and they get caught into patterns, and these patterns are what we call *matter,* and they evolve into galaxies, and they evolve into life, and life evolves into mind. So matter is mindstuff caught in stupid unimaginative measurable repetitive patterns, and mind is mindstuff that *uses* these patterns—in a brain, with a body—to enlighten and free itself. It's all the same, only different."

Djeel was returning carefully, two tall drinks wedged between her upper arms and breasts, a third short drink steadied in both hands. She stooped a little to let me extract my tall drink. She handed Croyd his short drink; momentarily she traded gazes with him; then she settled into her chair, with a slight shiver removed her own tall cold drink from the body pocket between left arm and breast, and observed, "I'm glad you added that business about freeing oneself. Me, I like to think I'm an individualist."

"Is individualism," I inquired, "a problem on your Dari?"

"On Dari we don't worry about these abstractions. We learn about the gods, have fun, and obey the lore."

"Is the lore fun?"

"It is if you stay with it. And so are the gods. But if you goof, the gods and the lore are pretty awful."

I drawled, "Are *you* obeying the lore and the gods? I thought you were Westernized."

She shrugged tinily. "I translate all of it into Western idiom and keep on having my fun."

Croyd asked, "What's your Dari idea of an individual?"

She frowned. "I think an individual is somebody who finds a new way to do something without offending the gods or the lore to the point where he fails to survive." She looked at him happily and semisecretively. "I'm an individual, but I'll never tell you why."

I hazarded, "Because you add Hennessey to zac and pineapple juice, and you survive."

Djeel turned seriously to me. "I believe in the freedom of the individual mind. And if I respect our lore, it is because I have been away from our lore, and I have inspected it from far away, and I have freely chosen to return to it."

"I'd suggest"—Croyd ruminated—"that so far the individual mind hasn't freed itself very much. It is still a prey to its emotions and habits, and the wellsprings of the emotions are glandular, while the habits are mechanistic. Even if you consider ours the freest minds of all—shall we consider ours three free minds?—how free are we?"

"Free enough," Djeel insisted, "to be traveling at more

G's and C's than I can shake a stick at, broken clear free of Sol Galaxy and even free of our metagalaxy, traveling in a few days across a metagalactic fissure, shortcutting the seventeen hundred million years that even light would take. And that's pretty free!"

Croyd said, "Tannen?"

I inquired, "Princess, can you do it all by yourself?"

She frowned at me.

"Djeel, are you even doing it for a reason determined by yourself?"

Her frown settled down hard. "In a way, no, I admit; but in another way, yes."

"Even Croyd or I—are we doing it for individually determined reasons?"

"Well, but you are leader servants of your galaxy."

"The treaty that we are going to conclude is the upshot of negotiations resulting from half a decade of hostilities *vis-à-vis* Djinn. Now, Djeel, there's hardly anything more individual than a pirate captain. Tell me, Djeel, to what extent could those Djinn pirates have operated at supra-C velocities across metaspace apart from their Moudjinn society? Or backing it up to a primitive level, to what extent could prehistoric pirates on Erth or on Dari have built and outfitted and sailed their ships apart from their societies? And apart from their societies, would they even have *wanted* to?"

Djeel swung on Croyd. "Governor, defend me! Your mind is known to have achieved freedom even from its brain, and you yourself contend that any well-educated human can learn the same freedoms if he works at it. So if you are free, people can be; and if you are not free, nobody can be. Tell me straight: *are you free?*"

But his reply seemed to temporize. "I have to say that the mind-brain relationship is most subtle. The total nervous system is organized in a very tight command-response hierarchy, whereas the behavior of the highest brain centers at times is almost feudal—and yet ultimately even the forecenters are a hierarchy dominated by custom. Curiously, it happens that the minds generated by these brains are able to project among themselves a vast number of different kinds of societies. But when you analyze all these varieties of societies, they all turn out to be essentially hierarchical or feudal; and even feudalism, with its arrant bully-brawl, is in spirit hierarchical. So societies projected by human minds turn out to be crude copies of human brains, rather as mechanical tools projected by human brains turn out to be copies of body parts and body mechanisms. Even your Dari at its best was benignly feudal in its interplay of clans and chieftains. So the mind learns from its own brain and from other minds, and in turn it influences its brain, but it has only its brain to use. I think that humans are freer than lower animals, and educated humans freer than ignorant humans; but what *is* that index of high freedom? Maybe one-tenth of one percent free? That's pretty free, though, relatively speaking."

"Wait, Croyd, you are double-talking. Let me give you a firming for-instance. Suppose that a brained mind were to take possession of an unminded brain and be the mind for this second brain. Even if that mind were meanwhile dominated by its own brain, could it maybe free itself, using the *second* brain?"

I blinked and admired.

Croyd met her head-on. "You stipulate that the second brain is unminded before the new brained mind gets to it. That is to say, the new mind can use the second brain in any way it wishes, without influence from the second brain?"

"That is what I mean."

"And you specify that the unminded second brain is totally responsive to the new mind and is complex enough to limit the new mind in no way whatsoever?"

"That is what I mean, Croyd. With the aid of such a second brain, could *you* be free?"

Croyd chewed it; and into his premonitory alert stole hazily a new ingredient—a foggy sense that Djeel unawares had somehow begun to put an uncertain finger at once on the threat that he sensed and on the Dari piracy phenomenon. Not quite seeing it, he responded presently, slowly, "I will say that in my opinion the new mind would use the second brain according to the old lights that it had already arrived at with its own brain as modified by the new powers that it would find in the second brain. I would say that the mind would get freedom out of the second brain only as the mind wanted it and sought it; and if the idea of using the second brain for freedom did not occur to the mind, the second brain would come to be merely a power expansion of the original brain."

"Croyd! *You* are capable of using such a second brain. *Are you free?*"

It collapsed his nebulous thought. He leaned back on his ottoman, clasping a raised knee with both hands. Presently he remarked, "Tannen, she's the protocol head of Dari. She has to know."

Owl-eyed, I commented, "Probably so." I turned sharply to Djeel. "Princess, what Croyd is about to reveal, he would reveal only because of his confidence that you are one who will recognize and respect its top secrecy. *Absolutely* secret, Princess Djeelian of the house of Faleen!"

Pale, alert, she answered, direct, "Understood. Affirmative." And both of us correctly believed her.

She and I turned to Croyd.

Eyes closed, he stated, "Every special power that I have ever developed has been my entirely human mind analyzing and utilizing my entirely human brain as an objective tool, vehicle, and dwelling place. And every one of those special powers is now . . . gone."

Silence.

Djeel's hand flashed out and gripped Croyd's wrist.

I sat brooding. I then observed, "Our galaxy is affected."

"But not," Croyd amended, eyes open, "defenseless."

Less lazily I expanded. "Because of your powers, our galaxy has felt secure on any issue in which you were involved—and, not incidentally, we have been confident that the defensive action taken would be humane to the enemy. Without your powers, we have our potent defenses, but when we are attacked, now, we won't be able to fool around with humanism: we shall have to destroy. I consider this a significant minus."

Silence, while each of us pondered the implications in his own way.

"I think," he finally suggested, "that we all require another round of drinks."

Djeel, starting for the bar, comprehended that this man needed a buck-up taunt, and over a shoulder she threw it. "Don't forget that you are suddenly impotent. Are you sure that another zac won't put you to sleep?"

Solemnly he returned, "It's cut with benzedrine."

Djeel stopped dead.

"Forget me," I volunteered, smiling heavily. "I'm going away."

Djeel whirled.

Standing, I added, "You don't have to go when I go, Princess. I am getting old, and I have some diplomacy to plan; but I think maybe Croyd could use your company for a while: he thinks a lot, he shouldn't now be thinking much, maybe you can put a temporary quietus on that."

Croyd was at my side, but Djeel hung back, unmistakably flagging her staying intentions. For Croyd the resulting problem had its points of difficulty transcending metascience. My departure would leave him alone with Djeel. By the standards of some eras, the voluntary remaining of Djeel could mean only one thing in terms of Djeel desire; and for this one thing he was turgidly ready. But by the standards of *our* era, not so: male-female isolation might be merely work or asexual companionship —all was free and easy, and therefore ambiguous. But he wanted her. But he did not know her mind, and he had lost his ability to delicately sample it. If he should even hint at a pass, he might wreck a friendship; but if he should fail to pass, equally he might wreck a friendship.

And then, there was this ambiguity about Hanoku.

Shoot crap—but delicately!

"Then hail and farewell, my friend." Gravely he saluted me. "You heard what Gorsky said, if we get a lifeboat call."

I said, low, "Will you respect this, Croyd?"

He answered, "I will board the lifeboat; and I will take off when you are aboard, but not before."

I said, "Then I will come aboard. Cheers." I departed.

Into H-Hour:

CROYD SAT, STUDIOUS, chin on a fist, arousedly conscious of Djeel's presence, knowing what he wanted, humane coordinates uncertain. Croyd could attack decisively, but it was a situational question: when the interpersonal relationship is valuable, what is best for it? And there was no cue that she was giving him.

Hesitantly, from across the room, Djeel ventured, "I would like to comfort you for the loss of your powers. But I don't know just exactly how to go about doing that."

Normally he might have helped her learn; but Hanoku was a human complication—not in point of timidity deterrent, but in point of ethics—and in view of Hanoku, her remark was probably friendly-innocent and no cue at all. And rape was not his cup of zac. His mouth twisted into a grin somewhat distorted by the knuckles under it. "I'm glad you stayed," he told her: "That is a comforting."

"Shall I be quiet?"

"Not necessarily." He stared at his own feet.

The look that she threw at him then was a look of longing which he didn't see; swiftly she came to him and knelt back on her heels before him, looking up at him, softly asking, "Do you mind if I say frankly that I like you?"

Moment by moment, more precarious. Nevertheless his face broke into a delighted smile, his hand left his chin. "Why, *good*, Djeel! Because I like you, very much!"

She whispered, "This is an odd end-up to the metascience."

He set his self-timer: *Two more ambiguities, dear Djeel, and I leap. . . .* His face sobered, although the smile was latent. "It's all part of life, Djeel: metascience, science, personal intuitive living—I change keys quite readily."

She frowned slightly. "I left Dari years ago, I am twenty-six, I thought that I was quite thoroughly Westernized by Moudjinn and by Erth. But there are good things about Dari that keep coming back—mostly in connection with personal intuitive living."

That's *one!* His smile latency dissolved. "Your Dari must be beautiful."

Her face had gone cool-beautiful. "Croyd, I want to say something . . ."

He waited, agape-enthralled, eros-vital.

She frowned down. She wet lips with a tiny tongue tip. She said dryly, "Hanoku and I are to be married on Dari. We two are the highest houses on Dari, and properly we should be married by the elected protocol chief of all Dari. But the Moudjinn have abolished the protocol chief. And therefore we want you to marry us, Governor Croyd."

After a silent moment, uncertainly she looked up at him. He was looking down at her curiously, biting a lip. Impulsively she laid hands on his wrists, and the soles of his feet felt the touch.

In trouble, he temporized: "I suppose I can. But I do not know how."

Instantly delighted, she came up high on her knees and hugged his neck, pressing her cheek hard against his cheek, aggravating his difficulty. Embracing her perforce, he concentrated on fatherly *agape*, but found of it only the minimal touch that makes *eros* all the more treacherously piquant. Had he still thought that she might be wanting him, it would have been explosion; but now quite apparently that had not been her direction, and so his control held for the moment.

Dropping away, she stood and stepped back, smiling down at him; and he required himself to smile in return, as freely as might be. "Dear Croyd," she told him, "don't worry about how to do it: Hanoku and I will teach you the ritual, and we are certain that when you know it you will bring it off with incomparable power. Indeed . . ." She took another step backward, looking all about her, up and around. "Now, here you have provided for me a perfect seaside Dari nocturne; and even though Hanoku is not here, we could rehearse it. Would you like that?"

He was beginning to be amused; the die having cast itself, he rolled with it (certain, though, that tomorrow or tonight he must go ship-prowling, now that one power had been tempestuously released by the failure of others). "It would be fun," he declared, "but you must lead."

"It is all very simple," she assured, "very easy—nothing elaborate, nothing like Western ritual, and even the small symbolism is as straightforward as it can possibly be. Let me see . . . you stand over there, Croyd, with your back to the bar; pretend it is the Holy of Holies." Smiling now, caught up in it, he stood and went toward the bar. She asked his back, "You wouldn't have a flake of Darian music?" Well, he did; he bent to the bar-panel console that controlled his cabin environment, the instrument panel wherewith he had fabricated the Darian moonlight and the surf susurrus and the eight-tenths gravity; and when he straightened, the room was mutedly filled with primitive strings and bongo drums in a teasing hula rhythm. And he turned to her in triumph and caught breath. At the far end of the room she faced him, radiantly nude except for a lemon-yellow lua-lua and a necklace of artificial yellow flowers.

Wetting lips, he essayed, "You seem luckily to have brought your own music."

"It is my bridal costume!" she cried. "Do you like it? I made it myself!" Then her smile hesitated. "And yet I feel difficult, seeing you there in your Western clothing. Do you suppose that you could . . . ?"

Suddenly *he* grinned; what a devil. of a child-innocent lark this was! "What would I wear?" he demanded; "a boy-type lua-lua?" She nodded, eager. "One moment," he cautioned with an upraised finger; he went behind the bar, poured a short one, downed it, stripped off his shirt, and (screened to the midriff by the bar) got rid of his other things; then he reached down to get something beneath the bar, and worked on himself, and emerged. Flaming crimson his gigantic bar-towel lua-lua was! Djeel applauded, screaming with laughter.

He stood erect before the bar, mock-solemn, intoning, "If there be here two young people who because of misinformation wish marriage, let them come forward."

Djeel too straightened and sobered as well as she could, although she kept blurping out little giggles, looking at his lua-lua. He kept his face straight, groin appreciating her bared beauty. And gradually she sobered entirely and stood proud, facing him at the far end of the room. And she said quietly, in a voice just audible above the drums, "We will have to teach you the ritual ..later, but for now you can just get the feel of it. I feel better now, Croyd. I am no longer laughing at your lua-lua; you are dressed right for Dari now; I am scarcely self-conscious at all now. Look, Governor, just stand there with the drums in your heart, and imagine that brown Hanoku stands here at my right, as tall and splendid as . . . as yourself, Croyd. See, I will have my right hand placed on his left forearm; no man will give me away, Croyd. I am a high princess, the last of my family, and he is a high prince, as you are a high prince. Now, catch the drum rhythm; to this rhythm Hanoku and I will advance toward you, like this."

With mounting pulse rate he watched her deliberately semihula toward him, lua-lua swinging, vital breasts rippling in delicate counterpoint, until she stood motionless not a meter away from him, gravely considering his hardset face. She told him serenely, "We are approaching climax now, Croyd. You must say, quote, 'According to the customs of your people, before you can be married, Djeelian must be deflowered by the chief of her clan. But her clan is all Dari, and under our new treaty the Governor of Dari is chief of all Dari. So it is I who must deflower her. Onu Hanoku, do you assent to this necessity?' End of quote for you, Croyd. And then Onu Hanoku will answer, 'I do!' For he and I both want our marriage to be thoroughly right, in accordance with the old customs of our people."

And then, for some reason her head went slowly down, and her wide-eyed gaze fastened on the subvoluntary self-assertiveness of his improvised lua-lua. Above her, his voice was harsh. "You and your Hanoku—*both* of you are honestly asking me to do this?"

Her face came slowly up to his; her face was all filled with concern. "Croyd, Onu and I have talked fully about this; we agree that you must be the co-father of our first child for his strengthening. But we realize that you are a Westerner; it would trouble you to deflower me in his presence and in the presence of others. But that will not be necessary, dear Croyd, if you can manage to marry us publicly tomorrow; the timing would be precarious but acceptable. Here I stand, we are alone at the rehearsal; what you do now with me before the gods will be valid for Hanoku and for all when Princess Djeelian reports it to Hanoku publicly for our people."

He cleared his throat loudly; nevertheless, his voice stayed harsh. "Believe that I want you; even with pirates, you never stood closer to ravishment. But I have to tell you what is true. As Governor of Dari, I am no more than a public servant reporting to President Tannen."

He waited, using all his human power, but only that power, to restrain his lua-lua and his heart.

She began to tremble. Slowly she sank to her knees and trembled at his feet, staring at his big bare feet.

She whispered, *"Tannen?"*

Her arms crossed themselves; her hands clutched her shoulders.

She told his feet, "You need not repeat it, I heard, I comprehend it; Hanoku and I faced this fact, we know it; only, we hoped that you would not think of this, or having thought of it, would choose not to mention it, and perhaps our gods would take it as merely an honest mistake and bless it. But you are one who has to be honest, Croyd, even at your own cost. And even this is a strengthening that our first child should have. But let this go, it has been said, now; this is what it must be, then: Tannen it must be."

Silence. He gazed melancholy down upon her, his lua-lua somnolent.

Presently her arms dropped, and her eyes came up to his. Gravely she informed him, "Nevertheless, I love you enough. *We* love you enough. Tannen be damned."

He stared down upon her, hands hanging loose, while her words penetrated his blood.

She caught breath; his lua-lua had catapulted itself away. Reaching behind him, he twisted a bar dial, killing the gravity; bending, he seized her upper arms, toe-thrust the floor, and rose with her into moonlit Dari midair.

She cried a high musical cry: *"Hoëné,* Croyd! *Hoëné! Hoëné!"*

Small bubbles of chicken blood in freefall scarlet-champagned their passional ballet in the Polynesian sky; she exulted and drifted, exulted and drifted, overflowing with his vitality, transfigured by this repetitious, wondrous defloration that should not be happening at all.

Something cacophonous was beginning to annoy his audio threshold. He ignored it. This was *Djeel.*

The noise kept going.

He found that he was listening to it. The emergency horn. *Lifeboats . . .*

It was an *insistent* hooting! It *convinced!*

. Resolutely he thrust her away from him; her head lay back, her eyes were closed, her mouth was open; she was totally unready for any sort of action other than one sort of action.

Twisting his own body, he drifted downward to the bar and manipulated the dial to three-tenths G; when his feet settled on the floor, he moved over and caught her, languorously falling. Laying her on the floor, he restored gravity to eight-tenths G and went into a rapid scattered-clothing retrieval. When in seven seconds he returned with her blue pants and yellow blouse and lua-lua and his own trousers (his shirt and their shoes were eluding him), she was up on one elbow watching him, but apathetic. He got her to her feet, encouraging haste; she responded with lethargy; for speed, he maneuvered on her lua-lua and blouse, and onto himself his own pants, and barefoot, shouldered her, barefoot, and prowled to his door, and palmed it open, and loped with her down the corridor to the lifeboat bulge, trailing her trousers in his left hand. I stood waiting by the bulge.

Djeel said urgently in his ear, "Let me down!" He swung her around and set her on her feet, his hands on her waist. Her hands on his shoulders, she demanded of his eyes, "This is a real emergency?"

He said, shortly, "It is. Get into the lifeboat."

Her hands bruise-clutched his shoulders, and she smiled hard and told him, "If this is real stuff, Croyd, you are wonderful, but I have to be with Hanoku." Twisting away, she turned and ran up the corridor toward the bridge.

Croyd ran seven paces after her, stopped dead, thought for a tenth-second, watched her disappear, swiveled, and came back to the lifeboat bulge. "Get in, Tannen," he commanded; "she's of age, and Hanoku will have a lifeboat"; and he thrust me inside and followed me in.

Two-G thrust sent us crashing over.

Viewplates opened. We stared at the image of the *Castel Jaloux*, football size in distance, floodlighted, diminishing.

The *Castel* converted herself into a solar flare and vanished.

Commandcom fell.

ON THE BRIDGE of the *Castel Jaloux*, Gorsky, flanked by Hanoku and a covey of crewmen, stolidly faced apparitions who seemed unaffected by the G forces.

Coldly she told the apparitions, "I believe that you omitted to salute the quarter-deck."

They were vaguely horrible, confusingly luminous, multifaceted, threatening. They held no evident weapons, yet they were clearly dangerous. Gorsky comprehended a reply within her mind—from one of them, or from all of them, no articulate words, but the following meaning: *Go to your quarters.*

Clearing her throat, Gorsky said, "Lieutenant Hanoku, you know what you have to do first. Do it now."

Hanoku successively pressed two buttons. Horning honking resounded through the ship, but with a bell undertone that signaled crew: "Passengers to lifeboats—but all crew stay aboard on red alert."

All of them felt the inward response: *We know that the signal will among other things send President Tannen and Governor Croyd to their lifeboat, which has standing orders to depart immediately both are aboard. We are allowing this departure, but no other departure. Go to your quarters.*

"They telepath," Gorsky observed, "but as yet they do nothing. I wonder if they understand us. Perhaps I should test. Hold still, Mr. Hanoku, I am going to let one of them have it." With unexpected speed she drew a sidearm and pressed the button. The shot disintegrated the bridge bulkhead. Into her mind came the alien comment: *We understand you. NOW, go to your quarters.*

Hanoku barked, "What is this—ghost piracy?" Gorsky silenced him with a warning look. "Very well," Hanoku snarled, "if that is how it is. Stand aside—you're blocking the exit." This blocked exit was now unusually broad, owing to the absence of a bulkhead.

Two of the appearances drew back; and Gorsky, followed by recalcitrant Hanoku and bristling crewmen, descended from the bridge.

As they moved down the corridor, pausing at the entrance to the admiral's cabin, not failing to notice the luminous weirds posted everywhere, Gorsky told her crew without lowering voice: "Go to your several quarters, and I will try to communicate via intercom. If you do not hear from me, all of us are on our own. Save the ship. Repeat: save the ship. That is all." She entered and closed her door.

Plodding to his quarters just ahead of two harassing phenomena, Hanoku turned a corner and caught running Djeel in his arms. He stood still, enfolding her, soothing her; the phantoms merely waited, blocking retreat. He told her ear, "Let's go"; and, cloaking her with an arm, he drew her into his tiny one-man cabin and locked the door. Nothing followed him through the locked door, but presumably they waited outside.

The man and woman sat on his bunk, he sheltering, she clinging.

"Why, Djeel," he mocked, "you are barefoot!"

She pushed herself roughly away from him and huddled beside him, staring at the floor, intermittently shivering. Concerned, but knowing her strength, considerately he waited.

She said, dead, "Do you know what they are?"

"I do not."

"Is it anything we can get out of?"

"I do not know. But somehow I think not."

Studying the floor: "I could have escaped with Croyd."

"But you did not."

"No. Because of you."

"I do not necessarily agree, Djeel. But I thank you—and endlessly I love you."

Silence. She had moved close to him; his arm cradled her shoulders.

She licked lips and told the floor, "The Croyd affair is consummated."

"Thank the gods," he said fervently. "What a co-father! Then he *did* miss the Tannen angle?"

She said, low, "No."

He considered that. His grip on her shoulder tightened.

She turned to face her lover fairly. Squaring her shoulders a little, she asserted, "He told me *first* that it would have to be Tannen. He was honest, manfully containing his own heat, and his heat was mighty. So I too was honest, and I told him that we knew this, but nevertheless . . . And so, then . . ."

A great cry of anguish burst from her throat; she clasped his torso and jammed her face against his chest and went into spasms of sobbing.

He held her, stroking her hair.

She found strangulated voice. "I was such an egotistical idiot, I was going to be an individual by twisting the lore for the strengthening of our child, and also for my pleasure, I will confess it to you, Onu; but the lore will *not* be used, I have called down death upon us."

"*How*, Djeelian?"

"Because Croyd it *should not* have been, by the lore; but Croyd it *was;* and now, if you are the next one, with Tannen excluded, the lore will be violated; but if Tannen is the next one, *you* will be excluded, Croyd and Tannen will be the co-fathers, and either way the lore will be violated; and therefore the gods have sent death upon us and this ship."

A playful smile began to steal upon his lips. "Djeel, never worry about what the gods may send, when our whimsical Dari gods have already sent whatever they are sending. Think, Djeel, do not our pleasant gods chuckle at the chicken blood?"

After a further sob or two, she was still. And presently her wondering face came up to his.

He said tenderly, "You are looking at it all backwards. You are imagining that two nights from now Tannen or I must finish what Croyd started. Whereas, in truth, it may well be that tonight Croyd finished what two nights ago *I* started."

She digested that. Her lips were wanly enlivened by the start of a small smile, but it quivered and vanished. "Even if that is so, Onu, the Tannen part remains to be consummated, and for the sake of the lore it *must* be consummated."

His own smile vanished. Slowly stroking her hair, he told the ceiling, "This talk about Tannen is academic; we are done with life. Through no doing of our gods, these phantoms are killing our ship, and we are powerless because they are not physical. They do not care about us two, they are after Croyd and Tannen, they are merely throwing us away. So we will marry ourselves now, on the strength of the strength that Governor Croyd has spent in you. And we will pass tonight and tomorrow night in prayerful chastity, praying to our benign gods that for the lack of higher consecration the Croyd passion has been not too much but just enough.

"If there should *be* for us a tomorrow night.

"Or a tonight. . . ."

In her cabin, whose instrumentation was a perfect replica of that on the bridge, Gorsky noted with interest that Croyd's lifeboat had embarked, presumably with Croyd and Tannen aboard.

Her attention was next engaged by the deflection upward of the *Castel*'s course.

Unfortunately she had no controls in her cabin; and, not for the first time, the need for control duplication crossed her mind. But in the name of Saint Stalin, hadn't she filed requisition after requisition?

Activating intercom, she announced, "Now hear this, all stations. This is the admiral. I do not know what these apparitions are. They have taken control of my bridge. The captain and I are separated and confined to quarters. Every station is ordered to reply if you hear me. Over."

She deactivated and waited for her visiphones to light up.

Instead, the entire *Castel Jaloux* lighted up. Externally, anyhow. She could see the fire in the viewplates.

It died. Metaspace darkness.

She tried calling Captain Czerny. No response. Evidently they had killed the intercom.

She tried for Croyd in the lifeboat. No response. The

flare had something to do with that; the *Castel Jaloux* was a total island.

A voice in her mind: *Your ship is headed for deep metaspace. It will dissolve out there. You are done; make your peace.*

She demanded, "Is Croyd your prisoner?"

He and Tannen.

"Why do you not take us where you are taking them?"

The rest of you do not matter. We are flushing you out.

Gorsky sat stiff in the swivel chair behind her desk. She inquired calmly, "Since we are all headed for death in metaspace, perhaps you won't mind explaining this to me. Who are you, and what is your motive?"

Since you are all headed for death in metaspace, why should we bother to explain?

"Curiosity," Gorsky bit. "Some of us believe in life after death. I don't, but I can be wrong. If I am wrong, it would be nice to remember later why we got the death."

If you are not one who has that belief, it does not matter.

Gorsky leaned across her desk toward the absent invisible phantom. "I am able to transcend my indoctrination if the arguments are convincing. *Is* there life after death?"

You must find some noumenon to ask. I am only a phenomenon.

Gorsky leaned back. "Then tell me, at least, why you spooks bother to stay aboard, since we are all done anyway."

I do not know. We have been placed aboard. We have not been withdrawn.

"In other words, you are all pretty stupid, just bohunks for some large character."

Perhaps we are just lucky.

Gorsky stated quietly, "I am now going to test you again. In my desk drawer there is an armed weapon. I am about to use it on you. Will you stop me?"

I will be fascinated to know how you will aim.

Deliberately making an assumption, Gorsky opened a drawer, drew a weapon, took aim dead in front of her, and fired. A wall disintegrated, revealing her bedroom beyond.

The voice said in her mind, *That wasn't where I was.*

Gorsky replaced the weapon, closed the drawer, folded her hands, and thought.

The uppermost thought concerned a dark young lieutenant and a semidark young princess. Gorsky was old and cynical; nevertheless, Gorsky was always irritated by the futility of young death.

ACTION AFTER H-HOUR:

MY BROODING HEAD WAS SNAPPED UP by the abrupt sharp commanding voice of Chloris. She asserted, "I know how to get out of here. I know how to rescue the *Castel,* if she exists. I need your help, Mr. President."

It chopped my yesterday reverie; on the other hand, already I had exhausted yesterday memories without finding any practical pattern. I inquired, "Will this involve also Croyd's rescue?"

"Possibly. And possibly also yours. I am interested in your omission of this thought. The *Castel* has first instrumental priority; your rescues depend on that."

I demanded, "How?"

"We are wasting time, but I see that you must know, and I will tell you crisply. Listen. They brought me down here, they bound me here; but at the moment they have forgotten me, and I am not bound. Internal inspection assures me that their beefing up of my velocity potential and my inertial shield has not diminished. I will hope to find and overtake the *Castel,* do something about her lack of self-control, and bring her down here to take care of you and Croyd. Must I waste further time in details?"

I ruminated.

Chloris, curt: "To confirm flight readiness, I need to have my exterior inspected. Will you be good enough to step outside and look me over?"

I was on my feet. "What am I to do?"

"Go out and look at my tail."

"What am I to notice about your tail?"

"My tail must be perfectly clean for perfect launch. If you see any foreign debris in my pipes, clean it out, then come back in."

"All right. Open your hatch."

"My hatch is open, sir; please act."

I descended into lush apparitional Gaza grass that had come positive again during my reverie. I went for the lifeboat's tail, which housed her repulsors. After extremely close inspection: "Chloris . . ."

"Mr. President?"

"You are clean."

"Wholly clean?"

"*Clean* clean."

"Good. Pray stand back while I test-blow."

"How far back shall I stand?"

"For safety, at least ten meters away from my flank, forward of my tail."

I turned and moved swiftly away from the lifeboat through luxurious grass in the direction of the Arcadian sea.

As I turned, I saw the blur of Chloris vanishing.

Chloris drove vertically upward at an acceleration which she maintained at maximum. Her beefed-up maximum was beyond her own credulity, and it kept growing.

As for her beefed-up inertial shield, it lagged somewhat behind her accelerative maximum, but she hoped that it would be enough to keep her own rekamatic structure from disintegrating.

Quietly she reminded herself that it would *not* have been enough to keep a human passenger from disintegrating.

Contemporary Action

PAN SAGITTARIUS

Days 2-3

You will need to apply all your skills to the solution of a most complex situation. Plan to do almost everything yourself, without help.

—A Representative Horoscope

HELP WAS ON THE WAY TO US, actually; had been on the way (if you are a fatalist) nearly four years. Whether it would arrive in time, or at all, would have been a problem had I known it was on the way; for Croyd, perhaps it was already too late.

The help was Pan Sagittarius. And this requires a bit of background.

In 2502, four years prior to the present brouhaha, our Sol Galaxy (whose economic hub was Erth) was attacked by invaders from a relatively nearby galaxy. The melancholy condition of humanity on Erth, at the moment of invasion, was such that only one man was free to counterattack. Luckily, that man was Croyd.

You don't single-handedly knock off an intergalactic invasion without somewhat unusual tools and aptitudes. Croyd deployed his; we have seen a sampling in action, before, grace to Childe Roland, he lost all of them.

His defense involved a complex system of maneuvers among several simultaneous probability spheres. In the course of these maneuvers, necessarily he left a Croyd probability body in each sphere that he visited. At the end it turned out that one extra Croyd body was left over, and also, one extra body for his friend Greta. These duplicates, if only to prevent confusion, decided to call themselves Pan and Freya Sagittarius.

"Admit," Croyd had remarked to Greta, "that this is a form of reproduction."

I permit myself a metascientific parenthesis:

If Croyd and Pan were physically and mentally perfect duplicates—both having one identical stream of single-person memories—then, subjectively, which was which? And if one of them should subjectively regard himself as junior to the other, what psychologically would happen to the junior? The same sort of question would apply to Greta and Freya. Some philosophers might offer the swift mordant reply: *What difference can it make?* But would that reply perhaps be too cheap?

For me, poignant is the concept of duplicates who are mature in their life histories *but somehow newborn,* trying to find their own ways as individuals. How much easier it would be for sons or daughters or even identical twins to find individualities! Each of them has a birth start for the search, whereas *these* duplicates had already matured in psychosomatic identity before they were split.

Newborn in 2502, Pan and Freya accepted a special heavy responsibility and went their ways.

In 2504 Pan departed that responsibility, taking Freya with him.

What follows is new material. I must, I think, take a moment or two over Pan's immediate action in 2504; but then we will be inspecting immediately pertinent events in 2506 ITC (Intergalactic Temporal Convention, a concord which permits synchronization to the day and even inexactly to the hour among galaxies). These immediately pertinent events begin on what I have herein labeled Day 2.

———— ▶◀ ◀▶◀ ▶◀ ————

OF THE TWO BILLION STARS IN DJINN GALAXY (an SBc-type galaxy, streaming in a simple S-shape, which meant, not that it was very old in accordance with the usual inference from the ancient Hubble classification, but rather that it was very young), only one star had interested Pan as he came in. This was Djinn, a there-unusual G2 Sol-type star not very far in from the tip of an S-arm; it had planets, and its seventh planet in particular arrested him—a giant belted with a rainbow girdle reminding him forcibly of Saturn. Instantly Pan named the planet Djinn VII frankly *Saturn;* and, acting on the double cue, he looked for life in the star system. Sure enough, an inner-on planet, Djinn IV, corresponded almost precisely to his own departed Sol III, or Erth; and it housed the dominant humanoid life in the galaxy. Its own name for itself was *Moudjinn.*

There was life also on Djinn III, or *Dari;* but Dari was known to be a sea of slave primitives islanded by enclaves of space pirates, wherefore Pan gave wide berth to that planet.

Pan formulated a tight problem for practical inquiry: how most efficiently to prey upon the civilized life of wealthy Moudjinn while establishing his own life at a leisurely level.

The solution hypothesis was related to Djinn VII, or

Saturn, terrific for visuals; and in on Saturn he homed in his metaspace yacht with semipassive Freya. (This yacht he had won by telekinetic cheating at dice on several planets, fleecing his purse with contributions from admiring and wealthy widows.) Bringing his craft into an orbit at a ninety-degree declination to the rainbow girdle, Pan deployed intricate robot equipment in space-platform construction. While that was in progress, he departed Saturn, touched down successively at about thirty strategic locations on Moudjinn (which on average was nearly as advanced as Erth despite a feudal politico-economy), got some entrées, distributed some cards (printed verkotype, which is to say, fried reonoffset), used charm and telepathy to get confidential dirt on a few key people, subliminally captured one or two by mind invasion, and departed for Saturn, leaving behind a number of irresistible promises.

Saturninn was the upshot (year 2504 ITC): a wicked hotel of gleaming metaloid, the plush Satan spot of Djinn Galaxy: a spheroid satellite of ten kilometers diameter, with 125 unobtrusive antipirate gun emplacements, with exterior viewports in all rooms, orbiting Saturn once in three hours at such an angle that the Saturn rings rushed up at you and receded from you and only for minutes were wholly invisible to you; and when you were right upon them (actually a few thousand kilometers out from them, for they would have been practically invisible had you been orbiting through their girdle), they were breathtakingly, sky-fillingly marvelous.

Saturninn.

Two new guests motored out one afternoon in 2506 (Day 2) from Moudjinn, an easy five-hour two-billion-kilometer run. (You hit light velocity at the end of the second hour, and spent the next three hours braking.)

There were three guest entrances: the Custom Entrance (for ordinarily or transiently wealthy people), the Ambassador Entrance (for VIP's), and the Rendezvous Entrance (for those of high or low degree who preferred to steal in, even though once inside they would go ostentatious); anybody could enter at Custom, but your card had to qualify you for VIP before you could make Rendezvous. It was at Rendezvous that the new guests berthed shortly after 1800 hours Saturninn time.

Had they seriously wished to be inconspicuous, they would have berthed at Custom.

A cab (antigrav) skimmed them inward a kilometer and let them off at an ornate foyer, where, rather than being coldly stood up for desk-clerk insolence in front of an impersonal counter with mail cubbyholes behind, they were greeted by a tailored blond receptionist who ushered them into a pleasant small office (it was almost a boudoir), seated them, seated herself, crossed sinuous bare legs, leaned forward a bit (ruffed choker collar, but a nice effect even so), and queried, "Would you prefer that I interview just one of you, or is both all right?"

The guest woman (darkly Junoesque and languorous, ornately coiffured, stoled in white virmin fur) glanced at her escort (slight, pale, aesthetic, asthenic, thin-moustached, evening-dressed). He informed the receptionist precisely, "Both is or are all right. You have my reservation?"

"We are holding precisely what you requested. I merely wondered . . ."

"Yes, we do have further requests. At eight, my companion and I will appear in the Starlight Lounge for cocktails, and there we should wish to be met by a man and a woman."

The receptionist took it quite matter-of-factly. "One moment," she said. She arose, entered a cubbyhole, and returned with two elegantly red-bound tomes. "You will wish to see samples and make selections. These are tri-d stills, but any that interest you can be projected for twenty seconds in limited activation on approval. The activation is, of course, perfectly discreet parlor action. This one is men, this one is women." She stood, intentionally indecisive, allowing the guests to decide which book each wanted.

The man took the women; the woman, shrugging, accepted the men. They riffled pages with disinterest, then almost simultaneously handed back the books. The man said, "Candidly, our thoughts were higher."

For the first time disconcerted, the receptionist stated, "While I hate to be sordid, I should make it clear that the time of each of these men and women is valuable and in great demand, and they for their part are choosy. To use one measure of value—they would lose money if they left here to become corporation vice-presidents."

The guest woman queried, "Would *you* lose money, sweets?"

The receptionist replied coldly, "Yes, although I accept very few arrangements." She turned and looked at the man deliberately.

The man said, cool, "We are interested in more than superficial pleasure. We are interested in personal force. I have the money required to interest two people who normally accept no arrangements whatsoever."

The receptionist went courteously distant. "If, then, you wish to make acquaintances among our guests, I am afraid I cannot be of assistance."

"Not among your guests. We had in mind Mr. Pan and Miss Freya."

The blond, already pale, paled, but lost not a drop of *sangfroid*. "They do not accept such arrangements."

"Possibly you misunderstand," the guest woman interposed. "Our interest in meeting them is . . . a gambling interest. If we give you our real nâmes, will you try to arrange it?"

"I know your real names, Duke Dzendzel, Princess Medzik."

"It is then arranged?"

"It is not. I shall have to let you know later. I am pessimistic."

The duke arose swiftly, the princess languidly. He asserted, "I will assume your success, because we came here only for the highest level of diversion. We will expect to meet Mr. Pan and Miss Freya in the Starlight Lounge at eight. Thereafter we will expect them to gamble with us at the game and stakes that we will name. You may tell them that I will stake one-tenth of my annual income from all sources for one year; what they are to stake will be confidential among the four of us."

"I said that I may fail."

"If you fail, have our cab and scouter ready at eight. Our rooms, madame."

"I assume," quietly said green-eyed ash-blond Freya, "that we will not be in the Starlight Lounge at eight."

The glowing rings of Djinn-Saturn swept toward them; their couple table nestled, with several other favored tables, in the bulge of the largest picture viewport in the casino of Saturninn—now, in 2506, the hard-established sin mecca of this galaxy.

The broad smile on the craggy-handsome face of auburn-haired Pan was merry-mocking, but the blue eyes were deep only in hue and otherwise shallow. "We'd miss entertainment if we didn't go," he told her. "He runs the Emperor, remember? And she's his second cousin."

Freya considered him moodily, chin palmed, long fingers tapping a cheekbone. She said then, "Until now, during ten years I have not been *paid*."

"We do not know that his game is you—or that her game is me. We do know that he will stake one-tenth of his one-year income. Have you tried totting up what that would *be*?"

"Purely for the information, what would it be?"

"Just the interest would build and operate a hundred Saturninns. Looking at it another way: with a tenth of his one-year income between us, you and I could buy what we needed in order to become the fourth- or fifth-wealthiest people on Moudjinn. Which is to say, our wish would be our command, forever. Monte Cristo, move over."

She said, "Between us there is a candle."

"Well?"

"Put it out. And don't pinch or blow."

The candle went out, apparently all by itself. Cool, Pan queried, "Well?"

"See those Saturn rings? I'm tired of their pale pink. Make them gold."

"No. What are you getting at?"

"But you *could* make them gold. And with powers like that, why do you need to play gigolo for any amount of money?"

"We don't know that this is the game, I said."

"I'm betting on it. And that's only the most distressing development in a spate of developments. Here's this inn, which is, you should excuse the puritanical phrasing for which there is no substitute, an iniquitous den of flimflam piracy."

"Freya, we don't hurt anybody except established masochists . . ."

". . . and your own fraternizing with the clientele, an unbrotherly fraternizing that is more like a permanent floating con game with erotic fringe benefits."

"All I do is to cheat millionaires of one sort of thing and husbands of another sort of thing. Let's go, Freya; we're due in the Starlight Lounge."

"The game," said Dzendzel over the second cocktail, "is a simple game, and one rule will be that either of us can cheat."

Pan gravely nodded; Freya watched narrowly; ample Princess Medzik looked bored. Pan commented, "We can get to the game and the rules in a minute. Quite candidly, your grace, I am more interested in the stakes."

Dzendzel incised, "I have announced what I stake—one-tenth of my annual income from all sources. What you are to stake, I have written on paper; it is in my pocket here. If you lose, I will hand it to you. If you win, you will not need to see it."

Pan said, cold, "No game."

Dzendzel studied his cocktail. Shrugging then, he produced a small paper from a small pocket and handed it over. Pan unfolded, read, raised eyebrows, and passed it to Freya. She read, crumpled the paper, and stared at Pan with brows down hard.

Pan told the duke, "These bets are uneven. You stake merely one-tenth of your income for one year; we are to stake our self-respect."

Insolently the duke stared at him.

Pan's face went faintly whimsical. "I see I can't bluff you. Tell me the name of the game."

Freya's face contorted. She kept expecting a telepathic communication from Pan, but none came.

Dzendzel told him blandly, "The game is coin toss. We do it here. I provide my coin, you provide yours. We toss three times. If you match me twice, you win. If you match me only once, I win. And we can cheat."

Pan said quietly, "There is only one way to cheat at a matching coin toss. The cheater has to know how the other coin is coming down, and he has to be able to make his own coin come down in the way that is best for himself. Since this is what you propose, you must be able to do that, and you must know that I am able to do that."

Dzendzel merely stared.

Pan turned to Freya, who was frightfully angry. Looking straight at her, he said, "Duke Dzendzel, there can be no trivial reason why you are willing to stake one-tenth of your annual income in the hope of enslaving Freya and me for a trifling year. I think you should tell us the real reason."

Oddly, Freya's anger began to dissipate.

Dzendzel said, cold, to both of them, while Princess Medzik toyed with her spent cocktail, "The slavery would not be sexual; if that were to be incidental, it would be voluntary. And neither of you would be harmed. Beyond that, I do not choose to give you reasons. Do you wish to play, or don't you?"

Pan suddenly grinned. It was a vital grin; it included his eyes. Swiftly he reached into a pocket, produced a coin, held it out in his palm beneath the thin nose of the duke.

The princess raised her face to stare at Pan. Then, gradually conscious of a counterstare, she turned her head to meet the amused eyes of Freya. After a moment of mutual challenge, the eyes of both women turned to the men.

Twice the coins spun high. The first toss was a match, the second not.

The four eyes of Pan and Dzendzel were snake-eyes interstriking.

Pan demanded, "If I win the next toss, how soon will I be paid?"

Dzendzel tonelessly asserted, "One-tenth of my last year's income is already on deposit in your Saturninn bank, to be released to you tomorrow unless I countermand by midnight tonight. If next year's income is higher, on my honor you will be paid the difference; if it is lower, there will be no penalty."

Pan glanced at Freya, was rewarded by a low-key smile, glanced at the princess, was invited by parted fleshy lips, and queried, "If I lose the next toss, what will be the action?"

The duke told him, "I will depart later tonight with Miss Freya; the princess will remain here at your disposition; soon I will send for you, and then you will do what I require."

Again Pan looked at Freya; her smile had gone hard. He smiled hard back. He turned to Dzendzel.

The simultaneous timing of their tosses was intuitive.

The coins rose to ten-foot height. They hesitated up there, slowly rotating in midair. They hesitated . . . and went motionless up there.

They shimmered up there for a period of seconds.

Both coins vanished.

Pan and Dzendzel matched eyes. Both women were numb.

Pan commented, "It seems to be a draw. I propose the following settlement. Princess Medzik will stay with me until she chooses to leave. Miss Freya will go your route until she chooses to quit you. I will be at your disposition until I weary of this. I will draw on your deposit month for month as long as one of us is with one of you."

The four eyes were coldly counterstriking serpents.

"Done," said Dzendzel.

Swiftly Princess Medzik looked at Freya, and was startled to discover that Freya seemed placid.

Freya had received no telepathy from Pan. But the final coin toss had told her why Pan could not risk telepathy in the presence of Dzendzel. Nevertheless, Freya was troubled.

Afterward Pan and Freya sat silent and somber in their viewport window. Freya ultimately challenged, "Pan, look, believe me, if it were *you, really* you, I'd accept it, I'd have fun with it—but it just isn't *you*, it's a *degenerate* you."

Now he was staring gloomily at the palms of his hands. "I thought it was just freedom. How is it degeneracy?"

"Well, because it—"

"Am I degenerating with *you*, Freya?"

"Come again?"

"Is my personal position with you degenerating?"

"No, but—"

"Are *you* in position to stone me?"

"*Yes!* I've had my little diversions, but . . . discreetly and selectively, not degenerately. And I've been disappointed every time, because you have spoiled me."

"And I, because of you."

"*Merci.*"

"They are, however, adventures, Freya."

"With me, dancing adventures. With you, sadisms."

"That is my degeneracy?"

She breathed deeply, resolved, said it. "No, it's deeper. Four years ago you took on a five-year personal responsibility, and I went with you. In two years you had the deal developing just fine. Then suddenly you blew out of there with me in tow, leaving your sworn charge weltering leaderless in nonspace. *Why?*"

He inhaled, and exhaled, and inquired of the table, "Then *that* is my degeneracy?"

She told the table, "Yes. The rest is just ornamentation."

"After two years of this, *now* you tell me?"

"I asked you about it two years ago. It was the only time you ever hit me."

Again he stared at his hands. "I'd forgotten that."

"Good."

"I guess I required myself to forget that."

"Still good. It was angry impulse. But it told me something about your state of mind, and I haven't seen any improvement."

"So I hit you during a cop-out two years ago, and ever since, I've been sliding down the drain. And yet, here you are."

"Well . . . yes."

"Why?"

"You know."

Silence.

"Freya, a while back you remarked that you hadn't done any fancy-lady stuff during ten years. What made you knock off?"

Her eyes were soft. "That was a good year, 2496. I met you."

"Who's *me?*"

She stared, beginning to catch his drift.

He pressed. "Both of us were born in 2502. *Four* years ago. *Who's me?*"

Now it was distressingly clear why during *more* than two years he had excluded her from telepathic sharing of his emotions, letting her see only the objective intelligibilities that he wanted to communicate, but coming nowhere near baring the nerve. She made the problem explicit: "You are trying to tell me that there are two of you, although there *can't* be two of you."

His smile had returned, but it was sardonic. "Also that when you look at me, you are seeing *me* during the past four years—and *him* during the prior six years."

It was Freya's turn to study her hands. She replied this way: "You and he were born one man. A lousy four years ago you and Croyd bifurcated while Greta and I bifurcated. And each of us four is full owner of all his prior ages. We four decided together for our paths. The existence of Greta doesn't trouble *me.*"

He looked as though he were going to respond tartly;

then he closed his mouth. Comprehending what he had in-hibited, she looked down, flushing.

But then his eyes came alive, and he leaned forward to take her hands in his, telling her, "As between us two, I regret nothing."

"You said *I*. You also said *us*."

.. His smile lost bitterness, brightening into a grin. "Didn't I, just!"

He sobered and dropped her hands. "Nevertheless, they are they, we are we. I accepted Duke Dzendzel's game for fun. I am asking you also to go along with it as a picaresque, and I will keep all the money for the sake of your soul."

"*Why?*"

"Somebody is on his way here to sign a treaty with the Emperor. And the intelligence of the Emperor is this same Duke Dzendzel."

"*Somebody?*"

He nodded. "Somebody from Nereid."

He had named the capital of Sol Galaxy—a small satel-lite of Neptune. Freya, frowning, bent her head low over the table. "You are suggesting that Croyd may be in dan-ger, then."

He said, low, "Yes, but my sense of the peril is deeper. Two galaxies are in some sort of hazard, and my unformu-lated sense of the threat is named Dzendzel."

———— ▶◀ ◀▶ ▶◀ ————

PAN:

Freya? Hi? Where are you?

In the duke's castle on Moudjinn. Where are you?

Still on Saturninn. The duke has a castle?

Pan, it's really something out of a nineteenth-century gothic romance! Do you have time to listen?

All clear, Freya. Give me the color.

He brought me here in the tonneau of a carriage be-hind four black horse creatures; their legs moved so fast that I couldn't count them, but there were certainly more than sixteen. We rumble-clattered across a moat draw-bridge under a portcullis into a courtyard. Ruffed pages attended us dismounting. Then—get this—courteously he poised his left wrist, and I laid my right hand lightly upon it, and in we went.

To his bedroom?

You may not believe this, Pan, but the duke has delicacy . . . and ideals. He took me to his dining room, dinner loosened his tongue, his conversation flowed with the wines; I helped it along, with polite listening, with an occasional delicate prod, and with a . . . what is it you call it?

With a subliminal aura of projective hypnosis?

That's good, that's very good. And the atmosphere was helping him, too: a small rough-hewn table in a small rough-hewn room with a log fire, the crystal service deployed by a single aging manservant. So then, after terminal brandy, he began to . . .

Come to the point?

Yes, but you aren't going to believe the point.

What is the point?

It's going to take me a little while to come to it. He asked me finally whether he could trust me.

Why would he think he possibly might, Freya?

Oh, he had plenty of doubts; he noted that he had won me transiently on a coin toss and that I seemed to be your woman; but he added that I seemed sympathetic and that I understood him.

I suspect that you have left a good deal of transitional material untold, but never mind. Go on.

Well, how do you answer a question like that? I asked if he could read my mind. Very courteously he said yes, but I would have to give him leave to enter. So I invited him in.

To your mind.

Exactly. And while he was in my mind, I engulfed him with mind love; so he learned nothing, but he did not know this. And afterward he trusted me; he gave me all . . .

I think maybe now we are coming to the point?

Pan, he has a dream of feudal-medieval empire for the total metagalaxy! Complete with knights and castles and jousting! And he wants me to be his fostering Lady of the Manor.

For the whole metagalaxy?

Right on.

Freya, for you that's a promotion!

Pray take note that he offered me . . . marriage.

Ve-ry good! This involves he should divorce the duchess?

Too long you've known Tannen. Yes.

To him did you say yes?

I'm in consultation with me.

Where would I fit?

He made that part of it explicit. The feudal standard is double. For him there will be Princess Medzik, and there will be others. But the Lady of the House must be gracious, uncomplaining, and . . . touchable only by the lord, and always by the lord at his will. In short, Pan, you wouldn't fit.

Then my answer is no.

I hoped so. What's with Princess Medzik, Pan?

She hasn't asked me to marry her.

Then I'm one up. Sorry about that.

Freya, you didn't ring me across two billion kilometers for small talk.

Not primarily. Dzendzel has a real big thing, Pan.

Tell me.

I saw it, Pan—in a kind of big well he has in a deep cellar of his castle; we leaned on a rail around it and looked down, and I saw . . . what I can't describe, like a dream indescribable. I'm afraid I'm not being much help.

Stop intellect-thinking it at me. Remember *it at me.*

Eh . . . Okay. Here, I'm going dreamy-reminiscent; you pick it up.

Prolonged period of direct mind-to-mind experience. Then, *Freya:*

Pan?

You have shown me what appears to be a loosely organized system of mind fragments interacting with the Rolandic fissure of a brain. What is it?

Do you have a good grip on the arms of the chair you're sitting in?

I am well in from the edge of the bed that I am lying in.

Who's with you?

Stick to the subject. What is it?

The duke says it is the metagalactic fissure.

The meta . . . But, Freya, that's only . . .

I know. I tell you what he tells me. And . . .

Go on.

The duke wants to convert the Djinn Galaxy to a pure feudalistic system—with him on top, of course, under the Emperor, and maybe on top of the Emperor. He knows he has a long way to go. Meanwhile, he says this . . . thing *of his, in the metagalactic fissure, is a pure feudalism of mind—with himself as its grand seigneur. When he gets it unified, he says, he can use it to bring about the perfected feudalism of Djinn in his own lifetime. Pan, I've given you only the first quarter of the picture, but pause now to digest it.*

I have it. A friend of ours named Croyd would be irritated. What's the next quarter?

Your friend named Croyd would be irritated also about you and a certain apostasy.

I repent me of that apostasy. I will do something about that. Afterward. What's the second quarter?

The duke's plan for the metagalactic fissure lacks one ingredient to bring off the unification. And ironically, that one ingredient, should it reach Djinn, would blast his plans totally.

Silence. Then: I can think of only one ingredient in the universe that would fit both specifications.

A friend of ours named Croyd.

So then he is in trouble, Freya! What will the duke do?

The metagalactic fissure is going to capture Croyd: it gets the duke his ingredient and prevents his obfuscation, all in one fell swoop. And don't shout cliché; *you got an apter line that's original?*

Freya, Croyd is uncapturable. As I am uncapturable.

You were capturable by a coin toss, Pan. As for Croyd, first they sneak in and knock out his special powers.

Silence. When Pan's thought resumed, it felt dead. What's the third quarter?

Dzendzel utilizes your enslavement to accomplish what he cannot use Croyd for.

She sensed his faraway pondering. He said then: It follows that he knows I am Croyd's duplicate. With all Croyd's powers.

Exactly.

But debased . . . and buyable . . . and, in fact, bought.

Exactly.

But also he knows that I can terminate the enslavement at will. Without apostasy, by the way, in terms of the bargain. How can he risk using me?

He is confident that you will find this unique enslavement remarkably power-attractive. You will end by wishing to exchange this enslavement for permanent high vassaldom to the duke.

In order to enrich the duke's power?

Exactly. And your own.

This would bring us to the final quarter, Freya. What is it?

It is that Dzendzel then captures the universe.

After prolonged thought, *Freya:*

Pan?

I can get into the metagalactic fissure fairly fast, without the help of Dzendzel. Meanwhile, you'd better make contact with Greta by I-ray intergalactic relay.

I agree. Who here has the sender?

Dzendzel has one. Right there in his castle. That well you looked into—it was a receiver; a transmitter must be nearby. Can you get at it?

Not until tomorrow. But . . . well, yes. And then?

Do you have the guts to follow me into the fissure, via the Dzendzel I-ray pullman?

Silence. Then: *That's a long way, down there. Around a billion light-years, down there. I could arrive with my head in an armpit. Or something.*

But do you have the guts?

Dzendzel does it. Can you arrange to meet me down there?

Probably not. I don't even know where you'd arrive, down there. That isn't the point. You know?

Silence. Then: *Croyd will be down there. In trouble. Maybe dying.*

Exactly.

So . . . I bat for Greta with Croyd, down there.

Silence.

Pan . . . do you mind?

That's the irony of the century, totally incomprehensible: if I did mind, I wouldn't know why I should. Do you have the guts?

Not to replace Greta. But I'll go. Cheers, Pan.

Cheers, Freya. What will you do about the duke?

Send him Princess Medzik. Out.

Phase Four

LORD OF THE FISSURE

Day 4

Among neurones in a brain, the vassal cells feed information into their lord cells—"information" that is really mere attention-competing, tonally modulated; the lord cell, so nudged in terms of its own biography and current mood, adopts an attitude; and each vassal, eagerly receptive to the lord's attitude in terms of its own predispositions and specializations, either co-thrusts downward or is passive. So it is at the level of middle nobility, and in several echelons therein. Only one major substitution is needed to make the analogy pat: the lord and its vassals in a brain control, not land areas, but functional spheres.

When we move upward in the brain to the level of the top lord neurones or neurone nets, ultimately we encounter a "democracy" with a limited aristocratic franchise, exercised among the "dukes"; and each duke comprehends (in a limited way) so much of the sways exercised by all the other dukes that he can in a pinch take over for any other.

The metascientific issue turns on an unsolved problem. Does this "council" of "dukes" conjointly settle all final questions by consensus? More searchingly, does it sometimes so bitterly divide on final questions that the soul schisms

into a dual personality? Or is there a "king"
cell (unlikely hypothesis) which settles all final
questions, although it is sometimes unhorsed?
Or (tertiarily) is there a *mind*, transcending all
the dukes, which settles all final questions and is
ultimately entitled by qualitative difference to
l'oint du seigneur—and which sometimes goes
mad?

> —Dzendzel, Archduke of
> 　　Moudjinn, *Memoirs* (2503)

CROYD STOOD ALONE, VAGUELY PUZZLED, on a back street that he somehow knew was near downtown in a well-known alien city; downtown must be to his right, he had urgency to go to a well-known intricate street web there, the web was *target*, so young he was, early twenties, a boy. . . . On a venture, he entered the left-hand alley; menacing low-brown characters male and female loitered all along the alley, they recognized him as Beige the Enemy, surly they closed in on him, two or three knives snapped open, one was at his ribs. Entirely sympathetic although in cold fear of death, he resolved to squeeze out of this situation whatever experience he could; he stood erect, eyes-to-eye-pairs in turn, asserting: "Your problems I comprehend, but there is nothing I can do for you until I know more; what will you gain by killing me?" They held tableau; then a rough man nodded at Croyd and head-jerked; the others did not fall back, but they let Croyd pass on, pressing against him until he was clear of them and had debouched from the alley

to find himself totally lost; it was not what he had expected, he was in a wholly different quarter of a possibly different city. Pan was with him, Croyd's twelve-year-old son; Croyd was responsible, Croyd had to decide for both of them; but small Pan, taking Croyd's arm and pointing back at the *single* alley mouth, counseled that they must have taken the wrong alley and shifted dimensions, they must go back through and try the other alley, it would surely bring them back *on target*. And because *on target* was ultimately urgent, Croyd, resolving to squeeze out of the situation all the experience he could,

reentered with his son Pan deliciously beside him, and they moved inexplicably into an artificially illuminated cul-de-sac whose blind ending was a neat Dutch kitchen with a single small high crisscross-mullioned window above a window seat. Entering the kitchen, Croyd chatted with the chubby man and wife while Pan explored; and Croyd was content there; but small Pan insisted, "We must leave by the window." At

Pan's word, Croyd clambered up on the window seat (being careful not to jostle bread loaves) and opened the window inward, and boosted small Pan through, and followed him out on to the street, and turned to look for the twin alley mouths

and gaped with dismay that they had *further* complicated the journey: there were neither alleys nor house; they teetered atop a hill street; the street declivitated below them. He and small Pan considered each other gravely; then simultaneously they grinned; in perfect psychic affinity father and son had agreed: *All the experience we can: we who are about to die keep our eyes open to watch and be amused by the manner of death's coming.* Croyd seized small Pan by the shoulders, and Pan gripped his waist, and they started downhill; and as they began to slide

all the downtown city opened up a mile below them: *Target!* As their tiny car gathered velocity on the rail declivity, Croyd gripped with both arms the waist of Pan on his lap and yelled in his ear, "Close your eyes!" But Pan called back, pointing, "Look down at the marvel!" Croyd looked down, and indeed the remote-below uprushing city marvel was groin-enchanting; yet again he screamed at Pan, "Close your eyes—we may crash!" But Pan gripped Croyd's waist-encircling forearms and cried, "All the experience we can!" And as the car rocketed to the brink of verticality and plunged over, joyously Croyd bellowed back to his son, "All the experience we can; we keep our four eyes *open*."

Whereafter there was confusion, and there seemed to be a high-velocity spill scramble; driving himself out of confusion, Croyd came into clarity standing erect in a quiet place of great complicated building clusters on many altitude levels but as though on the marge of a colossal roofed shadow, facing

a gray-eyed ash-blond goddess divinely taller than he, standing serene gazing down upon him as he in his black-white-checkered uniform gazed worshipfully up into her infinite eyes. Less a voice than a mind whisper came the voice from her motionless lips: *I love you. Follow. Follow . . .* The sense of her voice would lead him uphill, following her, to a trysting place nestling high on the hind hill of silvery hovels; she was all his desire, all his soul, Pan's mother, all his meaning

                          but to his right was the infinite darkling hollow, a vast museum hall new-built but unoccupied and bare of exhibits; and he swiveled, torn between the compulsions of the museum and of the goddess. Her comprehending mind plea was urgent: *Croyd, there is no time, Hanoku will be coming. . . .* He raised high his head: *All the experience we can . . .*

                               And he began to run; into the museum vault, faster and faster, fleet feet skimming floor marble, farther and deeper into the endless emptiness, hasting to know all of it and then return to her. Deep into the depths he ran, velocity beyond thought, all the way to the mile-wide rearward wall; swung right, sped along the wall to the end of it; swung right, rocketed forward to the open side; swiveled right just inside and skimmed back toward *her* who waited at the

                               stopped short: *soldiery!* Swiftly pressing on to his head his floppy, checkered officer's cap, slow-rhythmically he death-marched forward to beard the soldiery led by a tall ruddy-bearded young knight in flashing golden panoply. He resolved to squeeze out of the situation all the experience he could. . . .

But in fact the knight was back-flanked by only two spear carriers, and the eyes above the beard of the knight seemed puzzled and the knight observed, "By now, Croyd, you should be mad, but clearly you are not. I warned him that this would not work with you. I have kept noticing that whenever you have been on the verge of losing reason, the same single thought has braced you: *Let me squeeze out of the situation all the experience I can.*"

Grimacing, Croyd spread hands, noticing that his checkered uniform had dissolved, that he was clad just in the old trousers and bare above the waist and below the ankles; and the goddess was gone. "One has dreamed," he explained; "and all dreaming is conscious; and in a dream, even if one is action-decision-impotent, there are attitudinal decisions that have to be made."

The knight ejaculated, "But didn't I succeed in cutting off all your special powers?"

"*You* are the one who was in here?"

"Aye."

"Then how big are you, really?"

"Pardon?"

"Here you are somewhat taller than I, you make me think of a young Charlemagne, or a Roland; and in case you do not grasp the Erth references, they are complimentary. But in my brain, you must have been molecule-small. How big are you, really?"

"As I choose. You did not answer me."

"The answer is, you succeeded just fine. But a man without special powers can do a great deal with his own normal mind brain. Is it you, sir, who has been creating these masterful illusions—including the curiously Freudian illusion that my twin brother Pan was my preadolescent son?"

The knight coughed. "It was not I. It was my lord."

"Then I can forget tact and be candid. Every illusion from the instant we landed has been tainted by elements of nonbelievable circumstantiality. This fact says to me— if you will pardon my bluntness—that a powerful but essentially stupid intelligence is trying to blow the minds of Tannen and me. Am I warm?"

"Essentially *stupid?*"

"Excuse me, sir, you know my name, but I do not know yours."

The right fist of the knight closed on a waist-sheathed poniard; he drew himself erect. "Call me Roland. And what we do is by command of our grand seigneur. I am discomforted to hear that you consider him stupid. I would wish to test your assertion in combat, but it is for him to listen and declare me his champion. And now it will be necessary to kill you in the manner that my liege lord may elect. Will you go with me voluntarily, or must we paralyze you and drag you?"

"Sir, I am at your service. In any way you may specify. But as an enemy."

Slightly inclining his head, Roland stated, "Sir, I have been in there. I respect you as my enemy."

Then Roland added an odd addition, hesitantly, softly. "Sir, my allegiance to my liege is boundless. But it may be that after you have met my liege, I will wish to discuss with you your suggestion that he may be stupid."

THE CASTLE THAT ROSE from the gray plain (in place of the museum in the city complex) possessed,

Croyd noted, anachronisms. It was built in the architec-
tural-engineering motifs of a Gothic cathedral: with high
pointed arches framing broad doorways and windows (but
arches whose austerity was unrelieved by figurine lacery);
with soaring columns and ceiling arches and flying but-
tresses lofting the mass with the skeletal economy-genius
of steel girders in postmedieval skyscrapers or like the
spun-glass silicates of Croyd's own time in situations where
forcefield construction was impractical. There were only
two hitches: the architectural genius of Gothic architec-
ture had scarcely emerged, and was far short of this degree of clean sophistication, in the era signaled by the
superficially golden but actually brazen and fundamentally
crude armor of Childe Roland; and since the castle had
no mass, the mass-buttressing Gothic construction it did
not need.

This castle had no mass. Its appearance was massive,
but when Croyd smartly hand-slapped the facade, the
feeling he got was a familiar forcefield feeling. This castle
was, in fact, like the birthplace fantasies, a towering illusion—not in the mind of Croyd, but *required* of Croyd's
optic thalamus by stabilized mental direction *from outside*. And the form of the castle was due not to architectural evolution or to functional necessity but to someone's
aesthetic whim.

Suspicion grew in Croyd's mind that he had been
trapped in a grimly total antithesis of Dari.

Behind him, Roland courteously suggested, "We have
audience within."

Croyd whirled on him, but Croyd was thinking as he
whirled: thinking regrettably slower than his habit, thinking only at the peak speed that an ordinary human can
drive himself to. He was coming rapidly to a conclusion
that this metagalactic fissure was somehow under control
by an advanced human mind in a high culture located
somewhere else. If so, the organization of the fissure and
the form of its illusions reflected the quality of that mind—
either a mind formidable beyond what Croyd's *had been*,
or a mind deploying apparatus more sophisticated-power-
ful than anything ever at Croyd's disposal, or both. And
some of the motives and characteristics of that mind were
coming clear by inference. (He was halfway around to
Roland in his whirl.)

Obviously the mind admired feudalism, since the two
prime *stable* illusions that he had encountered—Roland

and this castle—were medieval-feudal in motif, although a
shade off tempo: medievalism had, after all, spanned on
Erth at least ten centuries of development; and, now he
thought about it, had spanned about the same duration on
Moudjinn. Croyd entertained a preguess that in the fissure
this mind—from Moudjinn?—had set up an approach to
pure feudal organization, complete with chivalric illusions.
He was beginning to think of the mind as *Lord of the
Fissure.*

Either this lord was historically so ignorant that he fell
into anachronisms, or, for aesthetic reasons of his own, he
brought together whatever he preferred to bring together,
disdaining possible charges of anachronism. The latter
was more likely. A third possibility, that this lord was
creating anachronisms out of whimsy, Croyd discarded:
as whimsy went, thus far it had all been a bit heavy-
handed.

Meanwhile, was Tannen safe? Eh, but Tannen was with
Chloris. There he was at least as safe as Croyd unprotected by special powers or anything else. As for Djeel
and Hanoku and Gorsky, though . . .

He was completing the whirl: the impassive face of
Roland was coming full into his central vision. Roland's
helmet-visor was up; his wide-apart eyes were calm-blue,
his nose was aggressive, his ruddy-bearded mouth was big-
sensual; under the beard his chin and jaw were square
and deep. Roland asserted, "Sir, courtesy requires that I
allow you to precede me; but since presumably you do
not know the way or anything else, another kind of courtesy seems to require me to . . ."

Croyd grinned. "You never told me how big you are,
really."

Having cleared his throat, Roland with dignity rejoined,
"You look as though you might wish to wrestle."

Croyd dropped arms. "Would that be good manners
hereabouts?"

"It would be more in order to joust."

"All right. I have a passionate desire to do *some*thing."

It won a grim smile from Roland. "Sir, evidently we
have something to talk about—later—if there should be
for you a later. But just now, we have audience within.
Pray follow me."

Brushing past Croyd, he strode into the castle. Croyd
followed, noting well the vulnerable target of Roland's
back (it was *very* old-fashioned jousting armor, backless,

trustfully designed for frontal clash); noting also with new respect that Roland disdained fear of a treacherous attack. But then, heigh-ho: Roland had been in there, he must *know* Croyd a little. Or else—and this was another sort of consideration—a physical attack would be quite irrelevant to this Roland.

This would be the first meeting between Croyd and Duke Dzendzel. There would be later meetings.

For Croyd it was a disconcertingly retrograde situation, taking him back to his boyhood on Nigel III (and then also he had possessed no special powers) when once in a long while his father, King Grayle, would find it advisable for disciplinary reasons to summon the youth into private audience in his great hall rather than in his private apartments. This hall itself was astonishingly a near-replica of his father's great hall (vast and stony and rough-raftered, anachronistic again in this much-later-type Gothic castle); and at the far end of it, there, perched on a low throne on a low dais, was

his father Grayle?

Catching himself shriveling, Croyd stiffened. Grayle had been small, tough-small; but *that* small figure was not Grayle, because Grayle would have been draped on his throne informally with arms and legs gauchely curling about his throne for comfort, whereas *that* figure was *poised* on his throne in approximately the manner of Gregory VII.

Forcing himself back into poise, Croyd advanced the length of the hall several paces behind Childe Roland, ignoring a thin but sufficient armed guard that flanked Duke Dzendzel; and although Croyd's feet were bare, he imagined that he could hear the old hard leather of his heels assaulting flagstones and echoing in the vault.

He noticed then, continuing to advance, that the feet of Roland were silent too. And this was totally irrational: the spurs of Roland scraping should have been striking sparks on the stones.

Roland knelt. On one knee. Head down. All of a sudden. Croyd froze.

At that point, the duke should have spoken carelessly to his familiar high vassal Roland. Instead, sharply he *commanded*, "Stand, Childe Roland, and stand to one side, and summon your prisoner forward." His vibrant tenor had a faint nasal quality.

That was when Croyd measured his man. The duke was dangerous. But also, he was pompous. And so he had no friends—only servants.

With difficulty Croyd required himself to kneel on both knees before the duke, bowing his head in submission.

He heard the voice. "You are Croyd, not Pan?"

"Yes, sir." The question was odd, unexpected, implicative of something.

"Address me properly!"

Croyd began to mumble something.

"Speak up, varlet!"

Biting a lip to repress a grim chuckle-blurp, Croyd said clearly, "Sir, I have not been instructed how to address you."

"Address me as your liege."

"Yes, your liege."

Electrostatic silence. The voice then seemed a bit strident. "Roland, instruct him how to address me."

Roland said—and, not daring to look, Croyd would have bet that the face of Roland was struggling for control—"When you speak to the duke, say to him, 'my liege.'"

"My regrets, my liege," Croyd responded. Then, unexpectedly, his face came up. "Sir, you know my name, but I do not know yours."

It froze the duke; to his credit, he held stiff on his throne, not rising or even jerking. Looking angry-direct down at Croyd, he incised, "Roland, this man does not appear to know who I am."

Roland said, dead, "My apologies, my liege. Croyd, this is Dzendzel, Archduke of Moudjinn, Lord of the Fissure. These titles are quite sufficient for him; he requires no extravagance. And I think he would prefer that you bow your head again."

Croyd ducked his face, telling the floor, "Lord Dzendzel, then. My lord, I crave permission to express an idea or two to my liege, after my liege has expressed the ideas that he may wish to express to me."

The voice went sardonic. "You are here. Your companions are accessible to me. After I have taken care of you, I may or may not bother to deal with them. There was a time when you and I might have been worthy adversaries; but we have reduced you to a most pitiable condition, and I really don't know why I trouble with you, unless it is because I am an admirer of your Marquis de Sade. Those are all the ideas that I wish to express, really. I shall not carry my sadism to grotesque lengths; I see you subject-powerless, that is almost enough; your obstacle to my dream is done. I think you said that you wished to express an idea?"

Up came Croyd's face, and on it he had schooled an expression of simple honesty. "I will not call you my liege, Duke Dzendzel, because you are not my liege: we are enemies. I acknowledge my total physical submission. I anticipate immediate death. Sir, is there anything— *anything*—that can prevent immediate death?"

The face of the duke was serene. "Your friend Pan might have prevented this, but unhappily, he has run away again."

That bit. Croyd suggested, "I would appreciate a detail or two."

"I can afford to spare you a detail or two. I need the powers that you have lost. I had a pact with Pan; I had counted on him to supply these powers. Had he stayed with the deal, I would simply have left you to languish with your friend in our nonspace Arcadia. But Pan has unaccountably disappeared, and so has his consort Freya; and while of course they may reappear, it is wisest for me to make do without them. So tomorrow, Croyd, I will be subjecting you to a brain scan, to recover from your brain the latencies of the powers that you can no longer deploy, so that I may deploy them myself. And the scan will be fatal, although not before it begins to be rather intolerably painful."

It threw Croyd into swift speculation. Suffering for two years over Pan's abandonment of a trust, yet implicitly comprehending the *why* of this desertion, he had kept private track of Pan; he knew all about Saturninn. That Pan should make a power deal with Dzendzel, this might be more of the same; but that Pan should run out on Dzendzel, totally losing himself *and Freya*—was this perhaps the *good* sort of runaway? Was there even a chance of a rescue operation? It was a great deal to digest in moments; and he concluded, like Dzendzel, to forget Pan. Unquestionably, during tomorrow's brain scan Dzendzel would be probing among other probings for whatever knowledge or speculation Croyd might entertain with respect to Pan; and this reflection caused Croyd instantly to

scramble his thoughts, hopefully beyond possibility of recovery.

He stood. "In that case, Duke Dzendzel, as governor
to duke, I express a last wish. May we perhaps pass an
hour talking politics in private—except, perhaps for the
presence of Roland?"

All in the room went taut. Duke Dzendzel, wiry-keen,
considered his prisoner. He said presently, "Croyd, you
have no powers beyond those of an ordinary man; and
while I do not *yet* have all the powers that you once
possessed, I have enough of them to reduce you to pain-
quivering jelly. Do you *really* wish to talk with me in
private?"

"Already you have intimated that tomorrow you will be
reducing me to pain-quivering jelly in the course of a
brain scan. I see no difference to my own comfort. Yes,
I wish to talk with you."

The duke sighed. "I would like that, too, because I
could take occasion to obviate the brain scan by milking
your brain with projective hypnosis. But the process would
be prolonged and inefficient; we can do it much better
tomorrow with a brain scan. And my mood now does not
incline toward theoretical discussions of political issues
that I have already settled for myself—and, now I think
about it, for the metagalaxy. So before I put you away
for the evening, do you have perhaps a *practical* question?"

Croyd glanced at Roland; the knight was frowning
down. Croyd then addressed the duke. "Sir, I know that
you are not unimportant on Moudjinn. I merely want to
inquire—what about the treaty? And what about Dari?"

Scornfully Dzendzel mimed the tearing and tossing of
paper. Placing hands on knees, he queried, "Any truly
practical questions?"

"Only a request, sir, not a question. I would wish to
have President Tannen and all aboard the *Castel Jaloux*
placed safely somewhere in Sol Galaxy, or in Djinn Galaxy, or in Andromeda, whichever is easiest."

Calm reply: "All of them know that something powerful and hostile is operating in this metagalactic fissure.
Consequently, they are dead."

Croyd's head went down. "Then I have nothing further.
I am at your mercy." Slowly he went to his knees.

Roland tugged at his beard; he seemed amazed. Then

Roland's mouth clamped shut, and he appeared stern and disappointed.

Dzendzel, standing, said, "Roland, pray conduct the prisoner to the dungeon keep. Croyd, inadvertently I have said the word *pray;* and if you have gods, I suggest you pass the night praying to them, because tomorrow will be difficult. Do not bother to sleep; we will keep you awake tomorrow—all day tomorrow—with a total and minute brain scan whose associated pain I rarely bother to block when I am watching. And when that is done, believe me, you will sleep."

Descending from the dais, he made an insolent point of bruising with his knee the nose of a Croyd whose head was far down in desolate submission. And he departed the hall.

The dungeon keep was not anachronistic, because it was cruel and therefore timeless.

Roland led him, this time between two guards with ponairds drawn, down many coiling stairways of pseudo-stone, debouching semifinally on a broad low-vaulted level whose floor was wet clay. (It was pseudowet, of course; the sophisticated illusion convincingly included even dank!) Paces ahead of him, in the floor, Croyd saw a hole. Roland went to it; the guards ponaird-prodded Croyd thereto. Roland turned, faced Croyd, and pointed down. Croyd looked down; he saw black.

Roland told him, "The floor of the keep is five meters down. We will let you down by your arms as far as possible, then drop you. If you grope for a while, eventually you will find bread and water; just don't kick over the water. You may also find neighbors; but they will not be human, so you may as well ignore them."

Their eyes met at a common level. Croyd remarked, "Your Lord of the Fissure *is* stupid."

After a moment, Roland, without turning, addressed the men-at-arms. "The prisoner's remark requires discipline. I prefer to do this alone. You are dismissed."

Oddly, they just vanished.

Croyd queried, "Are they illusions?"

"No more than I. They are my servants; I can make them vanish—permanently, if I choose. Just so, I am the duke's vassal; he can make me vanish—permanently, if he chooses. Do you not agree that it is an excellent way to run a feudalism?"

"I agree with my whole heart."

"Then why do you keep saying that he is stupid?"

"He refused to talk political theory with me on the ground that he has already settled all theories; he is therefore afraid of being outtalked. He refused to save my friends because they know too much; yet I guess that he has the power to extirpate their recent memories and still save them if he would wish. Apparently he has not grasped that I comprehend the illusory nature of this fissure realm, or he would not have trumped up the silly elaboration of this dungeon keep; he would simply have immobilized me somewhere. And . . . he has appointed *you* to be my guard."

Up came Roland's beard; his eyes were high.. now then Cryod's, looking down. "The last fact makes him stupid? Why?"

"From this last fact it is evident that he has not noticed two facts about yourself. You are a true knight, imbued with the high principles of chivalry, disdaining unfairness, noticing that his treatment of me and my friends is unfair. And you are beginning all by yourself to notice his ultimate stupidity."

The chin of Roland came down by a centimeter. "Sir, I am only probing you before I throw you in. I am not agreeing."

"I understand, sir. You have done well your knightly duty in my brain, and well are you doing it here. Be loyal to your sworn liege, no matter how stupid he may be, no matter how thoroughly he may have programmed you to believe in him. It is chivalry at its finest, for Duke Dzendzel has consecrated himself with *l'oint du seigneur.*"

Roland was angry. "I discount your blasphemy; you are an outlander. And he did not program me for obedience, he programmed me for intuitive interpretation of chivalric principles. I am a high vassal; there is a range within which I may feudally disobey him without violating his *oint du seigneur.*"

Croyd was cold. "Feudalism, sir, is merely a structure; chivalry runs deeper, it is an attitude, it is independent of feudalism. If you have a range of disobedience, I suggest that you exercise this range, sir; I suggest that you exercise this range."

"Give me leave to demand *how.*"

"By rejecting the concept that you are his because he made you. By asserting your individual manhood even

though he can annihilate you. As a high vassal, by asking
yourself questions about the validity of his concept of chivalry."

"Are *you* lecturing *me* about chivalry?"

"Sir, I had the honor on Nigel III to have been born
and bred as a knight in a *real* chivalry that evolved itself
through social interaction among strong and weak men
—and *not* in a contrived pseudochivalry designed to foster
one man's ambition. The truth of that assertion will come
out tomorrow in my lethal brain probe."

The four eyes were level again. Roland demanded,
"How is your claim related to *l'oint du seigneur?*"

"As follows. In *our* authentic chivalry, the king won
and held his kingdom by a combination of descent, manhood, and rightness in the judgment of his vassals. Whereas on Erth and on Moudjinn and on every metagalactic
planet I know that has chivalry in its history, *l'oint du
seigneur* has been superimposed by one or another schem-
ing king during a late period of chivalric decadence."

Roland said deliberately, "I should take pleasure in killing you."

"By illusion?"

"By force in physical combat."

"But, Roland, *can* you be physical?"

Slowly Roland drew his mouth open in a white-toothed
grin. And he demanded, "Can *you* be?"

Croyd's answering grin was rueful. "You, at least, are
not stupid. Put it this way: I can be as physical as you
can be, and I would like the combat; but I do not like to
kill, and this I would do only if I had to do it. Meanwhile
I am interested in the fact that I am not yet in that
dungeon keep."

Roland went intent. "Are you challenging?"

"If I were, would you be accepting?"

Roland went rueful. "No," he admitted, "because that
would be rash; I might lose, and that would be a disservice
to my lord. So I am afraid I must request that you enter
the dungeon voluntarily; and if you refuse, I shall have
to call back my two men, or if necessary seven or eight
of my men, to throw you in. The outcome is certain; and
since this outcome will be more comfortable for you in a
five-meter fall if voluntarily you allow me to lower you
in . . ."

Croyd studied Roland's feet.

Croyd said presently, "I wonder why I am not hurling

myself against your legs, knocking you over, paralyzing you with a stiff hand to the throat, and escaping."

Roland studied the back of Croyd's neck while Croyd, head bent, studied Roland's feet. "Since you have warned me, I wonder why I am not hammering the back of *your* neck. What would you do if you were to escape?"

"I would of course make for the lifeboat *Chloris*, to rescue my old friend."

"And would you get there?"

"Of course not. So, Roland, do you tell me the most comfortable way of dropping into that five-meter hole."

Now Croyd was gazing straight up into Roland's eyes. And Roland, looking down into his eyes, said wonderingly, "You realize that you have no way of getting out again, until we take you out tomorrow for the purpose that you know?"

"This I realize. Is there any proposition I could make, Roland, that would entice you . . . ?"

"No, Croyd. And this I regret."

"Why should you regret? We are strangers."

Roland said low, "I have talked with you. Also I have dwelt in your brain. You are no stranger to me."

Silence.

Croyd said low, "I do not say that direct acquaintance with my brain has anything to recommend itself. But if any man has dwelt in my brain and still feels reasonably congenial, that man has got to be my friend even if duty require him to kill me. In your position, I would be implacable; and I so understand you, Roland. Pray ease me into the hole."

Eyes level again, they considered each other.

Abruptly Roland extended himself on his belly in the damp clay, stretching out an arm toward the hole. "Get on your belly, clasp my arm, drop your hindquarters in. I will wriggle as close as I dare without sliding in after you."

Croyd silently obeyed; hands clasped arms above elbows.

Roland worked his way forward; Croyd slid in backward.

Roland grunted. "You are nearly as heavy as I. I dare come no closer."

Croyd, his armpits on hole's edge, his feet dangling above meters of black space, commanded, "Let go, my friend." And *he* let go.

Perforce, Roland let go. Croyd fell.

Roland waited. He wriggled to hole's edge, looked in, saw nothing. He inquired, "Are you all right?"

No reply.

Roland sighed heavily. He got to his feet, considered his beclayed armor, willed away the clay, ritually hand-brushed his front, considered the hole.

He leaned over this hole. He called, "Croyd, if you can hear me, remember what I said: you may find neighbors, but they will not be human, so you may as well ignore them."

No answer.

Somber, Childe Roland stalked away from the dungeon keep.

———— ◆◆◆ ————

WHEN, AFTER MANY dungeoned minutes, Croyd was fairly sure that Roland had gone away, he moved out of the cramped position that he had fallen into and lain motionless in, because he wanted to stop talking and think about (a) escape, (b) what practical outcome escape might lead to, (c) whether *a* would be worth the trouble in view of *b*. Unhappily, examination of his prison was going to be less than highly efficient, because, among the effective illusions of Duke Dzendzel, here the duke had established the illusion of total darkness. There was always, however, the sense of touch.

Cautiously making his way across dank clay with outstretched arms, Croyd encountered a pseudostone wall (pseudodank) and began to belly-crab his way along it, running fingers high up and low down. When after centimetering a couple of meters he had discovered no special feature on the wall, and could think of no way to make a tangible mark on the wall so that he would be able to tell when he would have come full around his cell, he decided on an assumption. Such a cell would be extremely unlikely to be more than fifty meters in perimeter, the concave wall curvature was such as to suggest more like fifteen, and his highly accurate mental clock (which long ago he had established before his discovery of more exotic mental possibilities, and which had therefore stayed with him) said he was progressing at a rate of one meter per minute; he would therefore

continue the scouting for fifty minutes, and this would
bring him all the way around at least once and possibly
three times.

At the end of five minutes, having discovered no re-
lieving feature anywhere in the wall, he narrowly missed
kicking over his bowl of water. He knelt to taste it; real
water—imported, probably; this you don't just illude.
Nearby there was bread. Considerately he set the water
a meter out from the wall so he wouldn't kick it again,
and positioned the bread near the wall so he would be
sure to kick it again, and moved onward. Fifteen minutes later he kicked the bread again, accurately validat-
ing his fifteen-meter concavity inference. In this circular
cell wall he had discovered no feature—certainly no hope
of an escape avenue—from floor to well over two meters
up.

On a chance—having apparently all night for this stuff
(if *night* was a term having reality here apart from the
diurnal rhythm established by Duke Dzendzel)—he made
one more circuit, leaping high as he went. When again
he met the bread, he had found no feature even above
three meters up. And he was momentarily winded.

Squatting, he ate some bread and drank some water.

Standing then, he began a shuffling, distrustful, cross-
pattern cruise of the pseudoclay floor; a lucky hole might
afford escape, an unlucky hole might drop him into itself
forever. (Fascinating how solidly and totally the Lord of
the Fissure had installed one-G gravity everywhere here!)
Since any hole less than thirty centimeters in diameter
would be useless for escape, he established his kinaesthetic
estimate of that width for his search pattern.

In almost precisely the center of his cell he found a
hole about ten centimeters in diameter. He had no idea
what use the duke would have for such a hole; Croyd,
however, thought of two uses, although neither was an
escape use. Having used this hole for one use, he pressed
onward.

He found no further hole. He felt his way back to the
bread. By placing his back to the wall, extending both
arms rigidly, and establishing his back as tangential to the
arc, he would be able to advance about four meters and
find the center hole again at any time when urgency
might suggest the second type of use.

He sat, nibbling the bread. The high hole above was
beyond his normal human jump reach.

This dungeon keep stank. Probably the stench was illusory; but as foolery went, it was pretty convincing.

That was when he was confronted by the panther and the python.

Quite evidently these animals were furious and ravenous, and each of them was oversize. It crossed Croyd's mind that the zoological poetry would have been better if there had also been an octopus.

An octopus joined them. It was oversize. All three were noticing Croyd.

He nibbled, examining them. Apart from their size and one other feature, they were a quite normal panther and python and octopus; and instant by instant, auditorily enlivened by the snarling and the hissing and the baleful octopus silence, they were drawing closer, the normal cell stench augmented by the stench of their breath.

The other abnormal feature was that they were visible in total darkness—visible in full color.

"Gramercy, Childe Roland," Croyd muttered; and casting his eyes upward, he gave attention to question *b*.

Should he somehow bring off escape—a possibility that now seemed as impossible as anything ever is—what then would he do? Three avenues suggested themselves. One was that he might lose himself in the fissure, and before dying of thirst or starvation (or perhaps of suffocation outside the artificially oxygenated area), somehow find a way to get to some galaxy—a process which would require, now he thought about it, around five quadrillion years if without a spaceship he could fly through metaspace at swallow speed. A second was that he might grope his way to Duke Dzendzel and kill him and release the fissure from thrall; but it was an outside hope that, having found the duke, he could kill him; it was no more than a random possibility that, in this chiaroscuro of illusory shifting, he could find the duke; and it was a god dream that, having found and killed the duke, he could discover how to disenslave a whole metagalactic fissure. (With his special powers, *maybe;* but they were gone.) A third avenue was—and he deferred this as third and last, although probably it would have been the first thing he would have tried—that he might somehow blunder into finding the *Chloris* and would rescue Tannen; but even assuming that he could find Chloris, she was immobilized here by the power of the duke, while the *Castel Jaloux* was googols of kilometers out into metaspace helplessly fleeing into annihilation with Djeel and Hanoku and Gorsky and the rest.

Escape, actually, was a pretty silly idea in terms of its possible consequences, quite apart from its nonexistent possibilities.

Perhaps, before departing Nereid, he would have been wise to contact Pan, giving him some checkpoints and checktimes. On the other hand, could he infer from Dzendzel's tongue slip that maybe Pan . . . He shrugged (heavily, with panther claws on both shoulders); Pan he had regretfully written off when Pan had welched on a duty and run away to Djinn for Las Vegas business. You keep on loving your brother who is your other self; but your brother is his own man, and you can't run him unless you want him to stop being his own man, and meanwhile you have your own life to live.

The panther had sunk its jaws agonizingly into one of his shoulders; the python was crushing his pelvis; lovingly the octopus was caressing his neck with a tentative tentacle, drawing blood with its sucking cups.

With his right hand he scratched the octopus gently behind the place where its ear ought to be, if it had one; with his left, he fondled the neck of the python; with his front teeth, playfully he bit the nose of the panther. And, as a purely academic exercise, he began to enumerate his possibilities of effective escape if he had not lost his special powers.

For example, since he was convinced that this castle, dungeon keep and all, was a system of externally forced illusion, he could have out illuded the illuder by converting the ceiling above his head into a circular sloping ramp down to the floor, whereup he could simply have walked out into the gray, seeking his friend.

Or, more simply, he could have located Tannen by projective telepathy and instantaneously teleported himself to his friend.

Alternatively and earlier, he might have avoided detention in the first place. Standing before Duke Dzendzel, he might have uptimed

to *when?* And to what effect? You can't change uptime. *Can you?*

Nevertheless, he might have gone uptime to the past instant (*gone power!*) when he and Tannen and Chloris, each experiencing illusions of his own birthplace, had realized simultaneously that these had to be illusions.

Whereupon Croyd could have lurked invisibly in Chloris, and at the instant of re-presentation of the present he could have called himself teleportatively back to himself.

No, that was silly. Had he possessed the power, then his action could have begun long before: at the instant when he and Tannen, whirled away from the *Castel Jaloux* aboard Chloris, had awakened to the fact that the *Castel* had been supernally boarded, Croyd by mind reach could have reboarded her and . . .

Absently he noticed that the panther and the python and the octopus had somehow departed. He rather missed them; he had come to like them a little. Nevertheless he returned to thought.

There was nothing valuable about this thought process, really, except an intuitive conclusion that it had led him to. If this elaborate system of illusions had been created at the will of Duke Dzendzel, who had exhibited in conversation challenge and also internally in his illusion system a mentality that was pretty good but not quite up to creating and sustaining these illusions all by itself—then the Fissure Illusion System was being created *and sustained* by a *brain* other than the duke's but executively bossed by the duke.

Furthermore, if this brain was more subtle and sustained than the minded brain of Duke Dzendzel, *someone else* had created this brain under command of the duke.

Childe Roland?

It was conceivable. Roland possibly had the intelligence, and Roland was obviously the duke's chief vassal here. A minor question—how an illusion like Roland might have arrived at creating a reality like the brain—could be settled later; meanwhile, here one had a working hypothesis that could be followed through as long as it would keep succeeding and could be abandoned if it should fail.

A circumstantial test occurred to Croyd, but the test could not be conclusive. If a brain were telepathically monitoring Croyd, then insofarforth Croyd must be in touch with the brain. And hence, if Croyd were to will with all his power a means of escape, possibly the brain would be influenced to . . .

During the following minutes, Croyd disciplined himself into a single-minded concentration comparable to the god-prayer-vigil that the Lord of the Fissure had recommended.

Nothing happened.

At length he abandoned this. The brain was under the duke's will control: the duke *thought* what he wanted, the brain found means to *do* what he wanted. The brain was putting consistent illusions into Croyd, efferently; but it had no readiness to accept impulses *out* of Croyd, afferently—except, natch, in terms of control feedback.

So then he was dead.

Oh, it would be a long tomorrow! They would intimately, agonizingly scan his brain, with Dzendzel standing by perversely enjoying his writhings on the rack; and when they would be done, Dzendzel would have all Croyd's knowledge, including his knowledge of his bygone powers, but Croyd too would be bygone—*i.e.*, dead.

Probably Croyd needed to be studying mental prophylaxes against tomorrow.

There were none available, other than the usual strong human prophylaxes. Against the scanning he could addle his own mind, but the remorseless scan would get what was in his brain; the addling would ultimately achieve nothing. The left Croyd with only normal human resources against extremes of agony that would have to be unbearable-uncontrollable. He could school himself to be Indian-stoic; unhappily, a sharp shot at his pain inhibitors would rekamatically destroy *that* possibility, mind or none. Or he could school himself to lie back and masochistically enjoy the pain; but this would work only until Dzendzel would catch on to the tactic and would correct it in Croyd's pyriform cortex. Or, finally, Croyd could abandon himself to God.

The last seemed the most meaningful course of action.

He embraced it, not being at all a total stranger.

Presently the pattern of his praying emerged into his consciousness, and what he confronted was sharply reorienting. He had a special time problem for *escape and rescue;* it must be brought off preferably and improbably within the next few hours; failing that, then tomorrow, or at the very latest in about seventy-two hours from last midnight—only a few more than forty-eight hours from now. For in sending him hallucinations involving his brother Pan as his small son, Dzendzel had wholly missed the *real* Freudian point. Subliminally Croyd was worried about *a* small son, male or female—whether he would be born, whether even his begetting would be completed; the Pan idea had intruded, that was all.

Here was the frustrating rationale. For Croyd to be co-father of Djeel's born child, the second impregnation must occur within seventy-two hours after the first; for otherwise, before the sperm journey would goal-end, the egg would die. Now, if two improbables should be butted end to end—that Tanner would find a synthesis, and that Hanoku and Djeel could be induced to consummate immediately after marriage—then, anytime ahead of forty-eight hours from *now*, Hanoku with Croyd could co-father the child. But because of the Faleen/Hanoku preoccupation with the lore, Croyd doubted that they would be willing to forget the prescribed forty-eight-hour chastity vigil; and meanwhile, he very much doubted that Tannen would arrive at a satisfactory synthesis. But if Tannen *should* find synthesis, while Djeel and Onu would cling to the vigil, then Tannen must perform the marriage within the next few hours; and that was simply impossible.

The last-ditch possibility was that Tannen, unable to find a synthesis, would nevertheless be able to perform the ceremony and (as chief) impregnate the bride within a few more than forty-eight hours from now; in which case there might be a child—but co-fathered with Croyd, not by Hanoku, but by Tannen.

In sum: Hanoku and Djeel must be rescued for themselves; but also, they must be rescued so that their marriage could be consummated somewhen between now and little more than forty-eight hours from now. If *now with synthesis*, then co-fathered by Hanoku; if *in two days without synthesis*, then co-fathered by Tannen; if in two days *with* synthesis—or later in any case—then Croyd would lose a half-child whom, now he thought about it, commandingly he valued.

Much as Croyd prized Tannen as a friend and as a man, Tannen's co-fathering would be not even second-best for Djeel and Onu, because Onu would be crowded out.

But Tannen would find a synthesis.

Wouldn't he?

Should he?

The voice of Dzendzel said, dead, "Croyd."

Gradually he returned from the infinity of his prayer state.

"Croyd," said again the dead voice.

He grasped that it came from above. He uttered, "You do not sound like God."

"Who knows how God sounds, or whether I am He? Meanwhile, my Djinn name is Dzendzel."

"That is what I figured." Croyd was all alert now.

"You are a remarkable man, Croyd. I confess that I could not resist coming to observe you in my favorite dungeon keep. I suspect that I can guess what your mind has been doing."

"Prior to my prayer, you mean?"

"You tried with the strength of your merely human mind to overcome your prison. Failing, you began to torture yourself with imaginings of what you might have done to your prison had I not stolen your power."

"Apart from your reversal of the time order, my liege, you are absolutely right."

"And so you have been praying, have you, Croyd?"

"I have been following your recommendation, my liege."

"Praying against tomorrow, probably?"

"Against tomorrow."

Hesitation. Then: "A while ago you suggested a debate with me."

"For me this would be a pride."

"It would be silly to debate; a purified feudalism is what I have settled for because it is the best social structure. Nevertheless, I would consider it an honor if you would consent to observe my purified feudalism in action." *

If you pray hard, you get an unprayed-for opportunity. Croyd murmured, *"Enchanté."*

Whereupon the ceiling above his head, at the silent will of Duke Dzendzel, converted itself into a circular sloping ramp down to the floor.

———◄—◆—►———

THEY FLOATED HIGH above a glowing metropolis of intricately interwoven streets and buildings, and the streets were clotted with glowing, swift-moving people.

The spreading of the city extended as far as he could see in any direction; its horizons curved upward in all but two directions, losing their upwardness in distance. Actual-

ly he was too high to distinguish individuals; yet somehow he *knew* that the multiplex darting glow on the
streets was small, busy people.

"They are," said Dzendzel beside him, "in a few cases
my vassals and the vassals of Childe Roland, and in all
cases my subjects. Contemplate the city, Croyd. Study
the city; it is feudalism perfected."

A voice profoundly sounded in Croyd's mind: *If you
can comprehend the city, you can rule us.* It was not
the voice of Dzendzel.

He concentrated on the city, trying to understand it
as an iridescent map. Presently his attention was drawn
to the main artery of the city with its curiously para-
doxical orientation. Hundreds of side streets were irregularly tributary to this boulevard; and every street that
he could see was tributary to a tributary or to a once-
or twice-removed tributary to this boulevard. The glow
of moving people on the side streets became dense
radiance on this boulevard. But whereas every place else
the city was concave, dishing upward toward horizons,
this boulevard through the valley of the city was convex,
curving downward until at its horizons it disappeared.

Was the boulevard with its brilliance and its paradox
another deceptive diversion? He felt that it was not, that
this was some kind of reality, some element of a prime
nature that he must know to find its place in the total
solution. To the Lord of the Fissure he remarked without
emphasis, "For beauty, it is thrilling; for feudal appreciation, I should descend closer."

"Done," said Dzendzel. The city began to rise toward
Croyd, or perhaps he was descending toward the city; it
was impossible to distinguish. Dzendzel added, "For this
while, Croyd, it is unnecessary for you to request action
from me; *will* whatever action you will, and your will becomes our action." And indeed, the mutual approach between himself and the city felt as though he were
willing it and therefore *doing* it. "When one walks, *how*
does one walk?" he asked himself with seeming ir-
relevance, only it was relevant; once having learned to
walk, just in this manner he merely willed to walk, and
walked—with his legs either thrusting his body toward
the goal, or turning his planet beneath him like a great

ball floating in water in order to rotate the goal toward him.

This boulevard should be explored systematically. Croyd (with Dzendzel tacitly assenting) therefore overflew it, or else like the planet ball he turned it, to one of the downward-vanishing extremities. The end of it simply petered out into gray; very few people were visible at this lone end; and as one of the people approached the street end, his glow rheostatically diminished until he lost visibility; perhaps he walked off, perhaps not.

It seemed important to return, overflying the length of the great boulevard. At a height of perhaps twenty meters (with Dzendzel silent beside him), Croyd went back over the entire length, intending to return more slowly at lower altitude. During this overflight, several gross features came to his attention.

First, at this height, the people seemed to be human; either Erth's *Homo sapiens* (which of course had spread to many planets), or his own Nigelian-human species known as *croyd Thoth*, or the Darian-human species called *Meria melens*, or some other human species. (He was thinking *human*, of course, anthropocentrically; and many planets had independently evolved species that were humanoid in that sense; in ethical definition, the term *human* transcended anatomy.)

Second, this boulevard indeed lay in a valley. The buildings (were they buildings?) on both flanks were nondescript gray; none of them rose as high as his altitude; their roofs were rounded rather than squared or pointed. These buildings looked soft; and they had no windows and perhaps no doors, yet people seemed to be going in and out of them at will.

Third, the brilliance of the collective people-glowing progressively grew until it crescendoed at what appeared to be about midway along the boulevard, then went into diminuendo as he moved on toward the far end, then reached a kind of pulsating secondary crescendo as he attained the peter-out into gray nothing. He recalled that the same sort of secondary pulsation had characterized the other end.

Fourth, the very long boulevard was divided into long segments—he had counted thirty-two. And yet the segments were not demarcated in any geometrical way—not, for instance, by tributary streets—but rather by a kind of people-clustering: one would say that there had been thirty-two people clusters.

He paused at the far end, at the edge of gray. He considered. There was something hauntingly familiar about this boulevard, its valleyness, its low-building softness, its thirty-twoness. It was like no city he had ever inhabited or visited; nevertheless, *somewhere* he had

Croyd remarked, "I want to retrace your boulevard, Lord—more intimately, this time."

Dzendzel responded, purring, "My pride. I am yours tonight; you are mine tomorrow."

Croyd descended to an altitude of three meters above the pavement, whence he could inspect individual people as they went about their incandescent pulsation and their convulsive business.

In this segment, as in every segment, there were uncountable numbers of people; and the glow of each person was like the glow of a firefly—dark for a while, then suddenly leaping into life, then fading.

He tried to pick out one person for study. At first it was hard to do because of the swiftness of their movements. At length he perceived that each person paused motionless for a moment and glowed, then moved a distance with great swiftness, then paused to glow; whenever there was a pause and a glow, two people were meeting. He had to consider them, not by ones, but by twos. Presently he picked a random spot on the boulevard to focus on, and waited for two people to pause and glow together in his focus.

By a method that many normally intelligent people learn, he was focusing his interior thoughts while scrambling his exterior thoughts so that the Lord of the Fissure could not easily discern by telepathy the direction of his central thinking.

Two paused and glowed in his focus. Their stomachs and intestines were gigantic and external, pendulous outside their bodies. They faded and moved on.

Croyd mentally blinked, and shook his head, and picked another spot. Two more glowed there; again, stomachs and intestines external. They faded.

None of these people paid any attention to Croyd or to Dzendzel above them.

Croyd made a cheap generalization that external viscera must be characteristic of these people Perhaps a sampling in the next segment would confirm it. He drifted, stopped, picked a spot, and waited.

Two people met, glowing. Their stomachs were properly unseen; what protruded was their pharynxes, outside their throats. They vanished.

Having checked one more case pair with external pharynxes, Croyd began to revise his hypothesis in rather an exciting way. Moving on to the next segment, he found that the people there looked commonplace except that their tongues were gigantic and protrusive. In the fourth segment, teeth and gums extended inches beyond lips. In the fifth segment, lower lips were Ubangi; in the sixth, both lips were vastly pendulous; in the seventh, upper lips hung entirely over mouths; in the eighth, astonishingly expanded faces were larger than heads; in the ninth, the noses were super-Cyrano; and in the tenth segment—the high point of the boulevard's brilliance, where people met most often and glowed most radiantly—everybody seemed to be suffering from a complication of ophthalmic goiter with optic gigantism.

Brows heavy-down, Croyd continued his deliberate overflight; and by now, in terms of his hardening hypothesis, he was *predicting* the deformities segment by segment along the boulevard. Successively he observed abnormal enlargement of brow, thumb, index finger, middle finger, ring finger, little finger, hand, wrist, forearm, elbow, arm, shoulder, head, neck, trunk, hip, leg, knee, ankle, foot, and toes. And as he returned to the jump-off end of the boulevard, at the gray-off place where he had started, the observed without surprise that the male and female inhabitants of this disreputable way-out quarter were loin-bare and possessed of the most magnificent genital spears or targets that he had ever seen; and he noticed also that their bright-glowing encounters were more intimate than those in any other segment.

And now his hypothesis was hard! He knew what the boulevard was!

His intuition had been right: the main boulevard was an essential part of his comprehension, but it wasn't all of his comprehension. The hinterland of small interlacing streets was just as important.

Any part of this hinterland?

Yes, basically; but best of all, *one particular part* of this hinterland.

To reach this particular part, which side of the boulevard should he penetrate?

On a hunch, he flew back arrow-swift to the second-last segment, where the people with the enlarged pharynxes dwelt.

He watched a number of encounters, examining with care the pulsations of their pharynxes. When a person is swallowing, each pharyngeal action stimulates a pharyngeal sensation reaction lower down in a wavular chain reaction. Then when two people would meet in this boulevard segment, it would be instructive to watch exactly where in their pharynxes the main enlargement would be. The stimulating person should have his enlargement a bit higher in the pharnyx then the person he stimulated. And if most of the stimulating people were coming from one side of the boulevard, while most of the stimulated people were coming from the other side, this would give Croyd the orientation he needed.

It was true. Most of the stimulating people came from one side. And *that* side he now wanted to examine in its hinterland.

But Duke Dzendzel intervened. "Back to jail, Croyd," he taunted. "And there you can tell me how you like my perfectly, feudal city."

The cell whither Dzendzel now brought Croyd was not, however, the dungeon keep; instead, it was a heavy-doored circular room in the third story of a lofty tower, with a barred window having no glass; full moonlight, arranged by Dzendzell flowed inward through this window, patterning on the stone floor in a cool white barred splash that was sufficient to make Dzendzel's face quite clearly visible. A cot chorded an arc of this wall, a pot dotted another, a crude table with a basin and pitcher gave dull character to another. Croyd and the duke stood facing each other near room's center, not two meters apart. Croyd demanded, "Why this instead of *that?*"

"Because Childe Roland admires you."

"Childe Roland issues orders to his liege?"

Dzendzel grinned. "Certainly *not*. My monarchy is absolute; it is the only way to run a feudalism. However, absolutism has its limits which a wise tyrant will respect. With a great vassal such as Roland, if one enforces every whim upon him, one loses that vassal's enthusiasm. He will continue to obey, but lethargically. I prefer that Roland obey with intensity, desire, and conscience. Therefore I usually grant his whims, and this is one of them. When occasionally I say no, he accepts, and we go on."

"Then, Dzendzel—since he admires me for some reason —he has expressed a whim to have me more comfortably quartered?"

"Somewhat more than that. Pray look out your window."

Having studied the duke's face, Croyd turned and went to the window, whose sill was at waist height. Moonlight made it unmistakable that the courtyard area below was a jousting area, complete with spectator pavilion and (in center court) the long rail-aisled lists in which lanced knights drove at each other. These lists at least were no anachronism; their time was matched with the Gothic motif of the castle, even though the level of relatively pure feudalism had long been superseded by the beginnings of anarchical nationalism at the time when lists had been invented.

Behind him, Dzendzel gloated, "Is it not admirably like the time of your King Arthur?"

Arthur had been an erthling, Croyd was not by origin an erthling; but even accepting "*your* King Arthur," authentic Arthurian it was not, but rather, thirteenth-century Malory Arthurian, seven centuries later than the short-lanced leather-armored bareheaded time of the real Arthur. Nevertheless, in politeness: "It is admirable," Croyd assented, turning. "Tell me why I am quartered above this admirability."

"Roland has requested a morning joust with you. Because of your modern inexperience with such matters, I thought it might be a favor to quarter you over the lists, where you could spend your night figuring out precisely what you would be facing in the morning." Dzendzel advanced. "Let me point out the details and what happens in terms of each detail."

"Unnecessary; I know the details."

Dzendzel stopped short. "You . . . *know* the details?"

"I know them vicariously, but thoroughly." *Vicariously* was a euphemism; Croyd had checked out this sort of thing in Erth's uptime; but since he hadn't really been there in its vitality, in a way his check-out had been vicarious.

Up came Dzendzel's chin. "Vicariously? Then you have not actually experienced the lists?"

Not these thirteenth-century-type lists. Much earlier-type jousting. Nevertheless: "I have not. But I understand them; you need not explain. In the morning I am to compete?"

"With Roland."

"He is dangerous?"

"He is invincible."

"This, however, will delay my scheduled brain scan?"

"Should you be subjected to brain scan tomorrow, I would have it intensified to make up for the delay."

"Why do you phrase it in the conditional?"

"Should you by some remote chance defeat Roland or fight him to a draw, we would grant you a boon that you would be able to enjoy until early the following morning; and *then* there would be the brain scan."

"I note that you phrase this also in the conditional."

"Of course. The possibility of this outcome is just nidderingly real; its improbability is overwhelming."

"I will have arms and armor?"

"Of your choice."

"And a mount?"

"Of your choice."

"My choice out of your stable?"

"Your choice absolutely. We can furnish anything alive out of any era of any planet."

"Nevertheless, I am sure to lose?"

"Whatever arms and armor and mount you may choose, the arms and armor and mount of Roland will be beefed up to equal them. It will therefore be equally you against Roland. And he will win."

"He may even kill me?"

"If he kills you, we have means to keep your brain entirely vital until the brain scan; but in such case, being actually dead, you would feel no pain—so for you it would be better to let Roland kill you."

"Roland would not want me to *let* him kill me. Or even to let him win."

"That is between you and Roland. I do not care. However it may come out, the spectacle will be diverting. I had not hoped for so much."

"Should he kill me, you would be deprived of the pain-subjective spectacle of my brain scan."

"I win one, I lose one; it balances—I end up winning. You have not told me what you think of my city."

"It is Plato's republic."

"I beg your pardon?"

"All the people in it are frozen at their respective statuses, and are happy in those statuses, each knowing that he in his own special way is contributing to the overall good of the eternal city."

Dzendzel purred, "You appear to be apprehending us perfectly."

"Is this your plan for the metagalaxy, Dzendzel—when you will have subjugated it?"

"Is it not perfect? Is it not eternal? Is it not exquisitely feudal?"

"It is all of these. But even in Plato's terms, there is an element that I miss."

"There is no missing element. What do you think you miss?"

"Ruling guardians."

"I am their ruling guardian. Roland is their ruling subguardian. There are other high vassals who are their guardians."

"Plato's guardians were dedicated."

"Roland and I are dedicated."

"Plato's guardians renounced power, wealth, individualism, and every pleasure except the pleasure of self-abnegatively guiding-guarding their city."

"Roland . . ." Dzendzel stopped, frowning heavily at his adversary.

Croyd asserted, "There is such a thing as a feudalism that is good and creative. Once upon a time, although a certain princess doesn't grasp this, it existed on Dari. I have not seen it, my Lord of the Fissure, in your fissure; here I have seen only the frozen forms of feudalism in frozen form. I do not recommend your version for the metagalaxy. But I do not suppose that my attitude makes any difference."

"It makes none."

"Then pray leave me to my vigil against tomorrow."

Dzendzel wheeled and departed, slamming the heavy door. Its lock was noisy.

Rather than brood on tomorrow's joust with the formidable Roland—since, merely by reaching back two centuries into his Nigel memory, he was memory-fresh in the mood and the practice—Croyd, crouching on his cot with hands clasped between wide-apart knees, gave attention to what he had learned tonight during the city overflight with the Lord of the Fissures. What he had learned was what was most practically important for the immediate and long-range future.

The city of Dzendzel was a *brain*. A colossal brain. And the boulevard that he had cruised was its Rolandic fissure —the center of control coordination at computer level, although this center fissure was only an instrumentality to the will and ego which was otherwhere and used it.

A brain he understood—Rolandic fissures of brains he understood—quite independently of the special powers that Childe Roland had stolen from him.

All the behavior of the little glowing deformed and specialized people on the boulevard was entirely consistent with this understanding. They were "people" only in a Pickwickian sense; actually they were ephemeral subjective impulses, each specialized in terms of a particular quality and orientation of impulse depending on his location in the fissure city.

Each meeting of two little people, each exchange between them, represented an exchange across the fissure between the brain's frontal interpretative area and the brain's parietal sensory area. That was why Croyd, a while back, had been concerned to determine which side of the boulevard was spawning the people who were stimulators. Having determined this, he had the brain oriented.

If somehow he could get loose in this brain, perhaps he could *use* it.

Was this mighty brain, occupying much of the metagalactic fissure created by the lobes of Galaxy Sol and Galaxy Djinn, the creation of Dzendzel—or of Roland under Dzendzel's domination?

Croyd thought either possibility so improbable as to be dismissable. More probably, the brain had evolved here through natural causes as a primordiality of cosmic action, and Dzendzel somehow had stumbled upon it and had found egotistical wit to enslave it and use it. So Dzendzel had once again illustrated a curious historical irony: it requires less intellectual intelligence to be a political executive than to be a high-level technician.

Perhaps there were morals to be drawn. But that was for later. At the instant, Croyd's problem was comprehension.

How had this brain grown into existence?

Perhaps (since basically a brain is energy organization, and only by gross organization spongy matter) its beginnings were the continuous photon stream from galaxy to galaxy that constituted the metagalactic surface tension. Gradually, while the current of the photon underlay on the inward metagalactic surface continued, responsive energy clusterings in the exterior fissure began partially to differentiate themselves into quasi-personalities. However, having no somatic bodies, but depending continuously and directly on their parent photonic-stream underlay, their self-differentiation could not approach the individualities of human beings. They developed therefore as collectively a social organism in the sense that Spengler had affirmed and Toynbee had denied: in effect, a brain.

But this brain had developed no function or purpose. Consequently it had never been able to generate a *mind* that would unify all its "people" while transcending all of them. It had no effectiveness. It received full sensory input information from all galaxies but had no reason to respond even with amusement.

Croyd suspected that Childe Roland had evolved as liege lord of this brain: *i.e.*, as prime coordinator of its sensory input and perceptive integration, but without yet having arrived at the concept of exercising directive will either to chuckle or to do. Roland perceived, and that was all. He was like the neural apex of a Hymenopterum who merely accepts stimuli and redirects them into suitable ganglia without entertaining any concept of doing something *new* about anything.

The dimensions of this brain awed Croyd, who had dandled concepts of mighty magnitude. When he had cruised this boulevard, chaperoned by Dzendzel, who had myopically assumed that Croyd would see only the perfection of feudal order and would not penetrate the *meaning*, Croyd had been moving with the swiftness of mind: the boulevard's length must be millions or billions of light-years. Nevertheless, Croyd reflected, with a brain the problem is not distance as such; the problem is swiftness of interplay, and while in a human material brain the speed of impulse propagation is relatively low (but practically instantaneous because of short distances), this metagalactic fissure brain propagated photon impulses at three hundred thousand kilometers per second.

Eh, but in this brain, that velocity had to be stepped up by a factor of billions. This, apparently, had occurred: evolution is spectacular, utilizing in bizarre ways every degree of freedom that natural circumstances may offer it.

As Croyd imaginatively visualized the appearance of the *whole* metagalactic exterior—not just the Sol and Djinn lobes, but *all* the millions of galactic lobes thrusting out in all directions—the external surface of the metagalaxy startlingly resembled the external surface of a human brain: lobes among fissures, fissures among lobes, convolution on convolution. And all was live energy. *Why shouldn't* all this have become a brain?

Conversely, though, *why should this* particular fissure be unique? The chances were that among the countless fissures between galaxies, there were numerous rudimentary-primal Rolandic fissures. Some, presumably, had attained high levels of evolution. The Sol/Djinn fissure was one.

Duke Dzendzel had somehow discovered its potential. He had taken charge of it. The minimal result was that this fissure, under the duke's control and with Roland's willing-dedicated-innocent aid, had swiftly ascended to a level that might be called *intelligent* if you included the duke's will and direction as the peak component in its intelligence. The chillingly possible maximum result was that *all the metagalactic surface everywhere was one brain under domination by the Lord of the Fissure.*

For example, Croyd did not now doubt that Dzendzel had used this brain to induce feudalistic Darian piracy as a pilot study. If a brained mind acquires possession of a second brain, the mind will not necessarily use the second brain to free itself; more likely it will invest the second brain with its own old preconceptions.

If, then, humankind (mammalian or otherwise) or any planet in any galaxy in this metagalaxy considered its will free, this was a howlingly laughable mistake. Duke Dzendzel, with his dandy extra brain, was in fact the *God of All the Metagalaxy.*

Duke Dzendzel did not, however, correspond perfectly to Croyd's concept of the *God* meaning.

(And then, again, there was prayer—for a speeding up of time; for a win or at least a draw tomorrow; for escape from the brain scan, not for comfort's sake but for rescue freedom; for some sort of inspiration that would solve this insoluble problem of rescue; for the continuing lives of Djeel and Hanoku and Tannen, at least until he could get at them; for the acquisition of some incredi-

ble sort of *control*. Control for the sake of the galaxy.
Control for the sake of a half-begotten son or daughter
intensely desired by this *croyd Thoth* who was sterile with
a *Homo sapiens* like Greta but who *might* have been able
to *half*-breed with a *Meria melens* like Djeelian.

(So very much depends on *time!*)

Phase Five

DUEL AT PHANTOM DAWN

Day 5

There was russhynge of sperys and swappyng
of swerdis, and sir Gawayne with Galantyne,
his swerde, dud many wondyrs. Than he threste
thorow the prece unto hym that lad sir Bors,
and bare hym thorow up to the hyltys, and lade
away sir Bors strayte unto his ferys.

> —Sir Thomas Malory, *The Tale of the
> Noble King Arthur That Was Em-
> peror Himself through Dignity of His
> Hands* (c. 1485) Ed. Eugène Vinaver

THE JOUSTING COURT was (Croyd wryly estimated) as long and wide as any particular person might please, irregularly walled by Norman-Gothic stone walls, some windowed, some crenellated, some high-turreted, with multicolor pennons everywhere fluttering in a breeze that only the pennons could feel—a court brightly illuminated now in midmorning, by an invisible sun that somehow cast no shadows. Along the wall of the castle facade had been arranged a long low pavilion that was filling now with _ ˙ˑ˙ dressed courtiers, male and female, all faintly glowing in a way that significantly reminded Croyd of the little people in the brain city. Croyd, ready but as yet unarmed and without his mount, stood inconspicious in a corner of the court where he could survey the pavilion; he had been given the armor that he had requested (light tough leather, perfectly replicating the sort of armor that he had learned well to live in two centuries ago on Nigel III); and they had promised him the mount he had requested, although this steed had not yet been given him. Violating protocol, he had ambled out of his dressing room to survey the grounds.

They all stood as the duke entered; they did not cheer, they merely stood. Ceremoniously, aided by servants, the duke found his front box in center pavilion, poised, and sat; and everybody sat. Heralds stood before the box awaiting his pleasure. The duke nodded once and clapped hands thrice. The heralds sounded a fanfare on long, straight *cire-perdue* trumpets hung with pennons.

Roland, walking, emerged from his dressing room beyond the pavilion at the duke's far right. He wore fifteenth-century golden armor, highly stylized and ornate, intricately jointed for maximum flexibility at knees and long-spiked elbows, fitted at right hip with a great hooked lance rest, with a spreading protective target plate in front of left shoulder and chest, where the enemy lance beak was most likely to strike, with the rest of his chest armor a single smooth-polished surface pigeon-breasted into a point so that lances would slide off harmlessly. In his left arm he carried his helm, which was a nearly opaque turret with long narrow horizontal eye slits and otherwise shaped like a beaked gander. Behind Roland walked his page, leading his mount, a great-chested great-hooved armored charger capable of juggernauting at high speed for distances up to a hundred yards and then perhaps yet another hundred, after which he would require a great deal of rest for the next hundred.

Croyd, meanwhile, was walking toward the duke's box, there to meet Roland. And from the stable at the duke's far left, a page led out Croyd's mount: a Nigelian graul resembling a tyrannosaur, only unmistakably mammalian rather than reptilian, prancing on mighty hind feet, pawing grotesquely with ineffectual foreclaws, bridled but not saddled, its shoulders towering several feet higher than the shoulders of Roland's horse.

They met before the duke; they saluted each other, Roland looking past Croyd to inspect his graul intently. Then Roland turned to kneel on one knee and bend his neck before the duke; while Croyd, who whimsically respected diversified protocols and saw no point in creating a scene that might embarrass Childe Roland, knelt likewise.

The duke said lazily, "Stand, Roland, good knight. Stand, Croyd, mighty enemy."

The combatants stood shoulder-to-shoulder, Roland cradling helmet in left arm, Croyd's arms hanging because he carried no helmet.

The duke asserted—and it was noticeable that he did not raise his voice enough for the spectators to hear— "You will ride up to three tilts in the lists. If neither is un . . ." (he paused an instant, glanced uncomfortably at Croyd's graul, and continued fluidly) ". . . horsed in three tilts, it is a draw, and Croyd may crave a boon until tomorrow morning. If either of you is unhorsed but still can fight, use secondary weapons until one of you can no longer fight; if Croyd wins, or if both of you simultaneously lose ability to fight, Croyd may crave a boon until tomorrow morning. Questions?"

"None, my liege," said Roland.

"None," said Croyd.

Now the duke studied Croyd's graul, allowing Roland also to study Croyd's graul while Croyd studied Roland. The duke commented, "The mounts appear unequal in Croyd's favor. Roland, do you wish to have the size of your horse augmented?"

Roland refused. "I am used to the size of my horse as

he is, and Croyd has indicated that he is used to his graul as it is. I would not wish a larger horse unless Croyd were willing to exchange his lethally inadequate leather armor for an adequate fitting of iron."

Croyd warned, "Roland, watch out. With this leather I can move faster than you, my graul has the speed of your horse and more momentum, and on my graul I will sit higher than you. I will keep my leather, but for equal handicapping I suggest that you augment your horse."

As Roland prepared to enter further objection, the duke intervened, "Perhaps before a decision is reached, we should examine the primary and secondary weapons."

Roland and Croyd wheeled back-to-back and bawled at their corners: "Weapons!" From Roland's corner, two pages marched out, carrying between them a fourteen foot hardwood lance beaked with brass; and a third followed burdened with a heavy sheathed two-hand sword. From Croyd's corner, one page emerged, easily carrying in his right hand a seven-foot hardwood splinter beaked with iron and in his left a sheathed one-hand sword.

Having inspected the weapons, Roland quietly told Croyd, "Perhaps I should shrink my horse."

"I rather suggest," returned Croyd, "that for your own good you shrink your lance."

Roland swung to the duke. "Liege, each of us has chosen his mount and his weapons. I will stay with mine, and I think that Croyd will stay with his. I ask only your full assurance that our arms and weapons and mounts and myself are temporarily reified so that we fight honestly as two knights able normally to fight and wound each other even unto the death."

The duke said, "Granted. Mount, and take the lists."

Croyd watched Roland mount, perforce aided by all pages, one steadying the restive mount, one holding a stirrup, one with both hands and arms straining-boosting Roland's rump up into final swing position; nevertheless Croyd nodded brief approval—the armor was enormously heavy, Roland himself had displayed strength and agility.

Then Croyd turned to his graul, stood under its neck (while it twisted head downward to study him with a bulbous eye), looked up at it as he stood with arms akimbo, told it quietly, "We're new to each other, so hold still and let's see what happens." The graul shivered all over; the nervous page who was holding the bridle dropped it; Croyd leaped, seizing the neck with both arms, swung himself onto the shoulders, and reached down for sword and spear, meanwhile with subtle knee pressures talking reassuringly to his mount. The graul seemed to get it: he semiquieted with a bit of prancing and snorting, while Croyd buckled on the sword and hefted the short lance, for which he had no rest.

Roland called, "My mount knows me. Take a little time to get acquainted with your own."

Croyd, saluting and smiling, called back, "Therefore my mount tires and you get to size him up." Then, at the falling face of Roland, who was not yet helmeted, Croyd amended, "Your pardon, I know you are honest. Yes, I wish to do this, thank you."

Roland and the duke for the next five minutes watched a virtuosity of graulsmanship all over the courtyard.

Then Croyd reined up at his end of the lists. "Childe Roland!" he cried. "Unarmed and on foot, we are equally matched, I am certain! Are you sure that thus armed and mounted we are equally handicapped?"

For reply, Roland, helmeted now, one-handedly guided his mighty horse into a complex of curvetage that equalled with major qualitative differences the display by Croyd and his graul. Then Roland took his place in the lists, raising the visor of his helm.

The duke, standing now, clapped thrice. The heralds trumpeted. The knights trotted forward to meet at the center of the lists. With one hand Roland raised his fourteen-foot lance to the vertical, while Croyd erected his seven-foot wand. They were closely face-to-face; their steeds held relatively quiet; they considered each other with profound respect.

Roland said, "Sir, I know you depend on agility to defeat me. If I may be forgiven a postmedieval twentieth-century reference, it is a tank against a jeep, except that I have no seventy-five-millimeter rifle and you have no bazooka. However, what I have can penetrate you, and what you have cannot penetrate me. May I prevail on you, at this last instant, to wear a helmet at least?"

Croyd said, "Thank you, sir. I have chosen my arms. They suit me, and once, a long while ago, I was used to them."

Over in the pavilion, the duke was exhibiting ill-restrained impatience, but these two knights were not noticing.

Roland said, "In the lists, it is customary to thrust only at the front of the adversary, since his rear is unprotected. But you must be sure to understand that if it should come to ground combat with secondary weapons, and should one of us inadvertently turn his back in the course of the fighting, the other might fairly thrust at his vulnerable back. This is our rule; if it were not for this rule, few of our fights would ever terminate in anything decisive. Do you understand this rule, Croyd?"

Croyd answered, curbing his graul, who had begun to dislike Roland's horse, "In my world it is different, but I am in your world. Roland, be sure that if you should turn your back while you were fighting, I would strike at your back. But not if you were running. I retract that; you will not be running."

."Nor will you. Shall we fight?"

"Before we begin, Roland, I want you to know that I am a conscientious objector to death combat. In the past, I have killed my share of men in fair combat; but that was a long time ago. I eschew it. A duel in which one of us would be temporarily disabled—and for the highest conceivable stakes—this I would welcome; but I have a distaste for killing you, because death has a way of terminating human options."

"Croyd, this is not shameful war into which the innocent are pressed, but an honorable duel of consenting peers."

"I do not really consent, Roland. I will fight you, but I do not want to kill you."

"If you do not kill me, I promise that I will kill you."

"To that I will never consent."

"Again, then, shall we fight?"

"Let's."

Roland slammed shut his visor; and the two knights cantered to the far ends of the lists and turned to await the trumpets.

In the first pass, they thundered down upon each other; Roland thrust viciously upward at Croyd's naked face, Croyd parried it to the right with his stick, which broke on Roland's lance but deflected it.

They turned to face each other at the far ends. A page ran forward to hand Croyd another short lance. There was no question of Roland's long lance shivering; Croyd was wearing nothing for it to shiver on.

In the second pass, Roland made for Croyd's leather-covered midriff; Croyd, parrying with nearly the hilt of his lance, managed at the same time to bring the beak around so that it thrust at Roland's vulnerable groin; but Roland's chain mail resisted the light beak, and his momentum drove Croyd's lance back through Croyd's hand, burning and bloodying the hand, while Roland earthquaked past, his groin in dolor but not really injured and not bloodied.

They turned again to each other. Croyd, grimacing, threw down his blood-greased lance and accepted another in his left hand; Roland with dignity was holding position in the saddle, and whatever pain contortions his face might be making were invisible within the gander beak of his helmet.

The trumpets bugled for the third and final pass.

This time Roland went muderously for Croyd's chest. Croyd ducked down on the graul neck at the last instant; the brass beak tore open his shoulder leather and skin as, passing Roland, with the hilt of his spear in his left hand, he jabbed rightward, catching Roland off-balance in the armored rib area and knocking him so far askew on his horse that armor weight pulled him down.

Croyd leaped off his graul, awkwardly drawing sword with his left hand.

The duke and all the people were on their feet.

By the time Croyd got to Roland, the knight had rolled over on his back and, visor up for visibility, was presenting the point of his great long two-handed sword. Croyd circled him cautiously, smaller sword ready in his left hand, which was nearly as dexterous as his right, unready to move in on the great sword, especially since Roland's front was practically invulnerable to Croyd's lighter blade. (He reflected, somewhat late, that his own sword was merely iron, whereas Roland's was doubtless beaten surface steel.) While he circled, Roland let go the sword with his right hand, began to push himself up off the ground with his left, had arm and wrist strength to parry a Croyd thrust with one hand, incredibly made it to his feet, and advanced on Croyd, swinging his neck-severing sword with both hands.

Desperate Croyd leaped and rolled at Roland's feet, his shoulders hitting Roland's brazen shins. Roland staggered but did not fall; and Roland raised his sword with both hands to bring its edge down on Croyd's neck. The

Croyd sword came up and dug into Roland's back down low; and the wounding deflected the Roland sword so that its heavily down-crashing flat crushed into the Croyd skull.

After a number of minutes it became clear to the duke, and presumably to any other people in the pavilion who might, like Roland, be more than phantoms, that neither man was now able to move, that both at least for a while would lie motionless.

The horse and the graul, bereft of riders, were together over on a far side of the courtyard, getting acquainted, beginning to see points of possible friendship value in each other. Unhappily, during this burgeoning, both of them vanished. So did the pages. So did most of the people.

Contemporary Action

INTERSPACE/NONSPACE

Days 4-5

This house of mine is vast and beautiful.
Even better, *its potentialities for new experience
are infinite!*

—*Dr. Orpheus*

SOMEWHEREWHEN in the spatiotemporal infinity of nonspace there brooded a solitary château that Pan/Croyd had long ago erected by psychophysical projections, reifying this house by directional fantasy out of the vitality that void is made of.

Because every point in real space is immediately adjacent to nonspace, Pan opened Croyd-rescue operations by going to this empty house, arriving there by means of an intricate midbrain act that did not clearly involve spatial body translation.

It would perhaps have been more direct to move instantly into Dzendzel's metaspace fissure brain whose image Freya had seen in a well that was actually the focal tube of an I-ray receptor. This, Pan might have done by the same method that had brought him here. But the most direct route is not always the wisest: you don't just waltz into a cosmic brain with hostile intent. Planning must be done; and the most congenial, most isolated, most concentration-fostering pace for swift combat planning was this nonplace, where (ruefully he reflected) Croyd certainly now was not.

This house consisted, symbolically perhaps, of two neo-Gothic-towering halves which rose eerily, separately out of a foundation of nothing; and these halves were linked by a lofty breezeway bridge like a golden spider skein across gray nothing.

Centered on this bridge Pan now stood, staring deep into endless zero, one fist gripping a slendering rail, the other slowly and rhythmically beating upon this rail. Already here his sensors had found the *Castel Jaloux* in metaspace at the instant of Croyd's ejection in Chloris—had penetrated Chloris and the brain of Croyd, had comprehended Croyd's power loss, had been unable to communicate, through Croyd's eyes had watched the *Castel* flare and vanish—and then abruptly had been *driven* out of Croyd and Chloris by an implacable-irresistible mind screen. He had tried again and again; he had failed even to find Chloris again, or the *Castel* either. For the moment he was impotent; and it harassed him to notice that in a way he was semiaccepting this impotence.

Pan/Croyd would be acting already. *Croyd* would be acting already.

In his split-off from Croyd, had he somehow left behind *will?*

No. Croyd will he possessed, fully—or Pan will, name it either way—but something within Pan was blocking it as effectively as the block by the hostile mind screen.

He knew what the *something* was.

He had first to kill the *inward* block.

To do this, he would have to confront the vitality of the block, even if that vitality should slay him.

The block was his two-years-abandoned responsibility.

In agony he catapulted a thought out into nonspace, physically shouting the thought as he thought it:

"KRELL!"

Freya sat in her private rooms in the duke's castle, nerving herself to attempt the adventure that Pan had asked her to attempt. Deliberately she infused her mind with abhorrence of the thing-complex that Dzendzel was creating; but precisely this effort sidetracked her into absorbed contemplation of the duke's impossible-possible feudal dream.

Feudalism! Not since college had she contemplated it. Or had she? Wait. . . .

What surfaced was an old bantering with . . . Croyd? Pan? How did one distinguish? *When?* A decade ago, nearly . . . no, only seven years ago. Eh, then Croyd it had been, and she had been Greta. Nostalgia weakened her with the blurred pang of the unreachably *gone;* nevertheless, Freya nerved herself to taste the saltiness of good remembering.

They had been studying plans for a ship of the line that he was projecting—a ship which (although this was a thing that Freya did not yet know) was to materialize as the *Castel Jaloux.* And she had remarked, "Castles are fun, grounded or airbone. Nevertheless, I took a D in early medieval history."

"Vague name for it, Greta. What centuries?"

"About third through fourteenth—I think. I remember something about the manor and the glebe. The lords and ladies huddled in the manor while the peasants got slaughtered outside in the glebe. They were always feuding, so we call it feudalism."

"You didn't earn the D. You flunked."

"What was it really, then?"

"Honest feudalism had pooped out by the tenth century. At its earlier best, a manor was like a big family. The glebe was where the peasants farmed, to feed the lord and themselves. In return, when trouble started, the lord moved all his serfs inside the walls for protection. And when things were peaceful, the bounteous lady of the manor went out and mothered the serfs. Rousseau and some others called it a social contract. We call it feudalism because *feud,* or *feod,* meant fee or fief."

"A fief was a fee? I thought it was a woman." Greta, who had actually earned a B, was playing stupid; this worked on Croyd the way tickling by an ant works on an aphid, and the milk was usually worth drinking.

"A fief was land, really," he told her. (Knowing her tactic, he invariably counterplayed stupid and *gave;* it was a private joke, and private jokes are high-level lovemaking.) "A big lord would give a little lord a title, and the little lord would pay for the title by giving the big lord his land as a fee—in fief. The little lord kept possession of his land, but now it was really the property of the big lord. That made the big lord the *liege* and the little lord his *vassal.*"

"Well, break my back! And here I always thought a vassal was a slave. How about the king?"

"He was liege to all the lords. They were all his vassals. I hope you realize I'm oversimplifying this."

"I take it you drew an A."

"I've been *there.*"

She had no question, she *knew.* He'd been uptime there—or then, rather; but much earlier, on his home planet, Nigel III, he'd grown up with the stuff. She suggested, "Take me there-then sometime?"

"Mm. Take you uptime on Erth, that is. My home planet isn't there anymore."

"But it was there *then?*"

"Of course."

"So take me there *then.*"

Silence. Croyd had gone thoughtful.

Greta brightened it. "From history, I remember that they stank. Did they? Did *you?*"

"No stench in uptime."

"True, but on Nigel III, when you lived there?"

"I never noticed anything that hadn't always been usual."

Freya suddenly giggled, and it broke the reverie, and inexplicably she found that the reverie had nerved her. Arising, she oriented her thought to the castle's I-ray transmitter which the duke had used several hours ago for descending into his hell-haven. Servants were about; she radiated projective hypnosis through multiple wall piles of thick rock: *sleep.* . . . When she *knew* that they slept, she quit her room and descended to the place where Pan had told her to go; and just as Pan had clairvoyantly known, there she found the transmission-reception cubicle of the duke's private I-ray pullman.

She entered this cubicle.

Just before she activated intergalactic relay, Freya experienced a patterning of comprehension. What had nerved her was a reverie about Croyd. What she feared was Greta. And this was totally absurd, because Pan *was* Croyd, and Freya *was* Greta.

Aren't we?

Behind Pan there was a nonhuman quiet cough.

Pan pondered this cough.

A chirring treble queried, "Is all well, Sirrah Pan?"

Slowly Pan turned to face with a semibitter smile a six-foot-high gold-armored decapod who stood as tall and erect on his four hind members as a decapod can stand, bending upon Pan all five of his eyes with a concern that the angles of his antennae expressed.

They contemplated each other.

Pan straightened a little. "You knew instantly that I am Pan, not Croyd."

"Instantly." The *chirr* did not come from the decapod's mouth; it seemed to emanate from vibrating chitin plates somewhere in the thorax—in one of the thoraces, anyhow.

Pan slumped on a thought. "I will not ask how you knew, and do not tell me." Again he straightened; and out of long practice (long ago) he chose the creature's second and fourth eyes to eye. "Then all the more you were good to come, Krell. How did you get here so fast?"

"I was here, just inside. We take turn about on sentry duty here. It is my trick."

"You do this for Croyd?"

"No. He has not been here often. He gives us no orders—not even advice. He listens to our reports, and nods, and goes. We have not seen him for months."

Emotionally Pan was in torment, wanting to ask about

Croyd, about Krell and his people; wanting to *tell* Krell about Croyd. No, this first thing had to be done first. Deliberately he said, "Four years ago I swore to Croyd that I would stay with you five years if need be. And I swore the same to you, Krell, and to your people. I called out to you first of all to stand here and tell you honestly that I ran out on my trust, that I bitterly regret running out on my trust. If you wish, you may kill me, Krell; I ask only that if you wish to kill me, you tell me so first, and let me answer before you strike. But I will not defend myself."

Taciturn Krell stared at Pan, and Pan waited. Krell could slay him with a snap or a blow of one claw.

Krell said deliberately, "I will take time to examine the nature of your trust. Our species was dying in Andromeda Galaxy. We gathered our pregnant females and crossed metaspace to invade your Sol Galaxy, to lay our eggs in humans and reconstitute ourselves as your masters. But you defeated us, sirrah. The trauma left our females sterile, so that we were no longer a threat to you in our small numbers, although we are virtually deathless; nevertheless, you would have been right to exterminate us. Instead, noble sirrah, you spared us; and because we were parlous unready to mingle with humans, you made an island for us in nonspace, and you and your Freya set aside five years of your precious lives to lead us into self-rehabilitation. What quarrel can we have with you for departing three years early?"

Somehow the six-foot Krell had become taller, not shorter than Pan, who responded eventually, weakly, "It was not I who defeated and spared you, it was Croyd."

"Sirrah, you are one of you, Croyd is the other of you. It would be totally impossible to determine which of you is which."

"*You* could tell."

"Only because you called to me in anguish. It was a good guess, because you departed us in anguish. If I may say so, sirrah, we have progressed in your absence, we have built on your early pointers; but we would profit now by your criticism, if you could spare time for a visit."

"Krell! Croyd is in trouble! That comes first!"

"Of course, Pan. Can we help in some way?"

Miserable, jaw-knotted Pan was beating a fist into a hand palm. "I had to confess guilt to you first. I had to get your reaction to that first. I have a painfully divided

mind about your reaction to that. Perhaps I hoped that
you would wish to kill me. Had you so informed me, I would
have asked for a delay until we could rescue Croyd; and then
I would have presented myself defenseless for killing."

"You have taught us, sirrah, that killing is an inhumane
act, to be reserved for ultimate exigency and thereafter
regretted. I fail to see here an ultimate exigency. I consider you my liege, and I prefer to serve you as a noble
vassal who is willing to say no and stand his ground."

But it didn't really help, although it quieted Pan a little.
He labored out the following: "It was Croyd and not Pan
who taught you that. This house is my birthplace and
Freya's birthplace. Croyd reified us here. Then we had a
conference, and I drew the chore with you people. It was
a sort of a family conference: Croyd was papa, Greta
was mama. Was I supposed to say 'Go to Hell, move
over, I'll be in command now'? Be a realist, Krell; was I
supposed to say that?"

Krell's face, if that was what it was, never wore any
particular expression; but the positions of his antennae
were revealing. Just now, both antennae were aimed
straight at Pan. "Of course not. You were supposed to do
what you did do instead. You were supposed to say, in
effect: 'Croyd, you and I have been one man for a long
time, but all of a sudden I seem to have become your
little boy. Okay, Father, I'll play the game, I won't kick
you off your rock; I'll accept your menial chores like
helping the Krell people get established in a new environment, and in return you will forgive me for being so
obsessed with your superiority and my own inferiority that
I end by turning my back on my trust and becoming a—' "

Krell suddenly went sprawling on the nonspace bridge,
felled by the sidesweeping hand and arm of Pan.

When, collecting consciousness, Krell could look up,
Pan was on his knees bending over him, and the eyes of
Pan were suicidal.

If now there was a faint blur in his chirr, Krell could be
pardoned. "Thank you, Pan. Now I owe you one. You'll
get it when you least expect it—at my pleasure. What
do we do now . . . for Croyd?"

Greta, pallid on Nereid, squeezed her chair arms, facing
the totocolor tri-d image of Freya floating free in the
receptor cubicle. She saw a mirror.

She said, "I have to go there."

"I know."

No, Freya was not a mirror image; such an image would present reversed objective orientation; instead, Freya *was* Greta, only Freya was over there. And, too, Freya was over there after a very long intergalactic transmission relay; where Freya was, apparently it was snowing.

Greta leaned forward, her fingers interlacing. "You and I were one, we were with him as one. Do *you* not feel an urgency to go?"

Freya bowed her head, covering her face with her long-fingered hands. She said soon, "This lousy language of ours does not have the prior experience for discussing the ridiculous situation." Her hands came down and slapped her thighs, her head came up, her eyes grappled with Greta's. "Pan has Croyd memories prior to 2502; but he has his own subsequent memories; and so do I, and they are with Pan. It is Pan, not Croyd, that I would wish to be with. And yet I would wish to be with Croyd also."

Greta's mouth approached a smile. "I would wish to embrace you. But even if it could be done, I would be diffident about that."

Freya's mouth approached a smile. "I suppose one does not embrace oneself, even though one is different from oneself. Nevertheless, I would wish to embrace you; but I too am diffident about that."

"Four years ago, we two were one woman."

"Yes."

"Four years ago, Croyd and Pan were one man."

"Yes."

Greta smiled playfully. "At least, if Croyd lives, he is not lonely. I happen to know about a Princess Djeelian shipping with him aboard the *Castel Jaloux*."

Freya smiled wryly. "For Pan, there has been a Princess Medzik. I give him that she looks comfortable." She grew serious. "Does this trouble you, about Croyd?"

Greta, gravely: "Of course not. If there has been a coupling with Princess Djeelian, it is a transiency. Croyd and I are not a transiency, and I must go to where he is. But it will take so long. . . ." She paused, then leaned forward. "How is it with you, Freya?"

Her eyes closed. "I am secondary. I am weary."

"Secondary to whom?"

"To you."

Greta studied her for a while. Then she articulated, "I

suspect that Pan too is weary because he is secondary."

Freya nodded.

Greta added, "But Pan is leaping into the breach."

Freya nodded.

Greta stood. "I have to go to Croyd, if only to preside over his disintegration. Our fleet has other ships that can clear the barrier, but it will take many days. And then, too . . ." She sank back into her chair, head down on a clenched fist. She muttered, "I seem to be temporary chairman of this galaxy. Croyd charged me with this, Tannen charged me with this. If I shifted it even to the next guy . . ." Her face came up; she was in trouble. "Freya, I am not at all sure that even a dying Croyd would welcome my presence, knowing that I had left this galaxy."

Freya was grave. "Perhaps what we need is a brief mind touch."

Greta: "Have you kept this skill?"

"Yes, but I have no notion whether I can project it over an intergalactic relay."

Greta leaned toward her. "Croyd could. *Try.*"

Silent communion.

Withdrawal.

Now the face of Greta was serene. And Greta said, "Do that, Freya. Be *me*, down there. We are *I* again; be me; I love him."

But Freya was weeping.

Greta, concerned: "Tell me."

Freya, brokenly: "I find now that I would wish to return into you."

Nonspace:

Pan and Krell stood on the bridge of a transparent spaceship out of Andromeda, a ship that resembled an oversize stick insect. On the pseudograss that Pan four years ago had created for this nonspace Krell colony clustered the decapod females. Like their males, these females were sterile; on the other hand, barring accident, they were practically immortal. That is to say, they had less biological need for progeny than most species; on the other hand, in the longer or shorter run their numbers could be whittled down to a point where these barren ones could have more need for impossible progeny than most species. Here in their nonspace exile they were dwelling in a sort of Ellis Island in preparation for ultimate galactic entry.

The grim expedition on which Pan was about to conduct Krell and the youngest, most vigorous of the male decapod adults promised, if it would succeed, to shorten their probation. On the other hand, failure could produce rather an abrupt whittling down of numbers.

"There will be no failure," Pan had told them last night; and he meant it. He had all of them plus Croyd plus Freya plus Greta plus himself on his soul.

Young Krell, golden-armored like Roland (only his was organic), crisp-chirred to Pan, "We appear ready for takeoff. Your orders?"

Pan, intently checking Krell's instrument check, murmured, "There is nothing you men wish to say to the women?"

Krell responded, "I have already made our speech to our women. I await your navigation and drive orders."

Pan absently scratched the bridge of his nose, gazing at the instrument panel. "I think you know, Krell, that nonspace is immediately adjacent to every space."

"True, sirrah. But is nonspace adjacent also to metaspace?"

"No, but space *is*, Krell—and I think that you yourself have penetrated both ways the metagalactic skin."

"I apprehend you, sirrah. We will move immediately to a point in space adjacent to the metagalactic skin, and use drive to penetrate the skin. Still I await your navigation and drive orders."

Pan stared at him. "Are you *sure* you have nothing more for the women?"

"Sirrah Pan, isn't it that Sirrah Croyd is waiting—if he is still able to wait?"

Pan's tone was queerly subordinate. "Krell, are you telling me just to take us off—just like that—*now?*"

Krell's antennae were straight down in front. Low he chirred, "You are taking us to rescue your duplicate Croyd whom for some irrational reason you consider superior to yourself. And you hesitate. Can it possibly be that you are . . . *afraid of succeeding?*"

Pan stared at him.

Pan snapped orders.

The ship vanished.

Where the stickbug ship materialized in space was midway between Sol and Djinn galaxies by ordinary light routes —roughly nine hundred million light-years each way.

Seven decapod officers, armored in various brilliant colors (as a cultural mode, they dye-dipped), thronged the bridge, their variously configured antennae interlacing, the five eyes of each warrior focused on the central Pan-Krell conference. Several dozen other kaleidoscopically armored males, back in the hull, at once watched the bridge and stared out through the transparent hull one way at Sol and another way at Djinn, both of which were small-magnitude stars among larger stars. All three ways at once—each warrior.

Pan said, terse, "This places us a parsec from the extreme inwardness of the metagalactic fissure. From the observations by Freya in Duke Dzendzel's Moudjinn castle, I have to conclude that we are directly beneath the prime fissure of the feudally organized brain that has captured Croyd and threatens the metagalaxy. That brain is so colossal that if now, from here, we were to direct all our hypernuclear weapons into the body of that fissure, allowing that any one of the weapons could annihilate a star, the entire salvo would do no more than give that brain a local and inconsequential thrill. So now we decide the next thing."

Krell remarked with some degree of suppressed wonderment, "I thought maybe you *had*."

Pan studied space. "Probably I should have, but I haven't. Maybe I had to be spaced here first, to appreciate the problem concretely. I do not know how to ruin that brain without rupturing the metagalactic shell. More concisely, I do not know how to ruin that brain. Finally, I do not know *whether* to ruin that brain; probably I would ruin Croyd along with it, and anyway, he may not want it ruined, he may have found a use for it. And I am tempted to go home with all of us."

Krell said concisely, "But you will not."

"I will not. Instead, we will enter. But we have to enter delicately. It is a bit like having to drill delicately through the impervious vault of a bank without knowing where within the police may lurk."

A green commander queried, "How can we enter? We are motionless here a mere parsec from the metagalactic skin; we cannot develop the velocity to punch through."

Krell turned to him, antennae frowning. "Thank you, sirrah. Pan will find methods, once he finds purposes."

Pan pursed lips. "Methods are easy; you are right, Krell. As for purposes—let me tell you what I think. . . ."

Somewhat later, the stick ship vanished.

Phase Six

ULTIMATE TEMPTATION

Day 5

Yes, let me dare those gates to fling asunder
Which every man would fain go slinking by!
'Tis time, through deeds this word of truth to
thunder:
That with the height of Gods Man's dignity
may vie!

—Johann Wolfgang von Goethe, *Faust*
(1808)/Baynard Taylor

So Jurgen shrugged, and climbed down
from the throne of the god. . . .

—James Branch Cabell, *Jurgen* (1919)

THREE ROLANDS gazed down upon Croyd, blurring in and out of each other; and the interweaving voices of perhaps five Rolands indescribably confounded Croyd's hearing. Feebly Croyd raised a hand; the five Rolands quieted, the three Rolands stayed. Croyd spoke, but he heard no sound emerging. Clearing throat and wetting lips, he spoke again, and his ears were assaulted by dozens of Croyd voices. He rested, thrusting himself into clarifying thought. One of the three Rolands clicked into unity with another; now there were only two. Hazily concluding that his voice might be all right even though his addled sensorium denied it, Croyd required himself to say deliberately through the addlebabble that his own noises were making, "Roland, I see two of you and I hear several of you and many of me. Is either of us really alive?"

The effort helped him; Roland resolved into a single semiblurred knight, and Roland's voice became an intelligible clatter. "Lie quiet, sir, please. You sustained a skull fracture and a severe concussion. We have repaired both, but you must not hurry the process of reintegration."

When Croyd had that comprehended, he lay back, closed eyes, and smiled wearily. "Thank you for repairing me. And I am glad you are alive, sir; I was afraid I had killed you."

"You did."

Croyd's face did not change. "Then during our fight you were playacting. You weren't really there."

Roland shook his head. "I was real in the fight. Your sword cleverly entered a kidney, and it appears that this wound was quickly mortal, because I died of physical shock. Once this had been diagnosed, the duke had me duplicated. While they carried my corpse off the field in one direction, I followed you in another direction and saw to the beginnings of your own recovery treatment. Then I went to preside over my own rites of disintegration, received orders from the duke, and returned just now. It appears that your treatment has succeeded."

With caution Croyd sat erect, swinging legs off the cot.

Feet on floor, he commented gravely, "It does appear that the work on both of us was well done, sir. Thank you for your knightly courtesy. And now I believe that I have earned a boon crave."

"And a boon collect, sir. The duke gave me explicit orders about this. But only, of course, until tomorrow morning, when we begin your terminal brain scan." Roland coughed and added, "I had some hopes of killing you, if only to spare you that brain scan. But on that score my thoughts were divided."

"I sense an ambiguity," Croyd declared, "but it is one that for now I will pass." He looked upward at the knight. "Sir, my boon is simple enough. Tomorrow I die; tonight I wish to taste the pleasures of your incomparable city."

The response was interesting: Roland, looking down upon him, went facially all guarded as he probed, "One wishes to prowl the boulevard?"

"One wishes to prowl the back streets."

"Those near the bright center, perhaps?"

"No. Those toward the far end, where the men and women display the most interesting anatomical specializations."

Roland had his great sword out, but only to lean upon its hilt; with its point grounded, as he studied Croyd. "I thought I had some reason to hope, sir, that you would opt for a less trivial final night. Nevertheless, I respect your manly needs; your boon is granted. Does it perhaps entail any ancillary complications?"

Croyd counterstudied Roland. Croyd decided to project a hint that would have to be transparent to a young-old man as astute and honest as this Roland seemed to be. He said deliberately, "There are a complication and a subcomplication. The complication is that the human-type distances in your city are rather great; I shall need, for my comfort, to be able on foot to traverse parsecs in blink-time without feeling hurried. And the subcomplication is that this kind of leisurely velocity on the boulevard will need to be maintainable on the back streets, at least during the short distance from that end of the boulevard to the center of my desire."

Having said this, he waited, watching Roland.

Presently Roland stood erect, slowly sheathed his great sword, and folded arms, frowning downward. Roland said then, "I shall have to come with you."

Croyd leaped to his feet with an eager smile. "Shall we start now, gallant comrade?"

He watched the polymorphic people all about him meeting and glowing, and very particularly glowing in the brave genital prominences that they externally displayed. During a long while he watched many encounters. Ultimately the stoic Roland, growing restless, inquired, "Sir, may I assist you in making a pleasant contact?"

Croyd turned to him. "*You* have no desire, Roland?"

"I have latent desire, but I have not chosen to release it. If you release yours, I will feel free to release mine."

"If I do not release mine, will this frustrate you?"

Roland was mildly surprised, all the while watching Croyd as though he wished to intercept any guarded facial or vocal cue that Croyd might choose to let slip. "I did not think that it was any longer a choice for you, whether to free your desire. I thought that I had stolen from you all those special powers, Croyd."

"Is this self-restraint a special power for you, Roland?"

"No, not for me; but I am—"

"I know what you are, Roland. You are lord of the Rolandic fissure of this brain that we stand in. This brain has evolved through aeons, and you have evolved as its liege lord, since a liege lord is a necessary outcome. Unhappily, you have given your feudal allegiance to Duke Dzendzel; and now *he* is the liege, and he has anointed himself with *l'oint du seigneur;* but you remain his high vassal, and you are of the quintessential mind substance that this brain is generating. But believe me, Roland, if you were wholly human like me, and without special powers, by the very power of your own minded brain you could if you chose *and insisted* inhibit any and all desires whenever they would seem inappropriate to your long-range interests. You would dislike it, but you could do it. So I." (In his mind he added wryly: *Usually, that is.*)

The men contemplated each other—Croyd calm, Roland going through an intricate intercombination of realizations.

Roland said presently—it was a question, but it sounded like a statement—"Then you know that this is a brain."

"Yes."

"And that I am . . . its senior outcome."

"Yes."

"Then where are we now, and why did you want to come here?"

"We are in the lowest extremity of a one-lobe Rolandic fissure, actually a bit in under the curve of the cerebral cortex—the extremity of this fissure that is devoted to sexual representation but also happens to be nearest of all to the commanding diencephalon. Roland, I have now told you a very great deal indeed. Will you tell me a thing or two, or will you instead paralyze me and take me back to the dungeon keep?"

Roland thought.

Roland said, "Through the offices of my brain I learned about the existence of the Djinn Galaxy. Again through my brain's offices, naïvely I went to Moudjinn because I was not an introvert and I wanted to establish relations with other intelligences. I had no other motive. The Emperor of Djinn brushed me off to his prime minister, who happened to be Duke Dzendzel. By hindsight I credit the duke as a man whose ambitions transcend galaxies and who knows opportunity when he sees it."

Croyd murmured, "It is beginning to come through. Dzendzel evidently appreciated what few do appreciate: an analogy between feudalism and brain organization, and very particularly, the efficiency-beauty of the Rolandic fissure which in its administrative transactions corresponds to an operational bureaucracy. And he seems also to have grasped a remote physical analogy between the walnut convolutions of the metagalactic skin and the walnut convolutions of a human cerebral cortex; and while the analogy in itself is fallacious, in this case it led him to a good thing."

"Precisely," Roland affirmed, gazing at Croyd with new appreciation.

"Only, Roland, *why* would you allow him to take over from *you?*"

Roland ruminated.

"Because," Roland finally said, "he had an idea about this brain that was higher than any idea that I had ever conceived. And because, sir, constitutionally I am a number-two man, a highest-level vassal—and a vassal requires a liege for his soul completion."

Two accomplished and rich-glowing belly dancers, wholly human in form, without any grotesque enlargements, were performing enthusiastically before these two men. Neither man was noticing.

Croyd tested carefully. "Lately I have felt honored by a certain interest in me that you have seemed to be developing."

"My lord duke is shrewd and subtle, his IQ is possibly one hundred and fifty if I may put it that way. This, sir, is an admirable IQ. But lately I have been giving some thought to whether it is enough IQ for competent feudalizing of a metagalaxy—recalling, sir, that true chivalric feudalism entails an ethos."

"Perhaps I apprehend you, Roland."

"Thank you, sir. But do not try to use me; I can kill you quickly."

"You are, I would almost guess, suggesting that my own IQ may be at least one hundred and fifty-one."

"However that may be, sir, I *am* suggesting that you may have a true sense of chivalric ethos."

"Roland, we are almost coming right out and *saying* it to each other."

The knight drew himself tall. "Then I shall be the one to say it first. I am going to give you tonight a full introduction to our fissure brain. If you're able to master our brain, you will be able to replace Duke Dzendzel. And even if you should master our brain, if you should then show signs of metagalactic treason, I would kill you— permanently. But if you fail to master our brain, I will commit you to the duke and the brain scan."

The belly dancers gave up and vanished. All around them, sexually protuberant people rebegan their boredom dancing, oblivious of the knight and his guest.

Croyd remarked, "This is indeed a fine locale for a night on the town."

"It is indeed, sir. And I have been here before, relaxed. It is for you to say, sir; I can give you this kind of guidance, if you wish."

"May I take a rain check, Roland? For a year from now, say?"

"Sir, what is rain?"

"I will answer that, Roland, a year from now, say. May we visit your hinterland, in the general direction of the diencephalon?"

Magnitude and velocity can be relative in more than ordinary ways, Croyd reminded himself, as, deep in the hinterland, Roland led him aboard an afferent axone whose energy shot them downward and inward. The pulpy rounded "building" bulges that lined and indeed created the Rolandic fissure and the far smaller inward-leading fissures were actually composed of quintillions of just such fibers. Had Croyd's eyes been able on the boulevard to discern one such fiber, it would have seemed an excessively fine gray hair; yet now, as they *entered* the axone, its thickness was many times their height, and it had no identifiable substance—only invisible energy at high velocity that caught them up and whirred them on. Croyd questioned, "Is it that we have shrunk, as you did when you entered my brain?"

Roland negated, "You are physical Croyd. I would not be able to shrink you so; but while we were on the boulevard, I exercised a certain control on your optical centers of cerebral representation so that your synoptic comprehension would not be overwhelmed."

And then, the distances and the velocities. If this brain had evolved into anything like a human brain (and the brains of all independently evolved mammalian-human species in Croyd's galaxy, at least, were roughly similar, this general form being apparently the one so-far most convenient for peak-energy competition survival), then the distance from the lower-inner sexual end of the Rolandic fissure to the irregularly planar surface between cerebrum and diencephalon was crudely one-third the distance from one end to the other of the unilobe fissure; and that same one-third distance, measured even in parsecs, was breathtaking. And yet, if this brain acted with ordinary high brain speed (which clearly it did), an impulse must traverse this intergalactic distance in microseconds! The physics of this demonstrable fact required study; it was extrametagalactic physics, which had not been anticipated by Einstein or even by Norstead or any of *his* successors. Possibly there was an analogy with I-rays.

Meanwhile, though, how about the relative duration of Croyd's own experience? That he had traversed the millions of parsecs of the Rolandic fissure in minutes last night with the duke, this he could put down to the duke's brain magic. But now he was experiencing a weird reversal; traveling with an impulse that traversed such parsecs in microseconds, he was finding time for all this thought and even for a bit of conversation with Roland.

Expressing this, he queried, "How?"

Roland replied, "Sir . . . think."

Croyd nodded. He started to give the reply. Roland interrupted with a terse "I apprehend you, sir." Roland, grace to his metagalactic fissure brain, possessed some of the powers that he had stolen from Croyd—among them, receptive telepathy. *He* saw that *Croyd* saw that Roland was exerting upon him something like a velocity-analogon of the Rolandic-boulevard effect; there, Roland had expanded the brain processes of Croyd so that he would see the relatively vast as the relatively ordinary; here, Roland had *accelerated* the brain processes of Croyd so that he would experience microseconds as minutes.

Roland possessed the power of receptive telepathy. At the instant, Roland was exercising this power, but only with respect to the mind content that Croyd was anyhow ready to communicate to Roland. And there was much evidence that Roland had not previously exercised this power, since Roland remained guarded about the intentions of Croyd. Then, with respect to telepathy—that is to say, with respect to mind privacy—Roland's ethics were like Croyd's. This reflection served to remind Croyd that pure chivalric ethics were at heart very much like pure middle-class ethics, even though most members of both classes might pay only lip service to either code. It was likely that Western nobility and bourgeois had originally evolved, in one culture or another, out of the same strong yeoman stock, possibly taking different directions because of primogeniture. Anyhow, the Roland-Croyd ethos was essentially one; and neither confined his service to his lips.

Middle class. That is, middle class accompanied by critical discernment between what is essential and what is mere taboo.

Roland warned, "We are swiftly approaching my own headquarters. Please be prepared for an abrupt debouchment."

THERE WAS NO SPECIAL VISIBLE FEATURE to the small cell that was Roland's headquarters as seneschal to the duke; indeed, Croyd (after his recent experiences with magnitude paradox) was not at all ready to judge that the cell had any special size. But the room was pregnant with sensa. They were in the air, if there was air; only, to Croyd they were not intelligible, and this was a vast pity, because a few days earlier, to Croyd they would have been intelligible, and he knew it. He grinned grimly at a phantom memory of a recent debility-interrupted foray into the Moskovian language; this was different, but the same. However, he merely queried as an opener, "This is where you locate yourself, Roland, when you direct your brain?"

"This is where I locate myself when I *intensively* direct *our* brain. The way you put it, Croyd, left about four considerations out of account. One is that this is a thoroughly mature brain, fully equipped with habitudes; routinely it regulates itself without direction."

"This I assumed."

"Another is that neither the duke nor I needs to be in his special brain place for purposes of minor direction; so this morning, without moving away from his pavilion, the duke by telepathy was able to produce instantaneously your graul and my reification—and, now I think about it, my duplication and your healing."

"So I assumed. And last night I further judged that when the duke by mental powers converted the ceiling of my dungeon keep into a circular ramp egress—"

"Your pardon, Croyd. A circular what?"

"Ramp egress. Well, when he did that, later when I thought about it, I judged that he had done it, not through any special power of his own minded brain, but rather through the power of *this* brain."

"I will not at this time assert that you are wrong." Nevertheless, the face of Roland was losing its poker; there was a nuance of growing confidence in Croyd.

"You were going to mention a third and a fourth consideration."

"The third is, Croyd, that when I do come here intensively to direct this brain, I direct it under the duke's guidelines. The fourth is that very often when I sit here *administrating* rather than directing this brain, in the course of excessively complex operations that are beyond my simple comprehension other than managing the detail work, Duke Dzendzel is in *his* place *beyond—really DIRECTING* this brain."

He waited then, clearly expecting a cross-question about the duke's place beyond. But Croyd ducked and counterthrust. "A while back, when I first awakened from my dolor, you mentioned ambivalence as to whether you wished me to live or to die. Is this ambivalence perhaps a fifth consideration that I am leaving out of account?"

Childe Roland took time to assimilate the question. While he did so, there came a remarkable change in him: the golden armor vanished, it was replaced by a tasteful-comfortable pseudocloth suit having a purple jerkin and pink tights—informal evening-parlor stuff, in no way self-assertive. Roland then appeared to relax into an invisible chair; Croyd, intuitively comprehending the *geste*, allowed himself to relax in the same way—into fortunately, another invisible chair.

It was the mutual decision.

To seal it, Roland extended a hand and arm sidewise; his hand was filled by a full wineglass. Croyd did the same and received the same; he tasted—it was a kind of Burgundy, just right, neither *brut* nor *douce*. He extended his glass toward Roland; they clicked; they sipped.

Roland asserted then, "When I *will* that this room not be bugged, it is not bugged. It is not bugged. I have judged my liege the duke, and I find him wanting in chivalry. Nevertheless, my provisional position is one of continuing loyalty. Meanwhile, I do not find you wanting in chivalry or in power of mind, despite my paltry pilferings. I was divided about killing you for the following reasons: if I should kill you, I would save you from the brain scan, and that would be good; but if I should not kill you, you *might* end by replacing the duke in my esteem—and that, should you pass all tests, would be better. You have now passed all tests of chivalry. There remains a test of intelligence—*projective* intelligence. Should you fail this test, I would use my powers to blank out your memory of this interview and commit you to the brain scan."

Croyd drained the wine and told him, "I am beholden. What is the test?"

Somehow the wineglass refilled itself.

After some orienting of Croyd to this featureless control room, whose operation fundamentally entailed that its operator be attentive to the *sorts* of impulses that might come in and peremptory about the *sorts* of impulses that he might wish to go out, Roland queried in an attitude of moderate interest that disguised eagerness, "Now, Croyd, what will your first action be?"

Croyd said instantly, "I wish to communicate with Chloris."

"Chloris?" Roland seemed disconcerted.

"Any questions? Any objections?" This was a demand.

Puzzled, Roland waved his wineglass. "Be careful. I am here."

In his mind Croyd called out, *Chloris!* And while he did so, he tried to visualize the entire metaspace region of the metagalactic fissure and beyond.

Faintly she responded in his mind, *Croyd, where are you?*

Roland was alert, monitoring. Croyd called, *You must give me your approximate coordinates to improve these readings.*

She responded, *I have moved vertically out of the fissure. Approximately eight hours ago I moved through and upward beyond the position where we quit the* Castel Jaloux. *I am searching for the* Castel. *Where are you, Croyd, and can you help me?*

His eyes were squeezed shut; he was concentrating on disciplined thought; he visualized and conceptualized the approximate position where she seemed to be; and then he commanded: *Say something to test signals.*

Louder and clearer: *That is much louder and clearer, Croyd. How well do you read me?*

He rapped: *Damn well! Stand by!* Opening eyes, he challenged Roland, "Can you give me visuals?"

Intent, Roland answered, "It is you who are test-directing the brain."

"Why, then," the Croyd voice lazed, "it is beautiful; with this magnificent instrument I *need* no special powers; this feels exactly like when my own ego decides to take a walk, and so my brain makes my body walk! As for visuals, though, this would require . . . well, never mind, Roland, because *any* communication in metaspace would require the same potential in your brain, so it must have it." He closed eyes again, and he *desired* to see the lifeboat Chloris.

She was clearly visible. But there was nothing else visible around her.

He opened eyes; still, over *there* in the indefinite space of the Roland cell, she was visible. And a fascinated Roland was looking at her.

Eyes open, Croyd thought at her: *Where is Tannen?*

Her voice, audible to him (and, apparently, to Roland),

was a thought callous. *Down there, somewhere. Him I had to jettison. Not enough inertial shield.*

Croyd swung to Roland. "Can we find and rescue him?"

Roland simply looked at Croyd.

Did you leave him where I left both of you? he demanded of Chloris.

Precisely, she affirmed.

You have not found the Castel?

I am on search course.

Stay on search course. I will be back with you shortly.

His eyes closed again, and he thought (image and personality): *Tannen.* I materialized before him, reaching upward for tree fruit, panting heavily, unaware of him as yet. He shot at Roland: "You see him. Can he eat and drink there?"

Roland gestured, meaning: "It is you who direct the brain."

Croyd mentally grated at the brain: *All fruit there is to be edible, with potable juices.* Then his soft thought projection entered me, jolting me: *Tannen, hold steady, don't say anything, think your reply. I am entering into some control, but stay where you are for now. Do you read me?*

I turned as though I were facing him—seeing, of course, only land and seascape. *I won't waste time muttering that I knew you would. Croyd, this is coming directly into my mind. Are you recovering your powers?*

No, there is another angle. Stay put. By a certain method I am opening a steady line of one-way communication with you, so that you will be witnessing all that I experience. You can eat or drink whatever you wish.

Good. I eat and I drink—and I stay attentive. Can you quickly fill me with nearly two days of lost background?

Hold tight; here it comes: the short form. . . .

Less than a minute later I had the subjective gist of all that had happened to him since yesterday when he had gone negative and vanished, together with enough symbolic footnoting to give me the intellective continuity. When it was done, I ventured: *Understood, I think. Later, when you have leisure, will you fill me full?*

IF we have leisure—indeed, if we have later. At least you can follow me intimately from here on in.

That is indeed a Blessèd Be He.

Tannen, have you arrived at a synthesis about Djeel and Hanoku?

Is there a point?

Conceivably you will need to use it. Just conceivably.

Because of Chloris?

Yes.

Well, I have one.

Croyd's face and voice became more passionally involved, in my vivid mind view, than at any time in my long experience of him. *Are you . . . sure you have a synthesis?*

I studied him. *I am sure. But I sought and found it mainly because to me it was important. To you it is also important?*

To me it is almost, you should forgive the redundancy, critically crucial.

I nodded once. *Then you should relax. I have a synthesis.*

Visibly Croyd relaxed, indeed sagged; and then he tautened, grinning hard. *Good. Don't bank on the use— but don't forget the synthesis. Out, old friend.*

Out, Croyd. Cheers.

I had no concept, then, that he was ambivalent about my synthesis.

Another subjective shift; Croyd was becoming fluid at this, it was like moving his eyes; room walls dissolved, all was metaspace nothing, he was floating in it—no, effortlessly swimming submerged in it; and full center in his visual field swam Chloris; he was following her, aft and slightly to port at an apparent distance of ten Chloris lengths. Before hailing, he swam past and around in front of her, although the subjective effect was as though he were manipulating Chloris; and he stabilized himself noses-on with her, half a Chloris length ahead of her, so that she could concentrate on him with just her central I-rays while all her others kept sweeping metaspace in search of the *Castel Jaloux*. From here she resembled a bows-on cyclopean fish. She looked petulant, although of course her mood was *not* petulant; rather she was intently driving herself at peak capacity, and the "expression" was built into the immobility of her metaloid structure.

They had already reentered communication, now in calm quiet conversation as though they were a gentleman and a lady seated just *tête-à-tête* in a salon. He told her, "I have Tannen stabilized; I am making some control progress in the fissure. To be brief, the fissure and its environing lobes and apparently a broad multilobed exterior surface of the metagalaxy are a brain controlled by a mind. I am not that controlling mind, I am only for the moment in partial control, I am not at liberty to say more. When you have completed your present mission, return as swiftly as possible. If we lose contact, and if still you can maneuver, touch down anywhere and keep sensors open. If I do not contact you, you are on your own. I do not know how to orient you to my position."

"Acknowledged."

"No trace of the *Castel?*"

"No, sir. I am persisting and sweeping."

"I know." He did not ask her about fuel; she was equipped to burn metaspace. "How far out are you now?"

"About two-point-five hundred million parsecs out beyond the lobe-end position where we lost the *Castel.*"

"Since when?"

"Since takeoff twenty hours ago."

"Then you have taken twenty hours to move outward merely twice the distance that they pulled you inward in five."

"That, sir, is syntax-faulty. First time in my experience of you."

"Slow time, Chloris!"

"I know. Even now I have been able to build up velocity only to a lousy hundred million parsecs per hour."

"Seriously, Chloris, *how?*"

"Sir, apparently they forgot to withdraw what they inserted in me. And I've always used normal space fuel; this metaspace juice is heady stuff."

"Are you in danger of structural collapse?"

"I experience no hazard indications, but at this acceleration, such indication might come simultaneously with collapse. My inertial shield is incredibly holding, but enough G's are coming through to slow my reaction time."

"Then reduce acceleration. Your velocity is high enough now; it needn't increase rapidly."

"Negative, sir."

"I beg your pardon?"

"Negative the command. I do not know the outward

velocity of the *Castel*. At merely my present velocity, she
could be years away."

"If she is years away, by the Heisenberg principle her
position is randomized and you have astronomically low
probability of finding her anyhow. Repeat: reduce acceleration."

Pause. Then: "Affirmative. But only just a little."

"If you haven't collapsed yet, perhaps just a little is
enough. Good; you are drifting back away from me; you
have done it already. Hold a moment while I stabilize. . . .
Now. Chloris . . ."

"Croyd?"

"If you find the *Castel*, what will you do?"

"I will seek means of turning her downward. I will then
seek means of bringing her under control."

"You will *seek* means? You have not *thought* of
means?"

Hesitation. Then: "No, sir." It would be a minnow
trying to influence Leviathan.

Croyd considered. He queried, "Why would you not
berth in her hull and seek communication with the admiral
as a first step?"

"The admiral may be unable to communicate, and in
any case, I might be phantom-swarmed and rendered helpless."

In the brain, involuntarily Croyd nodded. "Your IQ
stays up there."

"Only because my deceleration relief is indescribable."

"Chloris . . ."

"Croyd?"

"I think of only one way to turn her around without
internal cooperation, and maybe, even *with* internal cooperation."

Pause. Then: "I know. That has crossed my . . . well,
my brain."

"Your mind."

"Thank you."

"Are we speaking of the same thing, Chloris?"

"The repulsor ploy."

"Exactly."

"Affirmative, I think."

"Chloris . . ."

"Croyd?"

"That would be a damned ironical ploy. Should you

fail, you could return—but *only* you. Should you succeed, they could return—but *only* they."

"That's . . . how I figured it."

Between them, for the first time, there was a wordless emotive mental passage. Then both of them shut it off.

Croyd said, dry, "You have freedom to play it as you see it. If you return alone, I will count it as gain."

Chloris responded, dry, "I will play it as I see it."

"If you find the *Castel*, reopen signals with me immediately. If I can be there, I want to be there."

"Affirmative. Sir . . ."

"My name is Croyd."

"Croyd . . ."

"Chloris?"

"I feel human, sort of."

"You *are* human."

"How so?"

Croyd paraphrased a passage from the *Code of the Interplanetary Union:* "A human is one having sufficient neural complexity to use symbolic language in order to sublimate survival and reproductive interests in more complex levels of aesthetic development, individual or social, but without necessarily denying the more fundamental levels of living."

"Only the neural-complexity aspect fits me, Croyd. As for survival, I define it as survival until I will have completed a defined mission, which in this case is the turning of the *Castel*."

"That is a sublimation of survival interest."

"But I have no reproductive interest."

"But you wish to keep the crew of the *Castel* alive. That wish counts as sublimation of what would otherwise be reproductive interest."

"But I deny the more fundamental levels of living."

"You pay no attention to the continuing efficiency of your own reonics?"

Pause. Then, small: "I do not understand aesthetic development."

"Is that why you are finding the chase of the *Castel* boring?"

"It is not boring."

Soft: "And am I in your picture, a little?"

Pause. Then, stoic-small: "I find it a value to work with you for this while."

He told her decisively, "You are human. I pray that some god may bless you and your mission."

Long pause. Then, querulous: "*Could* it be maybe a goddess?"

He responded harsh: "Too long you have known Tannen. Chloris, I have to go. Cheers."

Promptly, and with odd exuberance: "Cheers, Croyd! Out."

He said quietly, "Cheers, Chloris. Out."

Her image rheostated out. Gradually Croyd became aware again of Roland; and slowly he turned again to Roland.

CHILDE ROLAND quietly told Croyd, "If I thought you were inclined toward feudal customs, I would kneel before you and clasp your mighty testicles and swear fealty."

Croyd, barely returning into self-orientation, gazed semistuporously at Roland. "Bypassing the rite you cite, I do not quite see why. Still, I have no special powers; I used your brain with my own minded brain, that is all."

"And tremendously do I admire your achievement. But I would not swear fealty to an achievement. I would, however, right gladly swear fealty to your conduct of the epochal conversation between yourself and the scouter *Chloris*."

Now Croyd's awareness was all back. He demanded, "How would *you* have dealt with Chloris, Roland?"

"If you had not dealt with her as I would have dealt with her, why would I wish to swear fealty to you?"

"Then do you swear fealty to yourself. And I will serve you, and put my hands between your thighs if you think it necessary for the swearing, until you have put all things to rights and got me and mine safe out of here."

Slowly Roland shook his long-haired, bearded young head. "I may have spoken too short. I would have dealt as you with Chloris if I had the imagination. But you thought of much that is beyond me, although, having listened, I agree. And this is my fundamental point, Croyd. I am a number-two leader, a solid and effective and loyal brain administrator. But I need a liege with imagination. Dzendzel has the imagination, but he deploys it for personal gain. You have even more imagination, and you deploy it on chivalric principles *just on the spur of the instant and without pausing to think about it*. Therefore it is you who should be my liege—*our* liege—and not Dzendzel.

"Let me put it baldly, Croyd. This metagalaxy exists and grows, and we have gradually been evolved by its energy mechanics, and finally we are beginning to realize ourselves as a brain for this metagalaxy that sorely needs a brain. We should be the consciousness of the metagalaxy; we should be its god. Unfortunately, we are only brain dynamics; even with me as prime coordinator, we are only brain dynamics. Your Aristotle named five human senses; he then added a sixth sense which coordinates the other five; but he insisted that finally a mind was required to use the sixth sense and accordingly direct a life. Think of me as our brain's sixth sense: *I* need a *liege mind*, Croyd. And Dzendzel has been my liege mind. But I do not want him anymore. I want *you*."

Having assimilated the might of this proposition, Croyd inquired, "If I were the mind of the metagalaxy, what would I be doing?"

"That would be for you to decide, being its mind. I have made an offer. It is your problem, and I should add that if you should accept my offer, there would be hazards from Dzendzel. It is a fundamental feudal principle that if one is to have, one must conquer and hold."

Silence.

Croyd cleared his throat. "I am not usually indecisive."

"This I comprehend."

"Forgive me."

"Forgiven."

"Although I often wish I could *afford* to be indecisive."

"I understand. So do I."

Silence.

Croyd said, low, "If I were to take command of the metagalaxy, Plato would applaud, recognizing me as the demiurge, confident that I would have to submit anyway to his eternal ideas. On the other hand, Dewey would make dark mutterings, until, perhaps, he would see that I as the mind would not be of the ivory-tower brain alone; instead, every galaxy in the metagalaxy would be contributing to the mind and influencing the mind in the process of being governed by the mind. If that were

the case, perhaps there would be no need for intergalactic
treaties; and in the special case of Dari, perhaps I could
revivify her in her old *genre* with a vital new synthesis
based on brain-analyzed reality rather than on the make-
shift perception methods of our alien team fishily scru-
tinizing the dead relics of Dari and trying therefore to
reconstruct the vitality of Dari."

Roland was attentive.

Almost whispered Croyd, "If this is to be my metagalaxy, show her to me."

Roland said, low, "This is your brain; use her. Take
your metagalaxy, and decide whether you wish to hold
her."

He was disembodied in a black star-punctuated cosmos.

The star points were all around him, outside and beyond him, semisurrounding him like a night sky watched
clear from an atmosphereless planet. He tried to turn, and
he seemed to be turning; but the panorastra turned with
him, there was no change.

They were not individual close-clustered stars, but wide-
apart galaxies.

At first he was bewildered at his understanding that
these galaxies were outside and beyond him; for he was
dwelling on the brain cortex of the metagalactic skin
which *enclosed* the galaxies as a convoluted walnut shell
encloses its kernel; and from this brain he must be looking
inward, for outside the brain there was only void. But
then comprehension came. If you were a box containing a
ball, and with eyes everywhere on your inner surface you
were gazing at the ball, seeing simultaneously all around
the ball with your multinocular vision, the ball would appear to be *all around you outside,* containing you. And if
you were *half* a box, the semicontained ball's convex hemisphere that you could see would again seem outside you,
concave, semicontaining you. Probably human vision
works like that in the brain: the diencephalon sucking in
external impressions from the eyes and registering them in
negative, with convex surfaces concaved and vice versa;
then the brain telencephalically reprojecting the scene,
and the mind grasping it in positive. Croyd, looking within
what was in effect his own enclosing metagalactic brain
rind, wherein the objects originally dwelt instead of being
reversed representations of what was outside, was auto-

matically projecting their images *as though they were outside*.

If his theory were right, convexities should be appearing as concavities, and vice versa. For instance, Sol Galaxy—to normal extragalactic vision a pancake with a central bulge—should now appear to Croyd as a doughnut with bulging periphery and central hole. He consulted the brain for indexical data: it pointed him instantly to Sol Galaxy, hinterminding him with a snide little footnote: *Named Sol Galaxy by its parochially ethnocentric Erth-based master race, although Sol, the star of Erth, is a mediocre G-type star out near the galactic periphery*. His smile at the scholarly stab waned into reflectiveness as he recognized that, without special powers and without the brain, he could unaided have located Sol Galaxy or any other major galaxy by mentally revising viewpoint coordinates.

Now he coaxed the brain's visual complex; swiftly it zoomed him in on Sol Galaxy, which was, as predicted, a doughnut. (He was convinced now that the basis of this brain's sensorium was I-rays.) To this brain's optic cortex he now issued a sharp corrective command: *Invert all percepts!* The doughnut instantly flipped into a star-coruscating pancake with central bulge; and he was ready to nose in and find Erth.

Not wholly convinced that he was God, he had nevertheless realistically to recognize that with this brain he was ready to do a god's job.

Perhaps, whether he wanted to do a god's job or not, he *should*.

Assuring himself that he did *not* want to do a god's job, purely for the sake of understanding the prospect he turned his back on Erth to nose in on the S galaxy Djinn and the Eden planet Dari.

What sharply brought him out of it somewhat later—just as he had pinpointed the eruption of piracy and was about to attempt a forward time tracing to *now*—was a delicate unrest in his control, a subtle sense that the brain was not wholly attentive to him-as-mind but was also beginning to attend to some *other* mind.

On the instant when he recognized the meaning of this sense, he shut off the metagalaxy and whirled in his own Croyd person to survey the interior of Roland's mind room.

Only, it was *not* Roland's mind room. Inattentive to

himself, engrossed in his metagalaxy, he had been sucked into a vaster mind room. In this room Duke Dzendzel, seated calmly on a capacious throne, held a supinely inert Greta across his lap with the small of her back on his knees and her legs dangling Croydward.

Eh, Greta it was not! on a nuance of difference in personality feel that could only be a difference in four recent years of memories.

Then it had to be Freya!

And the submissiveness of Freya struck Croyd as being unusual, apart from the unexpectedness of her presence here in the fissure. Checking about, he found Roland sitting in a chair, wholly shriveled, his glow diminished to pallor.

And in his mind Croyd heard the duke: *I thank you, Croyd, for your Croyd-Pan woman gift. I recognize that you are Croyd, not Pan, that she is Freya, not Greta; nevertheless, I have weakened your forces, and I will be invincible by the time Pan and Greta can array themselves against me. But it is unfortunate that you have traduced my Roland; he was the best of all knights. So much the worse for both of you: your mutual villainy has canceled out my boon gift, and tomorrow the brain scan will be bitter.*

For Croyd, the mind voice furzed in his own creeping mental and physical paralysis.

———— ⋈ ◀▶ ⋈ ————

INSTANT BY INSTANT, as Croyd and Dzendzel gazed at each other in bland challenge-counterchallenge (while Freya lay helplessly supine across the knees of Dzendzel and Roland crouched shriveled and glowless), Croyd felt the waning even of his normal human powers; Dzendzel had telepathically retaken command of Dzendzel's cosmic brain, and with it he had reduced Roland and Freya and was now reducing Croyd to ciphers of total passivity.

Croyd's wavering mind, though, knew with Dzendzel's that this was Freya, not Greta. There were attitude cues, even in her inertness. Nevertheless, she *had* been Greta. And somehow Croyd succeeded in formulating a Greta thought for Freya, shrouding it in a private mind language that they had known in order to prevent effective Dzendzel penetration. Croyd was unable to project this thought;

but *perhaps* Freya (beneath her overt apathy) had retained enough sensitivity to pull it in and possibly to reply in projection.

The thought was a question: *Are you total yet?*

Continuing to weaken, blurredly he received a reply in the same language: *Not yet.*

He got off one more signal: *Resist as long as you can, concentrate on that, I'll try to make a mind diversion.*

But then Dzendzel, catching the point of the unintelligible interchange, jammed the signal, knifing a cruel ultimatum through the jam in plain audible words: "Give up, Croyd. Soon you will be helpless, but I will hold you conscious and heart-sensitive so you can watch with full appreciation. And then, without desensitizing you and without awaiting tomorrow, I will start the brain scan."

Fuzzy-witted, Croyd comprehended that his only hope was a quarter of the fissure brain that Dzendzel would not have thought to control. And he issued to the brain—from this ultimately sensitive high place—a weak command: *Bring me back to Roland's place.*

Dzendzel and Freya and Roland vanished.

Still Croyd was in a gray place, but a somehow more circumscribed-indefinite gray place; he knew this place, it was Roland's place.

Now partially though not wholly screened from debilitation by the duke, he struggled into semiorientation, intercepting meanwhile the duke's angry, frustrated searching thoughts.

As a desperate emergency measure, he requested an inhibitor screen between himself and the duke's mastermind room. The mental snarling of the duke immediately blurred. In effect, the duke with respect to his cosmic brain was now in the situation of a mind whose control over its brain is marihuana-fuzzed; but this fuzzing was purchased at a price, for the lieutenant control of the brain by Croyd was fuzzed also, only Croyd was for the instant more immediately in touch with primary processes.

His own head was progressively clearing; he needed time: the duke possessed the sophistication to diagnose the trouble in his own brain and take projective telepathic countermeasures. There was, however, a rearguard hope: the duke's preoccupation with this problem, together with the brain fuzz, *might* shake Freya sufficiently loose from thrall so that she (having learned some of Croyd's powers at a more than rudimentary level) *might* further harass the duke, perhaps even releasing Roland. (Questions of how Freya had got here could be deferred; he did not even trifle with them.)

He could not, however, count on a Freya renaissance. He had to act effectively for himself, with the brain, from this inferior subcontrol position. Croyd kept shaking his head in hope of clearing it, knowing that the shaking in itself would do nothing except to challenge a sharpening of mental concentration.

Came a threshold-faint signal: "Croyd . . ."

He went alert. With all his power he called on the brain: *zero on that and amplify that!* Then he went totally receptive.

More clearly: "Calling Croyd. Calling Croyd. Chloris here. Chloris here. Do you read me? Over."

He answer-thought it intensely, subvocalizing it to harden his own intensity: "Croyd here. I read you faintly but clearly. Try to amplify transmission. Over."

With definition: "Croyd, I read you. I have sighted the *Castel Jaloux*. I am prepared to move in for critical action. I am prepared to do this alone, but I would do it better with you here. Can you assist? Over."

What a HELL of a time for *this!* Rapidly he intertwisted the conflicting skeins of action and counteraction, his head almost totally clear now, the muffled fumings of frustrated bloodhound Dzendzel drifting in as faintly distracting background.

And apparently the cosmic brain was helping him! Was it not surely this brain's frontal cortex that had to be the source of the following unexpected idea? *To the extent that our energies are concentrated on the problem of the* Chloris *with respect to Croyd, so much less can we be responsive to the disorganized commandings by our mind liege Duke Dzendzel.*

But that would be to leave Greta and Roland alone with the duke, at his uninterrupted mercy.

But were they not at the duke's mercy only to the extent that the duke retained total command over his brain?

This new action would have the effect of blocking the duke from his surrogate brain. The instant the duke would realize that he had lost control of his brain, he

would turn inward to concentrate on controlling Roland
and Freya *by his own resources.*

How potent were the duke's own resources?

Shoot crap!

Croyd mind-barked: *Augment the inhibitory muffler between me and the duke, remove the inhibitory muffler between me and yourselves. Respond to me. Concentrate
all available resources on Chloris and her vicinity, deploying at my direction. ACTIVATE!*

All the space was metaspace, and floating a hundred meters to Croyd's right was the port flank of Chloris, and
floating five kilometers ahead was the vast irregular bulk
of the *Castel Jaloux.* The distance between *Chloris* and
Castel did not appear to be increasing or decreasing; but
the *Castel* was tumbling slowly in metaspace, about one
complete rotation in maybe five minutes, which signified
an angular velocity approximating a hundred kilometers
per hour. On crew bow and stern, this would be rough.

Croyd mind-said quietly—and all the subsequent exchanges were quiet—"Croyd here, Chloris, on your port
flank, moving in tight. Tell me where you want me."

"For the instant, Croyd, come aboard. I am more ac-
customed to you when you are in here."

"At your instrument panel?"

"Deeper in. Where you can sense directly what I sense
directly. But not in control. Leave me my mind, Croyd, if
that is what it is."

"Good." Pause. "I am centrally located now in your
perceptual complex."

"Welcome aboard, sir."

"Thank you. I cannot salute your quarterdeck because
I am on it."

"Sir, was that a joke?"

"It was a friendly half-joke."

"Accepted, sir; I wish I had time to learn humor from
you. Do you see the *Castel?*"

"Affirmative."

"You have estimated the angular velocity of her tumbling?"

"Affirmative." They exchanged and reconciled estimates.

"Sir, I have already matched outbound velocities with
the *Castel.* I propose to move in on her tail, match angular
velocity with hers, then drift tail-on into her prime repulsor pipe. I will hover there until by reonic intertransmis-

sion I am satisfied that the internal engine adjustments are ready for ignition. I will then ignite, amplifying my own repulsor as a match. Does it sound feasible?"

Before replying, Croyd had to exert a great deal of emotional control upon himself in order to stay bland. Biting in the background was a phantom notion that there must be a better way; but the better way was not configuring itself, and he had to conclude that it was wishful thinking. Blandly he replied, "It does seem feasible. It may not work, but it is the best measure I can imagine."

"Sir, before you replied, you seemed to be wasting a great deal of energy on random subcortical activity centering in your thalamus. Would you mind explaining?"

His mind voice, replying, was not quite perfectly bland. "I was reflecting that if you succeed, you die. And because I like you, my thalamus was involved, and some of my energy was randomized."

"You . . . *like* me?"

They were drawing quite close to the *Castel.*

"That's right, Chloris."

Her reply was more dry than bland. "With respect to *you,* sir, if I had a thalamus, it would be involved; with respect to my own energy, I cannot at this time afford to randomize it."

"Thank you, Chloris. I shall remember you."

"Thank you, sir. At the last instant, if I succeed, I shall wish that I could have remembered you. And should I fail, I would depend upon you to guide me through the inevitable suicidal impulse into a sense of a new mission."

"This you can depend upon."

"Acknowledged. Croyd, are you now seeing precisely what I see?"

"I think so. You have effectively matched angular velocities with the tail of the *Castel;* we seem to be hovering motionless bow-on with the central pipe in her five-repulsor tail assembly. What now?"

"A problem, sir. I am not good at backing; my maximum perceptual field is three hundred and seventy degrees and weak at the rearward extremes; in short, I cannot see clearly to back into her. What can you do?"

Pause, while the phantom sense of *some better way* nagged him. Then: "I will relocate into your tail, utilizing the fissure brain for direct perception. But from there I will have no reonics for communication with you, and I cannot any more project telepathy. Can you reach back and pick me up?"

"I think so. Let us try it."

He directed the brain to locate him subjectively in the center of the *Chloris* tailpipe, looking outward. (Almost subliminally and fleetingly he was aware of background Dzendzel murmurings, and then he forgot this.) He spoke then. "Do you read me, Chloris?"

"Affirmative."

"Clearly?"

"Affirmative."

"Rotate axially at will, and I will report when our target comes into view."

For the best part of a minute there was no sense of motion, the uniform *nothing* view of metaspace giving him nothing to judge motion by. But then the left-hand arc of the *Chloris* tailspout began to include *something;* and he reported, "I am starting to see the *Castel.*"

"Good; I am slowing rotation. Report."

"Horizontally you are swinging in on her center pipe, vertically you are well centered."

"I am halting rotation. Report."

"You have swung seven degrees too far to your own starboard."

"Adjusting to port seven degrees. Report."

"Adjust one degree back starboard and two degrees downward, then back in slowly."

"Adjusted, backing. Keep reporting."

"You are on target, but slow it down." The great maw of the *Castel*'s central repulsor tube yawned to swallow him.

"Done. Report."

"Raise your tail half a degree and come on back at ten centimeters per second."

"In progress. Report."

The tube mouth closed upon him; there was darkness; just prior to darkness, swiftly he used the brain's hind vision to assure himself that Chloris would not even bump the tube edges. He snapped, "Cut power and drift—this tube is thirty meters deep."

Prolonged silence. Abruptly Chloris jet-braked. Then: "I am motionless relative to the tube. How far do I sit from ignition locus?"

"I would guess, about three meters."

"Too distant. I must come in a little deeper, but I must

not crush my own tube end. Is your judgment accurate?"

"Let me try the brain." His relationship with the fissure brain was much too new for him to understand its resources; and he felt about for intuition much as he would have done in his own brain. Presently a semiconviction came, and he ventured, "I have a sense that you could safely manage another two hundred and eighty centimeters."

"This is smaller than my perfect-control resolution power, but I will try. I am accelerating backward at a thousandth of a G for five seconds. I have cut power. I am braking. This is close, Croyd."

"I know."

Most prolonged silence.

A tiny *click*, a barely noticeable jar.

Silence.

Chloris, tautly: "One of us misjudged by a centimeter. Please finger my tube edges and report."

Croyd ran a psychic finger all around the rim of the tube that he mentally lay in. He reported, "There is no more than a one-millimeter inward annealing of the tube edge for no more than thirty degrees of arc. I would say that your matchfire ability is unimpaired."

"Good." The inward voice had returned considerably toward the bland. "I have now to establish reonic communication with the *Castel* engine adjustments to be sure that she is ready for matchfire. Croyd, I suggest that you return into my perceptual center."

"Why?"

Pause. Then: "Back there you will be double-incinerated by my fire and by her answering fire."

"In your perceptual center, Chloris, I will be incinerated *along with you* by her answering fire. And the delay from your tail to your nose will not be appreciable."

"Agreed. But in my tail, even if we fail and she does not offer answering fire, you will get my matchfire."

"Only mentally, Chloris. Remember that: I get it only mentally; you get it physically."

Pause. Then: "While we talk, I am establishing contact and getting sluggishly favorable results. Meanwhile, when you get it mentally, will it be fully subjective?"

"I suppose so."

"Involving your thalamus?"

"I suppose so."

"Painful, eh?"

"Probably. In more ways than one."

"Come up into me forward here, Croyd. I need you here, and there is no sense in having you incinerated by an unanswered blow from my tail."

Seeing the rationale, Croyd instantly moved forward to her perceptual center, informing her, "I am in here."

"Good. How do you perceive that I am doing?"

"Very well; the *Castel* engine automatics are responding favorably. But, Chloris . . ."

"Croyd?"

Still he was nagged by a dark sense that there must be a better way, some method that his mind should have found. He temporized: "For a last time, I suggest that you first try to find and awaken Admiral Gorsky or Captain Czerny or Lieutenant Hanoku."

Edgy: "I thought I had mentioned, in doing so, we might well excite the apparitions which invaded the ship in the first place."

"True. But . . ."

A psychic fist hit his mental forehead. "Chloris! For the love of any god or goddess, suspend operations until I have checked out something! I think I know how to beat this."

"Croyd, we are almost ready for matchfire; time is critical! Why should we delay now?"

"Chloris, no time to explain—I order you to hold! Hold, do you hear me? Hold! I will be back."

Turning all his attention to another quarter of the brain, abandoning Chloris for the instant, he demanded: *Was it this brain that activated the apparitions?*

Affirmative.

And sped the Castel *outward?*

Can we now deactivate the apparitions, arouse the crew, and inspeed the Castel?

Affirmative.

Then DO IT!

He felt it *done.*

Gratefully he returned to Chloris, arriving with profound soul shock into a radiant bee cluster of outwardly spreading atoms that had been Chloris before evidently ignoring his order she had matchfired and successfully ignited the disintegrative repulsors of the *Castel Jaloux.*

Shivering, he came into self-realization in the ambiguous room that was Roland's.

He sat there on something, gradually quieting.

A strong hand closed on his shoulder. A strong young voice asserted, "You can come back now."

He sat, bleakly experiencing the hand gripping his shoulder.

He laid a hand on Roland's hard hand. Slowly he arose.

The nothingness of the Roland room expanded into the more spatial nothingness of the Dzendzel room.

Before him was the Dzendzel throne. Freya sat on this throne, with the inert body of Dzendzel lying supine across her knees; and the eyes of the madonna in this *pietà* gazed at Croyd.

But then, over to one side of this room, a stick ship materialized, and out of it poured monsters who deployed themselves threateningly about the throne; and in the main hatch Pan appeared flaming, calling, "HOLD, DZENDZEL! TELL ME WHERE CROYD IS!"

And then there was ultimate silence.

In the midst of which, the eyes of Pan and Croyd met. And lingered together. Then the eyes of Pan moved throneward, considering the significance of inert Dzendzel lying supine across the knees of Freya.

The significance *to Pan*. The *totally ironical* significance to Pan.

Phase Seven

INTERPERSONAL CODA

Day 8 et seq.

The Leibnitz doctrine of *the identity of indiscernibles* was intended to dramatize a logical quandary: if no observer, no matter how thorough, can distinguish one entity from another entity, is there any good reason to insist that they are not the same entity?

This doctrine has been raped in recent centuries by probability physics. And I confess its utility in the abstract statistical work which is technologically the most practical. But in the final confrontation, the doctrine misses a crucial ontological point:

If each of the objectively indiscernible entities is a subjectively experiencing reality—a living org—can any observer authentically assert their identity or difference without first having dwelt in the moccasins of both?

—Nike Pan, *Plato and the Stars* (2318)

(Nike Pan was an earlier philosopher whose name Pan Sagittarius adopted for reasons of long-range admiration.)

ONCE MORE LADEN WITH *US*, the *Castel Jaloux* drove for the metagalactic barrier at the tip of the Djinn lobe; but on the third day after our mutual rescue between the perished hands of Chloris, and just prior to barrier breakage, there was time for a shipboard rite which had assumed in my mind an importance that in objective moments I tended to consider disproportionate.

Croyd was deep in a long-range black brood; nevertheless, urged by me, he joined me in beginning personal preparations nearly an hour in advance. In my private quarters, we peeled, showered, and dried; then each of us began to darken himself with a synthetic whose skin-browning effect resembled that of Darian nada-nut juice.

Midway through this browning, there was a discreet door knock; minimally draping myself, I caused the door to half-open, and I reached through to bring in with one hand our two costumes. Dropping them on a chair, I rejoined Croyd; in silence he did my back, then I did his; he donned his costume, I donned mine; we examined each other

and we broke up. And my own laughter was all the freer because this was the first free laughter by Croyd since the disintegration of the lifeboat *Chloris*.

But almost immediately his laughter shriveled; and later I would learn that it wasn't only Chloris. For here was this wedding rite; and already—synthesis or no synthesis, and with or without a chastity vigil—for Croyd it was too late.

We joined the assembled passengers and crew in the great balconied ballroom of the ship. The encircling balcony was thronged with crewmen and crewwomen, all who could be spared from stations (and that was half the crew at this time); the floor was packed with officers and petty officers and members of the Sol legations to Moudjinn and to Dari.

All without exception were brown, seminude, wearing only lua-lua and shell beads. If all the lua-lua and most of the shells were synthetic, nobody cared; they were ap-

propriate to a rite that mingled gaiety with solemnity, and
their primitive innocence represented a toylike triumph of
Western sophistication, having been turned out on one-day
notice by the ship's omnifabricators.

Amid the free chatter there was a general attention
trend toward the fifteen-meter open circle in the ballroom
center—a circle centered by a small grass-thatched hut
which at the moment was open all around but with rolled-
up screens that could close it.

Seated cross-legged on the floor of this hut was I,
brown and lua-lua'd and corpulent; explicitly, my belly
hung over the tie string of my lau-lua; I felt as *mal à pro-
pos* as a fat woman in a miniskirt. Standing behind me
was Croyd, brown and lua-lua'd and lean. The scene
shared the problem of every theater-in-the-round; it could
not play front-on at all times to all spectators; wherever
you sat, you discovered after you sat whether you would
be viewing mostly front or back; side seats were fair
compromises.

There was first a great musical business with a couple
of stringed instruments and some bongo drums; and twenty male and female dancers, hurriedly recruited and spot-
rehearsed, did an inexpert but enthusiastic Dari hula all
around the clearing (in, of course, eight-tenths gravity).
This was the only part of the ceremony wherein it did
not matter where you sat.

Peering into the peripheral shadows, I could descry
variously colored decapoda standing punctuative sentinel;
and, most inconspicuously, Pan was there, always with
Freya near.

Now the dancers disappeared, and the music quieted
(but continued); and Gorsky, surprisingly muscular in the
deminude (her breasts were military solid), stood before
me to announce the ceremony officiation by Captain
Czerny. Then the Czech, so thin in his scant-kilted brown-
ness that no shadow casting could be expected, intoned to
the throng: "I am favored to announce the nuptials of
Lieutenant Onu Hanoku, alias Prince Onu of the house of
Hanoku, and Miss Gilligan Flynn, alias Princess Djeelian
of the house of Faleen. If these principals continue to
wish marriage, they are bidden to come forward."

Whereupon people parted asunder; and Hanoku and
Djeel walked forward in a rhythmic walk that was a

kind of conservative hula, Djeel's right hand delicately placed on the sinewy brown left forearm of Hanoku.

They were the only people in the ballroom whose brown was not artificial; even the blacks and greens and blues and yellows and reds had made stabs at turning brown, but these two were for real. Djeel was tawny, Hanoku was burnt umber, they were exquisitely beautiful; and in her left hand the bride carefully carried a small opaque scarlet rhyton.

(Gorsky muttered in Croyd's ear, "Bomb in your lifecraft irrelevant."

(Her voice came to him from a very long distance away; he shook himself loose from distance, he attended to Gorsky, he reconstructed what she had said, he made no sense of it. He whispered back, "Pardon?"

(She hissed, "The bomb that was in your lifecraft during the drill. Irrelevant to the rest of the stuff. Planted by a paranoid second-class reonicist, he hates authority. In the brig now."

("Good," Croyd acknowledged. "Watch what is essential.")

Czerny stepped to one side. The young couple, together enthralled, rhythmed to the grass hut, stepped aboard, and quieted, standing before me, who was squat-seated beside a low altar.

And all was still.

Laboriously I got to my feet. And the couple knelt.

I stood wheezing for a moment. Sedately then I queried, "Onu Hanoku, do you wish life marriage to Djeelian Faleen according to the customs of your people?"

He intoned, "Aye."

"Djeelian Faleen, do you accord in a wish for life marriage to Onu Hanoku according to the customs of your people?"

She replied, "Aye." And all about us there was tension, for inevitably there had been ship gossip concerning marriage according to the lore of Dari.

Djeel was looking past me. Gorsky told me later that Djeel had been looking at Croyd; he had sustained her gaze for a moment, then had smiled with whole tenderness and had turned to meet the glowing eyes of Hanoku.

I asserted, "According to the customs of your people, before you can be married, Djeelian must be deflowered by the chief of Hanoku's clan; whereafter you two will pass two nights in chaste and holy prayer before this marriage may be consummated. But Onu Hanoku himself is clan chief, and therefore the deflowering must be accomplished by the protocol chief of these two highest houses on Dari. Now, that protocol chief must be chief of all Dari; and under our new treaty the President of the Interplanetary Union is chief of all Dari. So it is I who must accomplish this defloration. Onu, do you assent to this necessity?"

Thus I publicly and officially confirmed rumor. Never had the ballroom been quieter.

Onu, having glanced at demure Djeel, elevated his chin. "I do."

"Djeelian, do you assent to this ritual necessity?"

Noticeably pallid, she dropped her head. "I do."

Now I said clearly, "Onu and Djeelian, by rite you two have the say as to whether the screens of this hut shall be dropped for the privacy of this intimate deflowering; and if you two should disagreee on the question, then in this one matter Djeelian has the final say. Shall the screens be dropped?"

Onu and Djeel together raised their heads and cried sharply in unison, having rehearsed this: "No! Let the defloration be for all to see—complete with the sight of the precious blood that is the token of the bride's divine virginity!"

A sigh swept the hall. I sighed too, but for another reason.

I faced the bride squarely, and my breathing was heavy. "Djeelian, I am an old man, and I may not bring this off as neatly as your customs may expect. Are you prepared for whatever it will be?"

She gazed up at me openly, trustingly. "Tannen, you are a good chief. Whatever it will be, so be it."

Onu added, "I want my marriage with Djeel to be absolutely right. Do whatever you can . . . and whatever you will."

I paused, considering.

Croyd told me later that my face broke then into a radiant smile that was visible on the back of my neck. Reaching down, I grasped the pure white flower necklace of Djeel and wrenched at it, breaking it away from her. I raised this necklace high, examining it while small white flower heads fell away from it and Djeel and Hanoku knelt rapt watching me. I crushed this necklace to my lips with both hands, and I laid this necklace on the small rude altar beside me.

Djeel arose and urged wondering Hanoku to his feet, and they advanced to the altar. Considerately Djeel spilled the contents of her scarlet rhyton on the white flowers of the necklace: blood-red she stained the petals. Turning her face up to Hanoku, she passed the voided cup to him. Having kissed the cup, he laid it upon the flowers; and this action was his own creative response to my synthesis.

Onu and Djeel, clasping four hands, were looking expectantly at me. Behind me, Croyd's brood was soul-tangible.

I cleared my throat and preambled, "Since by this holy rite I have established for this princess her psychic virginity, which is the best sort of virginity, while spiritually co-fathering her first child by this prince in the presence of all our gods and particularly the friendly gods of Dari, now I claim the father privilege of saying a few words to this couple and to our child who will come.

"Onu and Djeelian, it is for you as lord and lady to lead the synthesis, to make the task of Governor Croyd progressively less necessary until he recognizes himself as a visiting futility and out of sheer ennui goes away from your new-vital Dari. This is the highest meaning of your marriage.

"As now you go into this endeavor, I call upon you and your descendants to be free and easy, respecting and loving your brains and your minds and the mindstuff that your brains and bodies and minds are made of. If something from the old time tastes good intuitively, then use it, but check with your brains to be sure that it may not be counterproductive for its own future. If a logical structure that your brain concocts appears eminently workable, taste it nevertheless with your intuitive minds to be sure that it may not be counterproductive for endlessly growing aesthetic experience; and use it only if it passes this taste test. Never forget that most of your subjects, particularly the least intelligent ones, are dominated by their brains, yet they have minds.

"Onu, be the highest lord of your Dari in a way that will be long-range good for Dari. Djeelian, be the fostering lady of the house for all the small good people of your Dari. Onu and Djeelian, together, in continuous council, *re-create* your Dari—so well that after your deaths, Dari will keep on re-creating herself.

"Let this creation grow out of your caring for each other. Let your caring spill beyond yourselves, let it overflow your Dari."

My part was ended then. And it all came over me that I had thought of no way to wind up this ceremony. Inwardly panicking, I called upon the Lord to end it for me somehow.

But Djeelian, gazing at me, feeling no sense of ceremonial trouble, was telling me, "Thank you, our spiritual chief. We shall count these luminous ideas as the substance of your spirited impregnation, and we shall teach them faithfully to the one who is conjointly our child and to all our children."

Hanoku, though, was gazing at Croyd as he added, "And in this one rare case, the gods of Dari have decreed that a lost deadline makes no difference. We shall burst with private pride whenever we look upon our first child, knowing secretly that in all Dari a tetraploid has never before been born."

Puzzled, I turned to look at Croyd. Most erect he now stood; and broadly he now smiled at Hanoku, responding, "I have caught the implication, and I bless it. Even when time is my enemy, still I praise Heaven for variability of sequence."

———————◆◆———◆◆———◆◆———————

WHILE CROYD WAS MINGLING with the happy crowd of pseudo-Darians in a Rollicking Rejoice that was fluidly facile by reason of endless flowing upa-upa and jango juice (turned out, like the ceremonial chicken blood and other commodities, by the ship's redoubtable omnifabricators), Croyd was arrested in midsentence by a *Thought*. Swinging accurately in its source direction, he saw Pan above him at a balcony rail. Pan nodded, turned, and departed. Croyd finished his sentence, creatively twisting the end of it into a bantering trivial reason for having to leave momentarily; and Croyd went to his quarters.

Pan awaited him, standing at room center, back to Croyd, head down, great shoulders drooping somewhat, although scarcely quite sagging. Bare, brown in his lua-

lua, Pan was a young god: this fact Croyd noted, although it did not then or later occur to Croyd that he was in fact admiring himself.

Croyd threw a thought: projective telepathy was the first power beginning to return to him after the Roland debilitation—in feebleness thus far, however; only Pan or Freya or faraway Greta could catch it.

But Pan elected speech. Without turning, he began, "You see how it is, Croyd? I drew on all the powers either of us ever had in order to bail you out of that fissure and beat down the duke. I might have saved my effort. When I got there, it was all done—done by your ordinary human brain and body, with an assist from a cosmic brain that any other imaginative and competent neuropsychologist could have figured out and used. Croyd, *who am I?*"

Krell, in the corridor, listened through a door that (owing to a reonic malfunction) had not quite closed behind Croyd.

Meanwhile Croyd was reflecting that his reply had to be as near right as might be. Perhaps telepathic directness? No, that would be salt in the wound; this, Pan had signaled by opting for speech. *Who am I?* Croyd probed: "As of what date?"

Pan turned to him a sober face. "I see your drift. But you be the one to say it."

"As of just before we were duplicated, we were one. As of just after, we were two, but we were absolutely identical. Just now, four years later, I am Croyd, you are Pan—we are different. I am what we were, modified by *my* four years; you are what we were, modified by *your* four years: you are *you*, is who—we were identical twins, we are now nonidentical twins. I fail to see why that bugs you."

"It bugs me because this twin is not *and can never be* the equal of *that* twin."

Croyd went grim. "You sound like a downcast son who notices that he is not yet the equal of his father, and therefore concludes that he can never be his father's equal. I would kick you in the teeth, Pan, except that you would guiltfully accept the kick and go deeper down into it, minus a couple of teeth."

Pan went grim. "I ought to storm out of here, Croyd. Instead I am trying to control my temper—normal human controls, Croyd—and keep channels open. Will you get mad if I hurl a system of counterinsults?"

"Of course. But I will try to control it."

"You are a goddamned prig. This means that *I was* a goddamned prig. I have revolted from you and from my old self. I am specifically trying *not* to be as good as you."

"It's a damn good revolt, Pan. I couldn't have done better myself."

"See what I mean, prig? Condescending, trying to persuade me that I *am* good."

"Tell me what you want me to say."

Silence.

Pan said queerly, "If I tell you, and you say what I want to hear, still you are a prig; but if you deliberately say what I do *not* want to hear, then you are putting me down. Is that it?"

Croyd waited.

Pan was studying his fingernails. "And since you tacitly assent to my analysis, it follows that you are a prig who is putting me down."

Croyd waited.

The door vanished; golden Krell strode in with lua-lua aswish, and, ignoring Pan, stood knightly erect before Croyd. "Forgive me, sirrah, I was listening. I ask you for just this instant to suppress all your ultrahuman powers and accept what I now do, decapod-to-man. Will you do this, Croyd?"

Eye-to-eyestalk with Krell: "Bypassing what this is all about, will you kill or cripple me?"

"No, sirrah. I don't think so."

"Your honor, Sirrah Krell."

With a self-telegraphing claw swing to a cheek, Krell felled Croyd, and, still ignoring Pan, departed. The closing door reappeared.

Pan stood looking down on Croyd, and the muscle play in Pan's face was unusual.

Rolling onto his back, Croyd opened eyes. "What was *that* for, Pan—do you know?"

Pan said, hard, "He was not trying to tell *you* a single thing. He was talking to *me* loud and clear. May I help you up, Croyd?"

"Pray do."

A moment later they stood facing each other: it was mirror stuff, except that their orientations were reversed.

Pan commented, "Good man, Krell."

"Damn good man."

"What are you doing about Dzendzel?"

"He is aboard ship, comfortably and securely confined. He will be conveyed to his Emperor; there is a relevant treaty clause."

"I want Roland reified; I will do it myself in our non-space house. I will take him back with Krell to the deca-pod colony. I will stay there until I have undone the harm of my negligence; I will then leave Roland as governor and depart. Agreed, Mr. Chairman?"

"I am not chairman. Greta is chairman."

"I suggest you do her the favor of resuming the chair."

Pause. Then: "I am committed to the Dari project. And just in passing—is the demand about Roland negotiable?"

"See what I mean, Croyd? I have made precisely two suggestions, and already on both suggestions you are preparing to say no to me."

"Pan, reflect: you have enough power to transform me into a frog. I repeat: is the demand about Roland negotiable?"

"What is your counterthought?"

"Leave Roland in charge of the brain; it can be useful to the metagalaxy, and Roland is now an incorruptible seneschal. After you have done what you consider to be your job with the Krell people, leave *Krell* as governor—he is quite the knightly equal of Roland, and he is one of them. Your comment?"

Pan's jaw muscles knotted. "Done, you bastard. How about the chairmanship?"

"Why do you want me to be permanent chairman?"

"To me it would be a mental hazard if I had to accept you as a fellow renegade. It would strengthen me to know that you were a permanent established prig."

"Then be easy, brother! I would be your fellow renegade if now I should run out on Dari; by holding course I establish myself as a permanent prig."

Their half-smiles were quite identical. Pan murmured, "Thus to eat one's cake and have it too."

Croyd added, "Nevertheless, I will tell you privately about a secret intention that I have. My Greta will not have to suffer the Galactic burden forever. As soon as Hanoku and Djeel are going the strong way I think they will go, I will hook in with Roland and his brain for a remote hot line of instant communication with Dari and reinforcement of Dari in her finding of her way. And that could be within a couple of years, even. And *then* I will run out on Dari."

Soberly now they were not-quite-identical twins, in tune.

Croyd queried, "What will you do after the Krell folk, Pan?"

"By that time, Croyd—or perhaps a year after—I will have come to decisions about myself. And then I will ask you to help me get *entrée* to those I will have to start with, whoever they may be, whatever it may be that I will be starting on. And that will be the last favor that I will ask."

"Instead, as my friend, please be free to ask when you need, leaving me free to say yes or no in terms of my coordinates."

"Done."

"Just by the way, Pan—your superior prig friend Croyd let his good friend Chloris die out of pure Croyd stupidity, even when he had at his disposal a cosmic brain."

"Equally by the way, Croyd—your good friend Chloris died heroically in the stupid process of refusing your order to hold action."

Pause. Then: "Still by the way, Pan—had *you* been the powerless prisoner of the fissure lord, and I the powerful rescuer—"

"It would have been the same in reverse. Erase all that."

"I have, Pan. Except the memory that you did come."

"Good. I too wish to keep remembering that I did come. And that I was unnecessary to you, Croyd. This is reassuring to me, when I look at it right-end-up."

"Then we are back in *rapport.*"

"Completely."

"We come then to the question of Freya. . . ."

GRETA AND FREYA AND PAN stood once again on the breezeway bridge of the Croyd-Pan nonspace house. The two identical women clung to Pan's arms, looking alternately at each other and at Pan. He peered into the nondescript gray. Curiously, the long dresses of the women fluttered as though there were an impossible breeze.

Greta said across his chest, "I think he has lost his tongue, Freya."

The other woman answered, "Reverse the positions,

Greta, and you would too. Are you *sure* you want me back? You'll be letting yourself in for some new and pretty rough memories."

"Any rougher than what both of us remember from the time before as one woman who met Croyd?"

Freya cat-smiled. "Not rougher, really. Higher level, too. More glamorous, maybe."

Greta cat-smiled. "Then I have no qualms."

Freya lost her smile, feeling hard pressure on her ribs from the right hand of Pan. Instantly the Greta smile went away also, and she gazed across Pan at Freya; and then she gazed at Pan, who was Croyd, really.

The women interchanged semidread thoughts: *Losing him, we gain him; gaining us, he loses us and frees himself; it is all weird, and friendship somehow resolves itself into an intermingling of identity and regret.*

Pan was catching the intermingled thought. (So, aeons away, was Croyd.) Pan broke it roughly: "Are you both sure that you understand the technique of this rejointure?"

Freya said sharply, "Pan, of *course* we understand the technique! *That was the wrong question!*"

He broke away from Greta and seized Freya and embraced her lovingly and bitterly. Greta drifted away, pensive; this was Pan, not Croyd; this was Freya, not Greta, and Pan was losing her, and she was losing him. As Greta, now, Freya would have Pan in Croyd; but Croyd was no longer Pan.

Suddenly and acutely Greta comprehended the whole developed individualities of the four who had been two. The loves were between Croyd and Greta and between Pan and Freya; there was no sharing or tempering, they were stark individual pair-loves.

Freya, must you leave me?

Listen, Pan, let me tell you again how it is.

Greta shivered, trying to exclude from her mind their naked mind exchange. Then she calmed and went open; soon she would be Freya also; she had to know.

Pan, listen. I am your woman as of four years ago; we were as much one as a man and a woman can be. You are one with Croyd as of four years ago, totally one with Croyd. Time gone is real; it is real totally for when it was. I am not leaving you as of then, but only as of now.

Do you love me as of now?

Bitterly. Please hold me.

Mind silence, while Greta suffered with them. Then:

Pan, if you are a self, know *yourself. It is not for you to have one place or one task or one woman. At the same time, know* me: *except for pleasant interludes, it is not for me to share my man. This is total and permanent divorce, Pan—for the good of my faithful soul, for the good of your roving soul.*

I will never stop loving you.

Thank God for that. I will never stop watching you and loving you. And then she flung an astounding thought past Pan: *Will we, Greta?*

Palsied, Greta thought assent: it was all she could manage.

And she blessed Pan for not letting go of Freya as now he turned to Greta. *You and Freya together are the woman I cared about from the moment I met you, and the only woman until four years ago. Since then, no matter what the appearances may have been, Freya has been the only woman I have cared about. When you two become one, I will suffer, because you will be with Croyd and not with me.*

Freya could not respond: mind-to-mind is truth. Greta responded sturdily, staying away from him. *Then when Freya and I are one again, you will love both of us wholly as one for what we two meant to each other four years ago, and you will also love Freya wholly for what she has meant to you during four years; and you will make this separation in your mind, realizing the impossibility of a jointure; and you will go on your roving ways knowing privately, as I will be knowing privately, that a four-year half of me loved Pan and not Croyd at all. And this knowing will heighten the glow of your new adventures for me and for Croyd—and for you.*

And as Pan's heart wavered, Freya's mind whispered: *I love you, Pan. So shall we get on with it?*

Greta mind-threw: *I will give a guest gift. Our name will be Freya, Freya.*

━━━━◆━◄━━━►━◆━━━━

THE SIGNING OF THE TREATY on Moudjinn was accomplished with imperial pomp in a contexture of intergalactic amity, with high Moudjinn nobles assembled. The eager young Emperor (who, on receiving the prisoner person of Archduke Dzendzel, had confined him to his castle on parole) somehow reminded me of Moskovia's Alexander I. I mentioned this to Gorsky; she bit, "I hope for all our sakes that he is more realistic."

Following rather a bizarre ceremony, at whose climax Croyd reluctantly but perforce accepted the title Archduke of Dari and in return swore modified fealty, the Emperor expressed desire to send the new governor to his planet at the head of a Moudjinnian space fleet swarming with marines. "You will encounter," he warned, "hostility—and not only from Darians." Croyd would have demurred in any event, having the *Castel Jaloux;* but now that the subtle brain of Roland had replaced the *Castel's* brute force, his demurral was fervent. The impression on Dari would be wrong, he said; it would be sufficient for the Emperor to inform the outgoing Moudjinnian governor that Croyd was about to relieve him, and to add a command that he inform the populace. Reluctantly the Emperor agreed.

After a week of celebration, the *Castel* departed with all her company; following a Dari stopover, she would take me home to Nereid and Erth.

Aloft in the *Castel,* Croyd went alone to his cabin and projected a thought. Still his projections were feeble, but they were strong enough to be picked up by a certain I-ray from remotely away and inward. Immediately he was in contact with Roland, who, in the fissure depth, had been tracking him constantly.

Croyd told Roland, "I have rather a complex request. Can you flood Dari with an aura of such-and-such a texture for Darians laced with such-and-such another texture for resident Moudjinnians?"

"Affirmative. Excellent."

"Can you then gradually, over a period of months, dilute this aura until by the end of a year it will be gone entirely?"

"I suggest, sir, that you retain this aura indefinitely."

"No, Roland. Eventually, in full possession of their own minds and emotions, the Darians must make their own decisions as to whether they continue to want me. I want only an early-on honeymoon; after that, if I lose, I lose honestly."

"My liege, I cannot agree. And my brain is feeding back logical disagreement."

"Acknowledged. Nevertheless, Roland, this is what I want."

"My liege, consider the aura established—and sustained —to be withdrawn at your pleasure. But I will withdraw it only as you may please and direct, and I will obey with reluctance."

Thereafter the *Castel* proceeded leisurely toward Dari, taking forty-eight hours for the short run.

Long before the *Castel* arrived, Dari and her environing space resembled an overripe apple being departed by swarms of pig-frightened fruit flies. These flies were space frigates and cutters and scouters, under command of the mortally and inexplicably terror-smitten governor from Moudjinn and numbers of his high vassals who had lorded fiefs on thousands of planetary islands, departing Dari permanently with their top vassals, leaving below their junior officers and soldiery and overseers abject with blue funk, and (on some fifty islands) unstrung Darian pirate lords wondering why their piracy.

Informed of this by Roland, Croyd told the knight to ease that ingredient of his aura so that miserable fear would relax into mere submissiveness, but to keep the feeling of mellow gold, for the while, warm in the heart of every Darian.

And it was so.

Gorsky and I remained aboard the *Castel*, which was parked in a five-hundred-kilometer orbit around Dari; we would descend next day for a visit, with me incognito because I did not want my own *oint du seigneur* to divert central attention from the new governor. Officers and men would follow in relays: shore leave all around before the voyage home.

Croyd, with Hanoku and Djeel and the thirty-nine civilian members of his staff—unguarded, and all dressed only in lua-lua—departed the *Castel* aboard the admiral's cutter. This cutter was equipped with a magnificent system of viewports on all flanks and above and below; and her bridge boasted a broad bay window. (The allusive poignancy of communicating with this commandcom was eased for Croyd, because the voice of this commandcom was masculine.)

They took several hours to circumnavigate Dari at a twenty-five-kilometer altitude, while Prince Onu and Princess Djeelian divided themselves between eager survey of their home planet and proud inspection of the delight on the faces of Croyd and his crew. It was indeed an islanded ocean paradise.

They came in finally on one of the largest islands—culturally the main island, the seat of the departed Moudjinnian governor, the island that had once been equally divided between the gently feudal power of the house of Faleen and the benignly feudal power of the house of Hanoku.

They came in on the seaside city—if an overgrown village can be called a city—that had been Onu's birthplace. Now forward on the bridge stood the triumvirate, Croyd and Onu and Djeelian: Croyd in the middle with his right arm about Hanoku's shoulders and his left hand draped over Djeel's left shoulder, while Hanoku's left arm encircled Croyd's shoulders and Djeel's right hand held Croyd's left hand.

Descending, they contemplated the largening city, whose wooden houses were lumping in sad desuetude; and central in the city rose a grisly anomaly—a fortified stone castle, the house of the departed governor—on precisely the site once occupied by the high wooden Hanoku house. But all the people were out, looking upward; and although their expressions could not be descried at this altitude, Croyd was satisfied that they were glad anticipatory expressions by reason of Roland's aura.

Hanoku tested: "Croyd, that castle is yours now."

Croyd countered, "Perhaps, but not as a dwelling. Whether it is to come down or be perpetuated as an eyesore museum for your people, I leave to your people."

Gratefully Djeel squeezed his hand, observing, "Pray take note, Onu, that if this governor fails, the reason will not be dishonesty."